SoWest:
Love Kills

SoWest:
Love Kills

Twenty-Four Original Southwestern Tales
from the Sisters in Crime
Desert Sleuths Chapter

Betty,
I hope the stories in this
volume — all Desert Slueth
members and each story reflects
a bit of Arizona — bring you
Many hours of enjoyment.

Claire

DS Publishing
Scottsdale, Arizona

Copyright Acknowledgments

"What Money Can't Buy" Copyright © 2021 by Shannon Baker
"Invoice Overdue" Copyright © 2021 by Mysti Berry
"Almost Dark Now" Copyright © 2021 by Meredith Blevins
"Tried and True" Copyright © 2021 by Patricia Bonn
"Turnabout" Copyright © 2021 by Lauren Buckingham
"Rules of Separation" Copyright © 2021 by Susan Budavari
"Ask Me Tomorrow" Copyright © 2021 by William Butler
"No Good Deed" Copyright © 2021 by Patricia Curren
"Seasons of Death" Copyright © 2021 by Meg E. Dobson
"Changing Woman" Copyright © 2021 by Beverly Forsyth
"Double or Nothing" Copyright © 2021 by Denise Ganley
"Fine Lines" Copyright © 2021 by Roberta Gibson
"He Had It Coming" Copyright © 2021 by Katherine Atwell Herbert
"Cooped Up" Copyright © 2021 by Tom Leveen
"Fade to Black" Copyright © 2021 by Susan Cummins Miller
"Creatures Of Habit" Copyright © 2021 by Charlotte Morganti
"Iris" Copyright © 2021 by Julie Morrison
"The Backpack" Copyright © 2021 by Claire A. Murray
"Notorious In Sedona" Copyright © 2021 by Kris Neri
"A Burn that Reaches Bone" Copyright © 2021 by Karen Odden
"Home is Where" Copyright © 2021 by R K Olson
"Night Shift" Copyright © 2021 by D.R. Ransdell
"Try Again" Copyright © 2021 by Kim Rivery
"Everything" Copyright © 2021 by Elena E. Smith

This is a work of fiction. All the characters, places,
and events portrayed in these short stories are either
fictitious or are used fictitiously.

Cover Designer: Maegan Beaumont- MW Designs
Interior Design and Formatting: Deborah J Ledford - IOF Productions Ltd

Print Format ISBN: 978-0982877487

For Nancy Dobson.
Rest well.

ACKNOWLEDGMENTS

We are indebted to our lead editor, award-winning author, Maegan Beaumont. A woman of tremendous talent and principle, Maegan not only provided the vision and determination needed to pull *Love Kills* together, she also found the time to create the cover. Of course she did.

Heaps of gratitude to our team of co-editors, Deborah J. Ledford, Meg Dobson, Roni Olson, Shannon Baker and last, but *never* least, Susan Budavari. Each of you brought your unique and deftly honed skills to the table, rolled up your sleeves and worked. Your tireless dedication and knowledge of the craft is unparalleled and your willingness to spread the wealth is recognized and very much appreciated—simply put, you ladies are rockstars!

To our authors—those who are within these pages and those who aren't—thank you. Thank you for putting your shoulder to the wheel and writing some of the most provocative and chilling stories we've ever had the pleasure of reading. In a time when it seemed as if the entire world had given up, you didn't and that is something to be proud of.

To our contributing authors—thank you for trusting us with your work. Your amazing talent and your willingness to learn and grow as authors made this an easy ride. Be proud of your work here and your place among these pages. You earned it.

Lastly, thank you to Lauren Buckingham, whose winning title idea helped spawn the concept for *Love Kills*, our first romantic suspense and domestic thriller anthology.

TABLE OF CONTENTS

WHAT MONEY CAN'T BUY   1
SHANNON BAKER

INVOICE OVERDUE   11
MYSTI BERRY

ALMOST DARK NOW   19
MEREDITH BLEVINS

TRIED AND TRUE   23
PATRICIA BONN

TURNABOUT   33
LAUREN BUCKINGHAM

RULES OF SEPARATION   41
SUSAN BUDAVARI

ASK ME TOMORROW   49
WILLIAM BUTLER

NO GOOD DEED   59
PATRICIA CURREN

SEASONS OF DEATH   69
MEG E. DOBSON

CHANGING WOMAN   75
BEVERLY FORSYTH

DOUBLE OR NOTHING   81
DENISE GANLEY

FINE LINES   91
ROBERTA GIBSON

TABLE OF CONTENTS

HE HAD IT COMING   99
KATHERINE ATWELL HERBERT

COOPED UP   109
TOM LEVEEN

FADE TO BLACK   117
SUSAN CUMMINS MILLER

CREATURES OF HABIT   127
CHARLOTTE MORGANTI

IRIS   137
JULIE MORRISON

THE BACKPACK   147
CLAIRE MURRAY

NOTORIOUS IN SEDONA   153
KRIS NERI

A BURN THAT REACHES BONE   163
KAREN ODDEN

HOME IS WHERE   173
R K OLSON

NIGHTSHIFT   183
D. R. RANSDELL

TRY AGAIN   193
KIM RIVERY

EVERYTHING   203
ELENA SMITH

WHAT MONEY CAN'T BUY
SHANNON BAKER

ROMAN stood with his arms folded, assessing the scene in front of him.

"Dammit! What are we gonna do? This is a disaster." Chuy always overreacted. He ran his hands through his already greasy hair, sweaty with nerves from his first big job.

They stood in the rundown warehouse in Tucson's outskirts. Just a cracked cement floor, a few messy stacks of metal and some welding equipment in one corner, a few ancient fluorescent lights to beat back the night. It smelled of decades-old oil and grease, though any hint of mechanics or vehicles was long gone.

Roman didn't need to feel for a pulse. Sitting in the highbacked chair, straining against the rope around his chest, head dangling from his neck, this poor slob wouldn't be talking.

And they needed him to talk. If he didn't reassure the drivers when they got here, there would be trouble. And if there was trouble, Frisco would be pissed.

Pissed enough Roman wouldn't get promoted to run his own crew. Maybe even pissed enough that Roman and Chuy would end up like this guy here.

Roman wrinkled his nose at the smell of death. It's a shame, really. A healthy young guy like this having a heart attack or something. Chuy and Roman hadn't even started to work him over. Roman pointed out the obvious. "That's what drugs'll do to you. Everyone knows you never sample the product."

Chuy continued to work himself into a froth. "Frisco's gonna kill us. We're dead."

"Take it down a notch, will ya? I need to think." Roman's gaze wandered to the chair next to where the dead man draped.

Her brown eyes watched everything without tears, barely blinking. Unlike her boyfriend before he'd bought it, she sat

1

quietly, no jiggling legs or wagging head. Not even a peep when the guy went into the seizure or whatever it was that ended in a white foam dripping from his mouth.

She didn't flinch when Roman reached out to remove the gag. Those eyes pinned him in place. He hadn't noticed much about her in the confusion of bursting in, fighting, tying them up, and then gagging her. But in the relative quiet, with only Chuy's hysterics, Roman noticed her big-time.

Gorgeous. That was the word for her. Flawless brown skin, black hair that fell in waves to the middle of her back. Her arms bound behind the chair emphasized some nice assets. The dead guy wasn't good looking or smart, just rich. Goes to show what money can buy.

Roman didn't care much for pretty women. In his experience, you either get beauty or brains. Looks had their charms, sure. But brainiacs turned Roman on.

Roman tossed the gag on the ground. Not expecting she knew much, he needed to at least try. "When's the shipment coming?"

She stared at Roman with velvety brown eyes and shook her head. "He never talks to me about business."

It hit him like a sucker punch. When he was a kid his mother gave him a puppy. She probably found it in a parking lot or someplace. He loved that damned thing. It went everywhere with him. Shared his bed on the folded-down passenger seat of that rusted out Chevy they called home. He fed it from his share of whatever they managed to scrounge for meals. Mom named her Juliet because she said he loved her so much they were like Romeo and Juliet, even though his name was really Roman. Juliet had these big, liquid brown eyes.

Like the woman in the chair.

Chuy stood over the woman. "You're lying. You know. Tell us, you lying c—" He raised his arm and started to swing toward her head.

Smack. His wrist connected with Roman's palm and strong fingers closed on it, yanking his arm down. "What the hell?" Chuy turned around, ready to strike Roman.

Roman gave him a look that was all the warning Chuy needed. He stepped back.

"Why you wanna be so mean?" Roman said to him before

addressing the woman and pointing to the dead guy. "He didn't mention anything about meeting someone? Ask you to take off?"

Her eyes widened even more. "Oh. Yeah. He told me I had to go stay with my sister tonight. He didn't say why and…" She paused and looked down, her soft cheeks turning pink in a way that made Roman want to stroke them. "I didn't ask. Asking always made him mad."

Roman nodded to Chuy. "There. You see what happens when you talk nice? We'll sit tight."

He could wait for the shipment that would make Frisco happy. Then Roman would move up the ranks. Make enough money to afford nice things for the first time in his life. Maybe even buy some love of his own.

"Take him into the office." Roman nodded his head from Chuy to the dead guy.

Chuy started to protest but probably remembered who Frisco had put in charge. He tightened his lips to show he didn't like being ordered around, but he untied the guy and dragged him away, taking most of the stench with him.

Roman eyed the girl and she stared back at him. He avoided thinking about how her night would end. "What is all this stuff anyway?" he asked, giving a quick chin jerk to the piles of junk scattered around the warehouse.

"He thought he was a welder." Her smile held a hint of a smirk. "An artist."

Roman pointed to the pile of metal in a corner. An acetylene tank stood nearby. "That?"

She shrugged.

He left her tied in her chair and went to a camping cooler next to a workbench. The cooler held a collection of beer and bottled water, along with a covered pie plate. He pulled out water.

Chuy shot from the office, panting and sweaty, smelling like he hadn't showered in two months. "We gotta get rid of the girl. She seen us."

She looked away from them and Roman hoped she hadn't heard. "She's less of a problem than you are if you don't calm down."

Chuy spun around, running his hand through his hair that now spiked. "She's a loose thread and you know how Frisco feels about loose threads."

The cold water soothed Roman's throat and he tipped the bottle back to finish it. "You think the delivery guys are gonna deal with strangers? They see her, know she's the girlfriend, and it's all okay."

Chuy shifted from foot to foot. "Shit. This ain't gonna work. We're so screwed."

Probably. Just when he thought life was looking up. There was a chance this still might work out. But Roman had never been very lucky. He reached into the cooler and took out a bottle of water and a beer. "Here." He handed Chuy the beer. "I'll talk to her."

Roman carried the bottle of water to the girl and sat in the chair next to her. He tilted the bottle to her lips and caught of whiff of flowers, soft and feminine. It'd be nice to nuzzle that silky hair and breathe in her sweetness. "Sorry about your boyfriend."

"Thanks." Her eyes flicked to the office and she shrugged. "The world's not going to miss him. Broke my arm once. Gave me more than one black eye."

How could anyone hit that face? Those eyes. "Come on, you could do better than him."

Her smile was sad. "I've had bad luck with guys. My dad kicked me out of the house when I was young because of the loser I was with."

Roman tossed a chin toward the office. "If he wasn't such a good guy, why'd you stay?"

"I got tired of being poor. It's not easy for a girl like me. Slinging drinks and community college isn't so great, you know. I planned on leaving him soon. Guess I won't get a chance now."

Like Roman thought. Just another pretty face looking for a free ride.

He was more disappointed than he had a right to be.

Chuy finished his beer and pulled out the pie dish. "Hot damn. Pie." He rummaged in the cooler and came out with a fork. He dug into the pie.

"There are plates in the bag," she said. Then exhaled in defeat as Chuy jabbed his fork in and shoveled another bite.

"This is good shit." Chuy's words came out garbled and he stuffed in more.

She gave Roman a sad look. "Chocolate. His favorite. But he

started drinking and snorting and, well, didn't get around to the pie."

"That's too bad," Roman said, wondering how stupid a man had to be to turn down homemade pie.

"Go ahead," she said. "Someone should enjoy it."

With his nerves on high, food didn't sound good. But she'd gone to all the work and he felt bad no one appreciated it. He sliced a piece opposite the pan where Chuy had gobbled, and ate it sitting next to her. If he never tasted another bite, which seemed like a good possibility, this was a good way to go out.

"So, you like to cook?" Roman asked.

Chuy bounced a look between the girl and Roman and shook his head at their conversation. He didn't dare say anything to Roman.

She nodded. "It relaxes me. I plan to open a pie shop someday."

"You'd be good at that," Roman said. He hated that she'd never get to bake another pie, let alone open that shop.

Roman never had a dream for his future other than scraping together enough money for a roof over his head and the next meal. Until he'd hooked up with Frisco. Now he had a chance at a decent life. Especially if he didn't screw up this job.

"What's your favorite pie?" she asked Roman.

He smiled at the idea. "Coconut."

They didn't speak for the next hour while Chuy paced from the window in the front door to the office and back, muttering and cursing. He eventually yanked open the door. "I gotta take a whizz."

The whole time the girl had sat with her arms bound behind her, a rope anchoring her to the chair and her ankles stuck to the legs with duct tape. Roman took his knife from his pocket and leaned over. "No reason for this." He sliced through the tape.

"Thanks." She stretched her legs. She glanced up at him, and he couldn't stop staring in her eyes. "Look, I know you're going to have to kill me. I get it. I played at the wrong table and this hand is a loser. But, thank you. Really. You could have made it a whole lot worse."

Her look, so trusting and grateful was just like Juliet. Roman had kept his pup for nearly three years when his mom hooked up with some two-bit drug dealer in Phoenix. Roman hadn't been able to save Juliet from that asshole. It was a weeping wound that never quite healed.

The door swung wide and Chuy burst in. "They're here."

Damn. He'd almost hoped the shipment wouldn't show up at all.

While Chuy hopped from foot to foot, running his hands through his sweat-spiked hair, Roman worked the ropes behind Julia. When she was free, she arched her back and rubbed her wrists.

Chuy shouted and motioned with his arms. "Get her up here. Come on."

Roman walked with her. "Open the door and tell them to come in, your boyfriend is in the can or something."

The sour tang of sweat billowed off Chuy and Roman waved him to stand close to the side of the door so he'd be behind the men when they entered.

Footsteps thudded on the cement and Roman positioned himself opposite Chuy. When the footsteps got close, Roman nodded at the girl.

She reached out and opened the door. "Come on in." She sounded so normal.

Two guys—one middle-aged and carrying too much weight on his gut, the other younger and bald, but with a dangerous energy—stepped into the warehouse.

The older one sounded tough addressing the girl. "Where's Tony?"

"Shut up!" Chuy yelled, waving his gun like a lunatic.

The two guys whirled around, already reaching for weapons.

Dammit, Chuy. So much for the element of surprise. Roman made his voice hard as granite. "Change of plans. Tony's not around so you're gonna unload here and drive away, nice and quiet."

The bald guy puffed up and flashed a nasty grin. "Don't give a fuck if it's Tony or the Jolly Green Giant. You got the money, you get the shit."

Roman fought the urge to check on the girl. He edged a few feet sideways to stand between her and Baldy, in case someone got an itchy finger.

Chuy danced from one foot to the other. "We get the shit. You get to live. That's the deal I'm giving you."

The older man spoke with authority. "Who the hell are you?"

"Frisco's man. *Capisce?*"

The hell? Chuy was going all Godfather.

Baldy shifted. Going for a gun? Farting? They'd never know because his movement was enough for Chuy to swing the gun around and fire.

Of course, he missed. But the older guy drew his piece and shot so quickly it sounded like a machine gun blast.

He missed, too. By then, I'd aimed and fired, sending Baldy to the ground. When his partner fell, the old guy had a split second to panic. His hesitation cost him as Chuy got lucky enough to hit something. In a matter of seconds it was all over and the delivery guys were dead, or would be soon.

Chuy turned his gun on the girl. "Where is it?" he yelled. His hand shook and his eyes had a crazy gleam.

Voice low she answered. "Where's what?"

"You know." He waved his hand. "Where is it?"

"I told you, he didn't talk business to me."

That didn't satisfy Chuy. He ran at her.

Roman took no time to regret his one chance at a future. The opportunity to be one of Frisco's main men, get some of the good things in life for himself. He gladly threw it away with the twitch of his finger.

One gunshot. Two stuttering steps until Chuy's momentum fizzled. He crumpled to the concrete floor, blood oozing to mingle with that of the delivery guys.

The girl spun around and ran to the office and Roman thought she was trying to escape from him.

He followed her. "You have to get out of here. Now."

Behind the desk she fumbled with boxes of supplies. She tossed aside several that looked empty and wrapped her arms around one box marked as shop rags. With a grunt, she hefted it. "Not without this."

Roman flipped open the top of the box. Stacks of cash banded in white paper. Fifties. How much could that box hold?

She didn't resist as Roman took the box from her and ran out of the office, hurdling Baldy and skirting around the old guy.

"Come on. No one knows you're here. Get as far away as possible and don't look back."

Her footsteps sounded behind his as he raced to her sporty BMW and threw the box into the backseat.

She sprinted to the driver's side and opened the door. "Come with me."

They wouldn't be sharing the front seat of a rusted Chevy. With the money in that box, they'd be making love on crisp sheets in a fancy hotel, drinking room service champagne.

But only until Frisco found them.

"I can't."

Those eyes zeroed in on him. "You feel it. I know you do." In a whisper she added, "You and me."

Roman had never wanted anything so much as he wanted to be with her. "Frisco will never let me go."

She flung her arm out to the delivery men's pickup. "Frisco has the shipment."

"He's gonna want the money, too."

She looked in the backseat, then focused on Roman. She was smart enough to know that if she took the money, Roman would be a dead man. She opened the back door, grabbed the box, and dashed back to the warehouse.

Roman chased her. "No. You need that. Start your pie shop. Live a good life."

She planted the box on the floor and grabbed Roman by the hand, dragging him to the Beemer. "I'd rather have you."

He dug his feet in. "You don't even know me."

"I know enough."

"No. I'm not worth your dream."

She put her hands on her hips and showed her temper for the first time. "I don't need his money to make my dream come true." She gave him a shove toward the car. "But I need you."

He climbed into the passenger seat and they drove from the warehouse district, turned north and kept driving until they no longer saw the lights of Tucson. She stopped the car on a hilltop, and they walked hand and hand to an outcropping of rocks.

They contemplated the gleaming stars over the desert. He buried his face in her hair and inhaled her soft scent. "I'm Roman, by the way."

She was silent for a beat, then tilted her head and let out a throaty laugh. All that dark hair tumbled down her back and her eyes twinkled.

A flush of embarrassment made him defensive. "What?"

The mischievous grin nearly stopped his heart but what she said next changed everything. "I'm Julia."

Roman couldn't stop gazing in those eyes until she closed them and kissed him with the kind of affection money can't buy.

† † †

Despite nearly daily declarations she's giving up writing forever, **SHANNON BAKER** has managed to complete not only this story but ten novels in three mystery series, a standalone dark suspense, as well as a few contemporary romances published under a pen name. A lover of Arizona sunsets viewed with a cold cocktail on her Tucson deck, Baker is, and always will be, a Nebraska Cornhusker. Go Big Red. Shannon-Baker.com

INVOICE OVERDUE
MYSTI BERRY

LIZZIE Street knew she was in a world of hurt the minute she logged into the South Mountain Community College virtual faculty lounge. The other instructors in her Health Science department didn't greet her or acknowledge her small talk. She knew as well as any of them that the first rule of Gossip Club is you don't talk to the gossip target, but before she could figure out why it was her turn to be the object of discussion, her phone buzzed.

BOARD CHAIR OFFICE ZOOM. NOW.

With a smooth hand developed over years of online instruction, Lizzie clicked out of the virtual lounge and requested entry to the Board office "green room," which was neither green nor a room—just a place in cyberspace to wait nervously for the Board chair, Dr. Ringel. Upon her arrival, the Health Science Board assistant nodded at Lizzie, eyes unexpressive above her mask, and then clicked her into Dr. Ringel's virtual office. Lizzie saw the Board Chair's perfect salt-and-pepper haircut and wondered how he'd managed it during the pandemic. She'd been stuck in a ponytail for months, waiting until it was safe. If it was ever going to be safe again.

Dr. Ringel made no small talk, but that was normal for him. He said, "Did you see the billboard this morning?"

She shook her head no. She hadn't driven her normal commute to the campus in months.

He said, "Someone put your name on a billboard near the campus, something about an overdue invoice? For fifty thousand dollars."

Lizzie laughed nervously. "Is the billboard a student prank?"

"Most of our students can't afford books, much less billboards. *Jah?*"

Lizzie's gut tightened. He only lapsed into German when he

was very, very upset.

Dr. Ringel leaned back and crossed his arms, nearly disappearing into his fake background of a cavernous room in the Berlin Library. "Go. View the billboard and resolve this. Until you do, your classes will be handled this week by Gary."

The meeting window closed without warning, leaving Lizzie feeling slapped.

Gary was the worst Health instructor on campus. Dr. Ringel's message rang loud and clear: if she didn't fix this, she'd be replaced, even if he had to use Gary to do it.

† † †

LIZZIE sat in her car, staring at the billboard, sweating despite the early hour. She rolled both front windows down since no one else was around, hoping the air would circulate a little bit. The billboard was off I-10, just before the Baseline exit. She'd had to get off at Baseline and circle back in order to park close enough to examine the thing. From the freeway, she recognized her own name and a red INVOICE OVERDUE stamp. The rest of the message was blurred columns of text and numbers, like a real invoice but with very small print. Now parked and able to see the billboard quite clearly, she realized the text and numbers were deliberately blurred. But she noticed in the corner of the sign, a modest logo for a podiatrist. The one she'd been cyber-flirting with since shortly after the start of the lockdown.

Guilt squeezed Lizzie, made her breath rapid, shallow breaths. She'd had just one physical appointment with him before the pandemic—they'd started flirting not long after lockdown. Well, more than flirting, if she was being honest with herself. But who could know about it, much less be so crazy as to put up a billboard? Not her husband Brian—he was a Luddite of the first order and had never cracked her phone or desktop passwords, she was sure of it. So, either the podiatrist had lost his ever-loving mind, or…his wife was on to them. Lizzie had spent a lot of time not thinking about Mrs. Dr. Sexy. He'd never said much about her. Would he have mentioned his wife if she was this crazy?

A woman's voice interrupted Lizzie's reverie. "Kind of shocking to see it in black and white like that, isn't it?"

A woman reached in the car to open the passenger door and slipped into her car. She settled into the seat as if she'd been invited.

Lizzie flinched. "Get out!" She frantically snatched her COVID mask off the dashboard and, fingers trembling, put it on.

The stranger's eyes crinkled over her own mask. Lizzie couldn't tell if she was smiling or sizing her up. The slender blonde intruder pulled an envelope from her back jeans pocket and dropped it in the console between them. Lizzie trembled in fear, dreading what was coming. She wanted to push the woman out of her car, and drive home, take a few sleeping pills and nap this nightmare away. But she sat still, waiting, dreading what came next.

The woman said, "It's all there. The amount of time you've spent with my husband online, the disgusting pictures you swapped, all of it. The billing time of my new psychiatrist at his rate, since our insurance doesn't cover it. And a modest amount to cover future shrink time for my son and daughter."

"What?"

The woman leaned close to Lizzie. "You cyber-dallied with my husband. You owe me."

"Are you crazy? We were just emailing and texting. I've never even met your husband."

The other woman leaned back. "So, are you as bad in bed as you are at lying?"

Lizzie snapped back, "If you had a better marriage, you wouldn't have to snoop in his private things."

The woman stared at Lizzie, eyes cold and hot at the same time. It terrified her.

Then the blonde shook herself and chuckled. "Did my husband ever tell you what I do for a living?"

Lizzie shook her head, silently praying that hog butcher wasn't the answer.

She said, "I work in cloud computing. I've told my husband a thousand times that nothing on the Internet is truly private. Now, on your drive home from your humiliating week's suspension—"

"How do you know about that?"

"I just told you, my day job is in the cloud. Think about all the digital trails your inappropriate, anti-feminist, dishonorable virtual affair with my husband are flickering in cyberspace. So easy to follow the metadata trail you left."

Lizzie said, "You have to take down this billboard. My career is at stake."

The woman laughed at Lizzie, a long, delighted laugh. "I don't care what happens to you at all." And then with the voice of an executioner, she said, "Pay your invoice, or those blurred words will turn into your text messages and 'love photos.' Everyone will know the nasty, disgusting person you really are."

The woman slipped out of her car and trotted away as silently as she had arrived. Lizzie watched her move away, never looking back, until she disappeared into a tree line beyond the vacant lot where the billboard loomed above her, shouting out her virtual infidelity. She sat for many long minutes, hearing nothing but her own breath through the mask, unable to think. When she got too hot, Lizzie fired up the engine and drove off, trying hard to convince herself it had all been a fever dream, a hallucination born of being housebound for so long.

One look at the very tangible billboard brought her back to reality. Everyone in town would see it if she didn't act quickly. Lizzie wondered what Mrs. Dr. Sexy really wanted from her. This couldn't really be just about the money. She'd glimpsed something in the other woman's eyes, something terrifying.

Lizzie had never felt this scared in her life.

As she left the billboard behind and headed toward home, she thought about her husband, furloughed, waiting for his assistant manager job to return when restaurants could open again. In the meantime, he watched an unending stream of kung fu movies and found new ways to cook hamburger. He was, she thought, just one spliff shy of being her very own stoner on the couch, like the Big Lebowski. No wonder she'd dallied, remotely, with the one man who'd touched her in the last year. Even if it was just her feet.

† † †

"HOW was your day?" Brian asked, the same as he greeted her after every workday—and lately just anticipating it set Lizzie's teeth on edge. She grunted out her habitual answer but thought about confessing her sin so she could ask him for help. She'd been telling herself all these weeks that a cyber-flirtation was no harm to anybody, especially during COVID, with half the city sequestered. She wasn't that into her husband these days, if she were being honest. But she didn't want to hurt him with the truth.

She begged off more conversation, complaining of all the work that needed doing this first week of classes, then dashed into the basement where she had worked since Brian lost his job and stayed home all day. In a frenzy, Lizzie deleted all of the texts and emails from Dr. Sexy, then cleared her browser history. She knew to do that much from watching *Forensic Files*. She couldn't relax though, knowing Mrs. Dr. Sexy probably had Dr. Sexy's text history as proof of the relationship.

Lizzie stood up and paced in her six-by-eight basement office, thinking. She didn't have the tens of thousands of dollars Mrs. Dr. Sexy was demanding. She probably knew that. Lizzie's throat tightened. It was very likely she wanted nothing but Lizzie's public humiliation. This kind of scandal could cost not only her current job, but risk other opportunities too, even in a city as large as Phoenix. How could she and Brian survive in the middle of a pandemic with a mortgage and no income? They'd spent their savings just getting the house.

Lizzie jumped when she heard a knock at her office door.

"Honey? You've been in here for ages. You have to eat something." Brian sounded concerned, which made her face flush with guilt and her gut churn from panic. She let him in after mussing a bunch of papers around to make it look like she had been working. He placed a tray of sangria and chips and salsa on the edge of her desk, and pecked her cheek.

He murmured, "You're so clever. I hope your students appreciate you as much as I do," and padded back out, pulling the door gently behind him.

Lizzie had never felt worse in her life. She wasted time on some guy she barely knew because he was something new in her dull days. Something slightly forbidden. Lizzie ate the chips and salsa but couldn't taste them. She guzzled a glass of sangria but it, too, was little solace.

Her phone buzzed, startling Lizzie. Then she thought perhaps it was Dr. Sexy, aware of his wife's wild behavior, a solution in hand. He always sounded as if he knew everything—maybe this time he did.

Lizzie opened her phone and saw, heart sinking, that it was an unknown number. Mrs. Dr. Sexy.

ARE YOU READY?

Lizzie's stomach soured. It was that woman again. She texted back:

CAN'T WE TALK ABOUT THIS LIKE GROWNUPS?

The answer was a screenshot of one of her racier texts with Dr. Sexy.

Lizzie thought a minute, then texted:

WHAT DO YOU REALLY WANT?

The reply came immediately.

YOU RUINED MY MARRIAGE. NOW RUIN YOURS.
TELL HIM.

As if it had suddenly come alive, Lizzie dropped her phone and kicked it across the room. She simply couldn't tell Brian about her virtual infidelity. She knew "virtual" was an excuse, and that she'd break Brian's heart when he had nowhere else to go, no other way to survive.

Her throat ached the way it always did before she started crying. To stave off the tears, she drank another glass of sangria. It hit her hard, that second glass.

"In tequila *veritas*," she mumbled to herself, realizing there was nothing she could do but tell Brian. She yelled for him through the closed door. With dread in her heart, she listened to him thud down the stairs. He opened the office door and she saw his sad, pudgy face blinking at her.

"What's wrong?"

Where could she start? How could she explain? Her tongue thick, all she could get out was, "I'm sorry. I'm sorry..."

Lizzie felt dizzy, and it was hard to breathe. Too much adrenaline she thought. When she could finally look her husband in the face, what she saw shocked her. Instead of her doughy, flat-gazed house husband, Brian's eyes glittered with excitement.

Like Mrs. Dr. Sexy.

His lips were a hard, sardonic line, not the soft lips curved in perpetual half-smile that she was used to.

Brian said, "Huh. I bet Maria a hundred dollars you'd do

anything to avoid the truth. I guess she knew you better than I did after researching your every move on the Internet."

"Maria?" Lizzie's slurred, dizziness turning into full-body nausea.

Mrs. Dr. Sexy, Maria, slipped into the office from behind Brian, grinning.

Maria said, "That husband of mine never even told you my first name?"

Brian put an arm around Maria's waist and pulled her into a lustful kiss. Lizzie wanted to jump up and shout her outrage, but she couldn't move. She could barely speak.

Lizzie managed to knock the tray of sangria and snacks over, and then stared at the mess.

Brian said, "Oh honey, I'm afraid you really can't do anything. Maria has fixed it so the only trail of contact is between you and the good doctor. Right now, he's dying from poisoned sangria, the same as you are, right Maria?"

She slid one hand up Brian's portly midsection all the way to his neck, and then kissed him hard. Performatively, Lizzie thought, pleased she could still remember the word.

Maria said, "There's some emails between you tonight—sprinkled liberally with your favorite words and phrases for authenticity. I've been studying your correspondences for a few months now. Your final email makes it clear that you two just couldn't stand being discovered."

Brian peered closely at Lizzie, who couldn't move at all now. "It's perfect." He went back to cuddling Maria and beamed at her as he pecked her cheek. "You're so clever."

Lizzie felt a little pang of jealousy as the phrase he'd said to her so many times now pointed to Maria. But mostly she felt a rage against death itself—a rage she was too drugged to express, dying from what she guessed were her own sleeping pills in the sangria.

Maria nuzzled Brian. "I especially like how she stayed away from the house so long today. We could finally consummate our own virtual romance."

Lizzie looked away, but still heard the sickening sound of them kissing.

Her heart beat slower, her breathing grew more and more shallow. Her body told her that opportunity was fading fast. She tried, but couldn't form the words to warn Brian that, if Maria was anything like the killers from her forensics shows, he was likely to be victim number three before another year was out.

She realized that she didn't hate Brian. She could see now, as never before, that her invoice had indeed been overdue. Not for the things Maria said. Lizzie had built the cage of her own unhappiness: she never gave Brian a chance to be a better husband. COVID isolation ground down on him harder than her, with her day job and therefore, more of her pride intact. She'd betrayed him with the flimsiest of excuses, telling herself that remote wasn't real. Of course, Maria and Brian were even worse than she and Dr. Sexy, killing their own spouses under the protective isolation of the pandemic.

How could the four of them have become so inhuman so quickly, she wondered, as the last of her reason flickered. Perhaps they had always been that way, hidden from their own monstrosity in the cocoon of a comfortable life.

† † †

MYSTI BERRY has an MFA in Writing from the University of San Francisco, but never lets that get in the way of a good story. She lives in San Francisco with graphic novelist husband Dale Berry. Her short stories have appeared in *Ellery Queen Mystery Magazine, Alfred Hitchcock Mystery Magazine,* a variety of anthologies, and has exactly one page in the upcoming *How to Write a Mystery* (MWA). She is also the editor of the *Low Down Dirty Vote* anthology series. Mysti is honored to serve as President of the Desert Sleuths chapter of Sisters in Crime. MystiBerry.com

ALMOST DARK NOW
MEREDITH BLEVINS

SHE watched him standing in the window, a pale figure fading as the sun wandered behind jagged hills. She had nurtured him, propped him up, and eased him into love. It was too much to see him now, swallowed by shadows. Eaten by his own expectations. Too fragile for life. It was, in short, time to call it quits.

He turned to her, just then, and he knew what she was thinking. (She had tried to turn away, but she wasn't quick enough.)

Vivianne smiled, just a small smile, and held out her hand to him.

"We'll be late," he said.

"I don't mind, do you?" she answered.

Richard didn't mind, not much, but it was an important evening for him.

The sky was streaked with stray threads of orange and pink, the tail-end of sunset, when their clothes fell to the floor. The McDowell Mountains peaked through the windows, spied on them, and they weren't even embarrassed. (Mountains are like that.)

Vivianne would make him forget what he had seen in her face. She knew how to do that.

Dark now, the room was almost dark now, as dark as it would get, anyway. They untangled and found their clothes and, still tender, they dressed each other. He kissed the patch of peach skin on the back of her neck. She held his fingers to her mouth.

He flipped on the lights. She walked to the closet, added a pair of panty-hose, and looked at herself in the mirror. Not great, but as good as it was going to get and, at least for tonight, it was all right.

"Is that what you're going to wear?" he asked.

Yes, it was what she was going to wear. This conversation wouldn't go well. She'd bend it around until everything was all right.

She said, "Is it too…?"

"Yes. It's tight."

She didn't care if it was too tight, but she would make him happy, happy for now. She could do that. She slipped on a different dress, it was silk, so slippery-fine, silk the color of ancient earth on the rim of the Grand Canyon. The color of a gorge.

Dinner with the other couple went the way she'd expected. Vivianne and the wife small-talked their way through four courses, and Richard tried too hard with the husband. Watching him in business conversation, desperate for investors, desperate for a lifeline, was like watching a drowning man. A man too far from the shore to rescue.

She had loved him in the beginning. In the beginning, she would have dragged him out of the restaurant, and out of his humiliation, if only for his astonishing beauty. That was a long time ago.

The two men promised to get in touch, and the two wives knew that they wouldn't. They couldn't even think of one word to say to each other as they waited for their cars. The valet bounced around and somehow remembered, without looking, which keys belonged to which couple.

Driving home, Richard performed an autopsy on the body of the evening. She kept her face relaxed so he wouldn't see the dance her small muscles did over her jaw.

The mountains were deep indigo, slashed with gray ridges and dotted with cactus. She so admired the cactus's will to live. The way they had changed to save their own lives. Turning their leaves into spines, over time, to keep the sun from sucking their juice. She understood, 100%.

They pulled into the drive, the round, long driveway of their home, tucked into the hills north of Scottsdale, tucked into a pretense of well-being and comfort.

He dropped the car keys into a bowl that sat on the cabinet in the entryway. "Vivi, do you think I pushed too hard?"

Around other people, he called her Vivianne. When they were alone, he called her Vivi, as if shortening her name was an act of intimacy. When they were alone, she called him Richard. When they were with other people, she called him Rick.

"Richard, I thought you were splendid. Truly." She wasn't telling a lie. He had looked splendid. It only went to hell when he talked himself into corners and couldn't get out. If only he had been an artist. No talking required.

She poured him a glass of wine. It was a good bottle. (She'd opened it before they went out, giving it time to breathe, time to absorb the taint of toxin.) He upended his glass and gestured for more. Faint light caught a hint of sadness as Vivi poured. Faint light caught her resolve.

He sighed, ran fine fingers through his hair—it was going gray. "Sometimes I think I should have stuck with painting, Vivianne. I feel lost in my life. Sometimes I feel lost, Vivi."

Sometimes he did feel lost, and she was amazed when he said that. It was so real. Just then, he almost shed his shadow-bitten edges.

He said, "Why don't we spend the weekend in Sedona? We need a getaway. Let's have a getaway. No talk of business."

"I would like that." She said it and she meant it and right then she wished she hadn't poured him a glass of wine, of strangely tinted wine. She wished she wasn't the one who had made the dough, hadn't bought the swanky digs. She wished she could take it back, take all of it. Back.

Richard said, "Maybe we can stop into that gallery, the one that wanted me once."

"They might still, you know. They might still want you." She wanted him, and she thought of calling 911.

Slowly he slipped to the floor, soft as a memory, right through the tile. That's what it looked like to her as she eased herself down with him.

She cradled his box-bone head and imagined what might still be inside it, inside that lovely vessel.

Richard said, "Vivi, I'm tired, so tired."

She told him he could sleep, he could rest. She rocked him, stroked him.

Richard opened his eyes, he opened them wide just then (it surprised her, startled her a little), and he saw her, really saw her. It had been a long time. "Vivianne. I want to roll your name around my tongue as if it's wine. I do."

She smiled, just a small smile, and he understood what she was thinking. What had happened.

"Thank you," he said, almost a deep purr. "Thank you."

And then Richard closed his eyes, as if in prayer. She wondered if he could see her still, could see her as he drifted away.

A sliver of moon was pinned above them, a crescent that looked like a silver smile, floating on a black sea, surrounded by star-glitter. The moon pulsed little light on the intractable-irascible desert, that holy midden, that sacred ground. Vivianne wrapped her arms around Richard, shielding him, protecting him from stillborn dreams shaped like broken wings. Wings unable to fly.

† † †

MEREDITH BLEVINS has been a marketing queen, college professor, and writer of mystery and fantasy books. She is currently writing travel and playing with an erotic mystery series. Meredith has lived in the southwest since dinosaurs roamed the earth, and believes in saying *YES* to just about everything. She is married and has a bunch of kids and grandkids, a tangible result of the *YES* factor. MeredithAndWinBlevins.com

TRIED AND TRUE
Patricia Bonn

"**A** silhouette against the dying sun, the figure on the bluff, buffeted by the ocean breeze, embraced the coming darkness as a balm for a troubled soul. The island held secrets…"

"What a load of horse shit!"

Madeline swallowed her own obscenity as she peered over her glasses to her ninety-five-year-old twin sister, Caroline. Always the diplomat of the two, she smiled to hide the murderous designs she carried most of her life for her sibling.

"What seems to be the issue, Sister?"

"A cheesy opening for one thing. It reads like a juvenile romance novel instead of the intro to a world-class mystery. For God's sake, where do you get such drivel? It's a wonder we've sold any books at all."

Quite the contrary, the sisters had been *New York Times* bestsellers for the past thirty years. Their awards included every recognition obtainable in the mystery genre. Extraordinary since their collaboration commenced when widowed in their sixties. More curious was their success despite the siblings' lifelong hate/hate relationship.

"It's called foreshadowing, Sister, to hook the reader to delve further into the story for answers about the person on the bluff and the island secrets."

Caroline was not in the mood for mollification. Truth be told, she was never in the mood. "Who the hell cares about a silhouette? Let's kill off some poor unsuspecting fool. Action's what we need to draw the suckers who buy our books. A knife in the ribs. A blunt object to the head. Mowed down by an Uzi. Get the message out there in the first sentence. There's a murder mystery to be solved."

As much as the sisters were loath to admit it, neither would have been a bestselling author without her sibling. Opposites in personality, Caroline's masterful plotting and Madeline's inspired use of language blended into one bestseller after another. The process of writing, however, was one filled with its own threat of violence.

"Very well, *Caroline*. How would you suggest we dispatch the victim on the bluff? The tried and true? Push him or her into the rocks below?"

"*Madeline*, a shove off the cliff is overdone and boring. It's a cliché. I must conceive a shocking death to grab the reader's attention."

"A gruesome death would work if we wrote a thriller."

The sharp-edged commentary continued like a tennis match between the two diminutive women hidden behind their large computer monitors. Their desks faced one another to accommodate hearing and vision loss which manifested itself in their eighties. An unhappy compromise between two people who preferred to work from separate rooms, frankly different continents, but whose volatile relationship proved essential to success.

Despite, or perhaps because of hours of harping, swearing, and general verbal mayhem, the first draft of chapter one was saved. Like boxers returning to their respective corners, the sisters retreated to their bedroom suites at opposite ends of the single-level home, a pattern established early in their lives. Identical twins who couldn't have been more dissimilar. They were as strangers somehow linked at birth. Even when quite young, they chose separate paths. Different high schools, one West Coast university and one East Coast institution. Visits to the family home on the southern slope of Camelback Mountain in Phoenix occurred as necessary with husbands and children in tow. Widowhood forced each to face unpleasant financial realities.

Their mother had recently passed in a care facility preceded by their father who died a decade prior. The house could be an investment to fund the future if sold or a secure refuge as the sisters faced an uncertain future. They reluctantly chose the latter.

CHAPTER FIVE

CAROLINE opened her eyes to see Madeline poised at her bedside with a pillow grasped in both hands.

"What the hell are you doing, Sister?"

Without hesitation, Madeline replied while fluffing the pillow, "You snored louder than the coyote howls. I assumed an extra pillow under your head would help."

"I'm sure that's why you're in my bedroom at three a.m. Nice try but suffocation with a pillow is passé. Good night, Sister. Close the door on your way out."

Madeline dropped the pillow at the foot of the bed as she left the bedroom. *Too bad, it worked so well in our third book,* Murder Under the Sun.

† † †

THE arrival of the sisters' housekeeper and personal assistant set mornings in motion. The employment agency's grueling search to find two individuals who could handle the sisters' idiosyncrasies threatened the agent's own sanity. The tasks these women performed were straightforward. The housekeeper, María José, spoke only Spanish in the house and ignored any attempts of communication in English, a strategy to avoid conversing with her fractious employers. Fluent in three languages, including English, she added Italian in anticipation of planned travel to Italy. Annie, the personal assistant, was so perpetually cheerful she lapped up the insults as if she were a goofy Lab and the ugly words were praise.

"*Buenos días, señoras. ¿Como fue el escrito?*"

"Goddammit." Caroline looked from her perusal of the newspaper obituaries. "Why don't you people learn how to speak English? Never mind, you don't understand me anyway." She returned to reading as María José smiled and went about her duties.

"Sister, please. Don't speak so rudely." Madeline sat at the opposite end of the long dining room table. "You know how difficult it was to find her."

"Huh, there's a million like her crossing the border right now."

"STOP!" Madeline's sharp rebuke caused her twin to clench her fists, the newspaper crackled in Caroline's hands. "As long as I live in this house, you will treat our staff with respect." *What a relief it would be if Caroline would only die and leave her in peace. It would not look suspicious to stop writing at her age and in mourning. Ha! Mourning, as if.*

The door opened and heels clicked on the parquet floor. "Oh God, here comes Mary Sunshine," Caroline muttered loud enough to draw a sharp glance from Madeline.

Goddammit, what I would give to be free of these three meddlesome women. If it's not the goofy lab bouncing around then it's the immigrant with a knowing smile. And Madeline, good God, why can't she just slip into a coma or something.

Annie bounded into the room like a lab puppy just off leash. "Good morning, ladies. I have the edits of yesterday's chapter and I must say it is one of your best. We have some business to attend to this morning, interview requests, book signings, contract stuff from the publisher. I'll be in the office when you're ready."

The office was the former family room converted to accommodate the business of writing thirty bestselling mysteries. Annie knew what the sisters wanted in their creative space and kept the room organized with research materials on one wall and filing cabinets on the opposite. Prior to widowhood, Madeline had moderate success in writing mystery short stories and toyed with the idea of a novel-length manuscript. Caroline discovered the outline and declared any idiot could write an intriguing whodunnit to appeal to mystery readers and publishers. The gauntlet thrown; the twins had a draft for the chilling mystery which would become their first bestseller. Neither expected to be writing thirty years later. Each believed the other would have died by now.

Annie efficiently led them through the business side of authorship and then left them to battle out the next chapters. The storyline included another victim of the killer and the sisters disagreed on how to get rid of him or her. Caroline's most recent suggestion was particularly gruesome, and her sister objected.

"Our readers don't want that level of violence." Madeline read from a page of their research notes, "Hmm, we've used poison, gun, knife, asphyxia, the generic blunt object, hanging, and pushed from a height, in front of a train, or other speeding vehicle. We seem to be out of murder ideas."

Caroline harrumphed. "There are unlimited ways for human beings to dispatch one another. You have no imagination."

CHAPTER TWENTY-SIX

THE sisters took a customary break mid-afternoon for tea and a snack. They were in good health despite their age but fatigued after hours in literary battle. Madeline brought a plate of cookies to the kitchen table where Caroline sipped her tea.

"Sister, try these. I saw them in the case at AJ's and they looked delicious."

Caroline picked one absentmindedly and opened her mouth before she closed it abruptly. She sniffed as she held it under her nose.

"Madeline, is it possible these cookies have nuts?"

"Oh dear, I didn't think. I'm so sorry. I forgot about your nut allergy."

"Anaphylactic shock skipped your mind?"

"It was an honest mistake and I said I'm sorry." *It wasn't a mistake and I'm sure as hell not sorry.*

† † †

DAYS of creative mayhem passed as the sisters worked their way through Caroline's intricate pace and plot. Madeline considered her twin's plot machinations convoluted but couldn't argue with success.

Annie bounced in every weekday with edits, results of research questions, and other minutiae of writing. Madeline questioned why Caroline insisted on setting scenes in locales to which the sisters had never traveled. Without a doubt, Provence and the Outer Banks of North Carolina were lovely, but she had to rely on Annie's research to supply the visual details.

The manuscript was coming along nicely. Long, hot summer days didn't allow them outside to enjoy the lush landscaping or the vistas from their elevated position on the mountainside. The sisters had attained a point where the story would drag if they didn't keep it fresh. To avoid the doldrums, they took a week from writing. They could afford an executive car and driver to take day drives out of the valley to Sedona, of course, individually and on different days. Madeline enjoyed a spa day and later in the week a visit to the Phoenix Art Museum followed by lunch at Durant's. Caroline binge watched true crime programs, using María José for her personal room service. The following week they were back to work.

† † †

"IT'S time for a bathroom break, Sister." Caroline stood and stretched to her full height of five feet nothing. She removed her glasses to massage the bridge of her nose and walked to her bathroom. Madeline mirrored her sister's action only to turn back when Sister was out of sight to exchange their glasses. Like all else, their prescriptions were vastly different. They returned to the desks, grasped their eyeglasses and Caroline stepped away. She routinely did a few tai chi movements to loosen her muscles. Her sister's glasses distorted her depth perception, and she lost her balance.

María José carried fresh water into the office when she saw Caroline stagger. She lunged for her and wrapped her free arm around the nonagenarian's waist to save her from a nasty fall. Safely seated at her desk, she removed the glasses and shoved them in Madeline's direction.

"Nice try, Sister."

Madeline shrugged.

CHAPTER FORTY-ONE

OCTOBER was a perfect time for Thomas Butler, their New York agent, to visit the authors. No fool, he waited for cool weather to golf and swim at the resort's pool to his heart's content. His meetings with the sisters were strategically planned to be short and focused. With most of his clients, he enjoyed lingering conversations with highly intelligent and articulate individuals. The sisters met the standard, but irascible Caroline and competitive Madeline made for encounters destined for a migraine. Truth be told, he was afraid of them. Their small stature and advanced age hid a frightening reservoir of cunning. The innate trait manifested itself in thirty bestselling murder mysteries which, of course, reflected well on him. There was something Edgar Allen Poe creepy about them. His contractual duty completed, he bid the sisters adieu and fled back to the East coast.

† † †

AFTER their agent's departure, the sisters settled in for the push to finish the manuscript. However, Madeline had difficulty with her focus on the outline.

"Sister, I do so enjoy our young man's company. East coast polish in a handsome package. My, if I were a half a century younger, I'd jump his bones."

"God, Madeline, what an image. Why don't you apply your wistfulness to the task at hand?"

"Sister, I'm impressed. *Reader's Digest* improving your vocabulary?"

Caroline stilled. Madeline waited for the explosion of obscenities which failed to come.

"As much as I'd like to engage in *conversation* with you, we need to complete the chapter in which our protagonist, *remember him*, fails to achieve his objective. The story hangs on the verisimilitude of his crisis, another Jeopardy word, so let's get the hell to work!"

Madeline smiled. "Sister, I'm so glad you added that last phrase. I was beginning to worry about you."

With her usual obliviousness to the tension between the sisters, Annie bounced in gushing about the agent. "It was so nice to see Thomas again. I always enjoy his visits and I learn so much about the publishing business. He's generous in sharing his expertise."

"I bet that's not all he shares," Caroline muttered.

"Did you see the new cover? It captures the essence of the story without giving anything away."

"*What new cover?*" Madeline skewered her sister with a look.

"Oh, I thought you knew, Miss Madeline. During your summer break, Miss Caroline had a new idea for the cover and it truly is extraordinary. It will catch the eyes of readers who are not already your fans. I'll let you ladies get back to work."

"*How dare you!* What gave you the right to decide without even the courtesy of telling me? My name is on the cover, too."

"Don't get your panties in a bunch, Madeline. It was a simple marketing decision and does nothing to interfere with your writing contributions to the book. I assumed you wouldn't mind."

"Of course, you didn't." *If Caroline imagines she can push me aside, she has another thing coming.*

CHAPTER FIFTY-SIX

IT was mid-afternoon on a beautiful day in late October. The patio doors were open, and a light breeze blew in through the screen doors.

"This cooler weather has increased my appetite. I think I'll make myself a snack." Madeline stood and walked into the kitchen. She carried a stepstool to a cupboard, climbed to get a cast iron griddle.

"Sister," she called out, "would you come and help me?"

Swearing, Caroline entered the kitchen to see her sister standing precariously on a stool and pulling something heavy and black off a shelf.

"Goddammit. Why didn't you ask María for help? I should let you kill yourself."

Madeline watched her sister move to stand beside the stool and place her hand on her back to steady her. The griddle slipped from Madeline's grasp to drop in the direction of her sister's head. Caroline spotted it in her peripheral vision. She let go of her sister and fell to the floor, landing on her butt. The griddle landed with a thunderous whack that reverberated through the kitchen. It settled precariously close to Caroline's brittle legs.

"Oh, God. Sister, are you all right?" Madeline remained on the stool clinging onto a shelf.

The commotion brought María José running into the kitchen.

"*¡Ay Díos mío! ¡El comál!*"

Speaking rapidly in Spanish, the housekeeper lowered Madeline from the stepstool and sat her at the kitchen table. María José turned her attention to Caroline and gently pulled her to stand. She walked the diminutive woman to the table to sit opposite her sister, and then placed her hand on her chest as if to calm her own panic.

"*¿Señoras, qué pasó?*"

Caroline eyed her sister with true malice. As if she were clueless to the intent of the incident, Madeline looked sheepishly at the housekeeper.

"I wanted a cheese crisp and didn't want to bother you. I guess the griddle was heavier than I remembered."

"Cheese crisp? Ah, *una quesadilla.*" María José busied herself with the task of making the snack.

The sisters sat at the table in silence. Madeline blithely ignored her twin's palpable hostility. *Sure Madeline, look innocent. You've never used a griddle in your entire annoying life. I am mighty weary of her bungled attempts to do me harm. She is necessary in the short term to finish the manuscript. After that, we shall see.*

† † †

THE holidays came and went as the sisters completed the manuscript. As they waited for the galleys, they went about the business of writing with conference calls with various staff members of their publishing house. Annie assisted with the details of a book launch. Caroline and Madeline didn't travel so book tours were impossible. As bestselling authors, an event at The Poisoned Pen in Scottsdale would be enough to promote the latest in their murder mystery series.

THE LAST CHAPTER

THE sisters owned a Lincoln Town Car and, by some miracle, they both had restricted drivers' licenses. It had been a year to the day since they faced off to write the latest novel. Each sister went about her daily routine without regard to the other. One of those routines included collecting the mail. The mailbox chimed when the postal carrier delivered mail. The box was located at the end of a long, steep driveway which ended at the curve of their cul-de-sac.

One sister walked with a cane by the pool and took the brick steps at the front gate to the mailbox. Another routine, her twin drove to AJ's for something sweet. She backed the big car out of the carport and aimed it to the street below. Gas pedal depressed, the car hurled down the incline toward the mailbox. The ninety-five-year-old with her cane was no match for the bulk and weight of the Lincoln. When hit, she was airborne before she landed in a crumpled heap in the street.

Behind the wheel, her sister pushed the hands-free phone button.

"Nine-one-one. What is your emergency?"

A hysterical voice answered, "Oh my God! What have I done? I was confused…and I pressed the gas…I…my sister, oh no, she can't be dead!"

"Ma'am, assistance is on the way. Try to remain calm. Can you tell me your name?"

Between sobs, the dispatcher heard, "Caroline."

Oh, Sister. What did you make me do? Run down by a car. Trite, but tried and true. Madeline, you would have enjoyed the irony.

"Ma'am, are you okay?"

"I can't...catch my breath. The...pain, my chest..."

"Ma'am? Caroline?"

† † †

PATRICIA BONN is a native of San José, California, and has lived in the Phoenix area since 1969. For the past 10 years SinC/DS has been a perfect home for a writer working by fits and start toward the ultimate goal of a novel manuscript. Also, one whose style is in search of a genre. A playwright as well as an author, her original plays on topics of social justice have been produced locally. She was awarded Second place, Arizona Authors Association 2007 Literary Contest in the Short Story category. "Never Left Behind" appeared in the 2015 Desert Sleuths anthology. AuthorPatriciaBonn.com

TURNABOUT
LAUREN BUCKINGHAM

"GOING somewhere, Mom?"

Emma Blaylock turned and sighed. Her son didn't miss a trick.

Connor glanced up from his calculus textbook and looked at her with suspicion.

Emma shifted her gaze to her purse and fumbled with her keys. "I'm going out for the evening." She looked over at Connor. "Will you be okay here?"

He nodded. "I'll be fine." He paused for a moment. "Will you?"

"Yes." She hesitated, unsure of what to say next. In not so many words, Connor had made his sentiments known how he felt about her dating again so soon, and about her dating Lance Pearson, in particular.

"What is he, anyway, like thirty?"

"He's...in his thirties." Emma clenched her jaw. It was times like this that she wished she hadn't raised her son to be so inquisitive.

"Uh-huh," Connor muttered and turned back to his schoolwork.

"I get the feeling you don't approve, but—"

"I never said that."

"You didn't have to."

If only Connor and his friends hadn't stopped by the food court at Scottsdale Fashion Square while she and Lance were having lunch. She'd tried to choose a place where she wouldn't run into anyone she knew, especially not Connor, who disliked Scottsdale with a passion. He claimed his friends had wanted to hang out there for a change of scenery, and she had no reason not to believe him. He looked shocked to see her there on a date with Lance, or on a date with anyone, for that matter. Not that she could blame him, considering it had been a mere eight months since he'd lost his father. In some ways, it was as though more time had passed, but in other ways, it might as well have been yesterday.

She reached down to straighten her dress. She hadn't worn this dress, a clingy navy blue satin, in a while and was surprised it still fit her. It was perfect for tonight—alluring enough to capture Lance's attention, but not something she, a middle-aged mom, would be embarrassed to be seen wearing. She fought back tears, recalling how Brian used to tell her how this dress brought out the blue in her eyes.

"If you need anything tonight, please get hold of me, okay?"

Connor shrugged. "I won't be interrupting something?"

Emma smiled and swallowed hard. She moved into the living room, where Connor sat on the couch. She touched his shoulder. "I'm never too busy for you, sweetheart, you know that."

He nodded then looked away.

Emma took a seat on the couch next to her son and put her arm around him. "No matter what, no matter who else may come into our lives, I'm always going to be here for you."

"Thanks, Mom, I appreciate that." He half-smiled. "So, when will I get to meet Mr. Wonderful?"

Emma chuckled. "We'll see how things go tonight, but you don't have to do anything until you're ready."

"Fair enough." Connor stood up from the couch. "I think I'll drive over to Brad's house to study. He's really good at calculus, and I'm kind of struggling with it."

"It's fine." She stood and gave him a hug. She smoothed his hair, mindful of the jagged scar just above his left temple.

For an instant, she considered calling it all off, telling Lance to cancel their date tonight. She would stay home with Connor and try her best to help him with his homework. But, no. Lance was already expecting her, and if she really wanted to move forward with her life, tonight would have to be part of it.

"I'll see you later." Emma turned to leave and gathered up her purse from the coffee table. She turned to Connor and smiled. "I love you."

"Love you, too, Mom."

His words echoed as she stepped out of the house and locked the front door.

She would carry those words with her, especially tonight.

† † †

"Thank you for suggesting this restaurant," Emma said.

"Did you have any trouble finding it?"

"No, not at all." Emma took a sip of wine. "Between your instructions and my GPS, it was pretty easy to locate."

"Well, good, I'm glad you didn't have to waste a lot of time looking for this place." Lance grinned at her, a twinkle in his vibrant amber-colored eyes. "That gives us more time to spend together." He reached for the bread basket at the center of the table. "You know, if you'd let me pick you up at your house, we could spend even more time together."

Emma sighed. "I know, I know. It's just that my son's there, and, well, he's still getting used to the idea of my dating again."

"Understandable." Lance nodded. "This can't be easy for him, any of it."

"No, it isn't. Sixteen is a difficult enough age, then add to that everything else he's been through."

Lance gave her an empathetic nod, his eyes fixed on hers. "If you don't mind my asking, what happened to your husband?"

Her head tilted downward, and her eyes grew moist. Memories came flooding back to her. Emotions overwhelmed her whenever she allowed herself to think about the rollover accident that had killed her husband and left her with a few minor bumps and bruises. And a whole lot of survivor's guilt. The heartbreak when she recalled Connor waking up from the crash and asking about his father. Having to tell him Brian hadn't survived. After regaining her composure, Emma told Lance the full story.

"Oh, Emma, I'm so sorry. I had no idea." He gently clasped his hands over hers.

"It's all right." Emma slowly nodded. "I can't change what happened. All I can do is to keep going and be there for Connor, just as Brian would have wanted."

"How is Connor doing?"

"Physically, he's recovered quite well, but emotionally? That's hard to say. He says he's all right, but some days, I'm not so sure."

"Those would be some horrible memories to deal with at any age, but I imagine more so for somebody so young."

"I'm thankful Connor doesn't remember anything about the accident." Emma sniffled and bit her lip. "And I hope he never does."

"I hope he doesn't, either." Lance shook his head. "I suppose it would bring closure to you both if you could find whoever hit your car."

She stared at him, struggling to keep her emotions at bay. "It would help."

Just then, the server stopped at their table, a pizza plate in her hand.

"You ordered the fig, rosemary and gorgonzola white pizza, correct?"

"We did." Lance turned to Emma. "Trust me, you're going to like this."

Emma forced herself to smile. What she wouldn't have given right now to trade that fruit topped pizza with its cracker-thin crust for a thick crust pizza piled high with every topping on the menu, including anchovies, at her favorite pizza place in her neighborhood's strip mall.

The server set a plate in front of Emma. "Enjoy!"

Emma didn't hold out much hope but resolved to keep an open mind.

"Ladies first," Lance said, as he handed her the pizza cutter.

"Thanks." She began to slice through the brittle crust.

"So, you work in a law firm, right?"

Emma nodded, her concentration still focused on slicing the pizza.

"What exactly do you do there?"

"Research, mainly." She shrugged and carefully eased a wedge of pizza onto her plate.

"Research? That sounds interesting."

"It isn't, really. It's actually quite boring at times." She propped her chin on her hands and grinned at Lance. "Honestly, I'm more interested to hear about what you do. Tell me, how did you manage to build such a successful consulting business in less than five years?"

Lance chuckled. "I know it sounds like a cliché but, from the ground up."

He proceeded to describe in great detail how he started by

helping a friend grow a struggling sports bar he'd just taken over. That had been Lance's first taste of success in turning around failing businesses. He expanded his operation over the years. Considering how much Lance liked to talk about himself, getting him to boast about his life's work was the best decision she'd made all evening.

"That's quite a remarkable story," Emma said. So remarkable, she couldn't help but wonder how much of it was true.

Lance beamed proudly. "That it is, and it's the story of my life." He motioned to the nearly empty pizza plate. "Do you want the last piece?"

Emma shook her head. "You have it."

He scooped the slice of pizza. "Thanks." He looked back up at Emma. "You know, I had a really good time tonight."

She chuckled. "You almost sound surprised."

"No, I mean it. I really don't want this evening to end." He leaned forward, eyes twinkling. "Maybe it doesn't have to."

† † †

I'M glad you thought of this," Emma said. She flashed a smile at Lance. In the moonlight, she could see his broad, confident grin. He was staring straight ahead at the dimly lit path they had taken through the park.

"Sometimes, I come out here when I need to clear my head."

Emma nodded. "I'm sure it isn't always easy being you."

"Not always easy, but it's great being me." He laughed aloud. Emma caught a whiff of alcohol.

"Are you sure you'll be okay to drive?" she asked.

"I'll be fine. I haven't had that much to drink. I can hold a lot."

"Famous last words," Emma muttered under her breath.

Lance sighed. "I can understand your obsession with drinking and driving. Can't say I blame you. Someone drives after downing a fifth of gin, kills your husband, and badly injures your son."

She stood still for a moment then spun around to look him in the eye. "How did you know the driver who caused our accident was driving drunk?"

Lance froze but recovered quickly. "I just assumed so."

"I don't believe you. No one would have known for sure the driver was drunk. They definitely wouldn't speculate *what* the driver was drinking, or how much." She glared at him. "Unless, they were there."

He stayed silent.

Emma sneered, "I guess when you've been drinking, you tend to say—and do—stupid things. Like let things slip. Or drive drunk."

He curled his lip. "Are you happy now? That's what you were hoping for, wasn't it? To trip me up to prove I was the hit-and-run driver?"

"You can't deny it." Emma pointed a finger at him. "I saw you. Only for a split-second, but I remember you. I'll never forget your face as long as I live."

"And I know all about you too, Emma. You don't just do research at a law firm, you're their lead investigator." He grimaced. "If only you had stayed off my radar, hadn't gone snooping around, calling body shops, used car lots, trying to find my vehicle..."

He inched so close she could feel his voice vibrate through her body. "You must have thought a golden opportunity had dropped in your lap when you met me in the grocery store and I asked you out."

"I knew all along you intended to try to eliminate me as a problem. I had to take that risk if I hoped to make sure you paid for what you did." She looked him in the eyes and gave him a savage smile. "Now I have you."

"No." Lance grasped her shoulders. "Now I have *you*."

She reached for her purse, but Lance forced her hand away. He ripped the bag off her shoulder, then tossed it into a nearby patch of bushes.

"Too late to call for help, Emma. No one's going to save you now."

In an instant, Lance put his hands around her neck. Her heart pounded. She gasped for air.

He tightened his grip, his voice a menacing whisper. "You should have let it go, moved on with your life. Ruining my life won't bring your husband back."

Emma dug her nails into his hands and tried to pry his fingers from her throat. She struggled to breathe. Seeing Lance's face, lit only by the moon, and backlit by the faraway glow of the Phoenix skyline, was tragically familiar. Reminiscent of the glimpse of him in the headlights that night, when he slammed into their car and sent it tumbling. She felt it all again. Fear for the ones she loved. A sense she had only moments to live. Her life flashing before her eyes.

The pressure around her neck grew tighter.

She spotted a shadow. Not a shadow. A person.

She tried to scream, but only a muffled wail came out.

"It's almost over, Emma," Lance taunted her. "Soon, you and your dear Brian will be together again."

The figure came closer. Close enough for her to see who it was.

Her eyes grew wide with panic. Why was he here? Or was she hallucinating?

"Don't fight it anymore," Lance whispered. "You can't win."

Dizziness enveloped her. Her vision blurred. From the corner of her eye, she saw the figure pick up her purse and pull out her pistol.

The sound of two gunshots pierced the night air, and Lance's grip on her neck weakened. She peeled his hand back from her neck and broke free. He crumbled to the ground.

She steadied herself. Connor dropped the pistol and rushed to her side.

"Mom? Are you all right?"

Emma rubbed her throbbing neck and stared down at Lance's lifeless body. "I will be."

"It's over, Mom. I'll call nine-one-one," Connor said.

† † †

"**HOW** are you, Connor?" Emma sat down at the kitchen table. She clasped a mug of hot tea in her hands.

"I'm all right, Mom. Shouldn't I be asking you that question?"

Emma delicately touched the scarf wrapped around her neck. Underneath it were angry purple bruises, a reminder of Lance's hands on her neck, her struggle to breathe, and watching Connor take a life in order to save hers. The bruises would go away soon, but she was under no illusion the memories would go away anytime in the near future. She had dreamed about the attack for two nights straight and anticipated the nightmare would invade her sleep tonight.

"Nice scarf." Connor pointed at the beige scarf, accented with subtle gold leopard spots.

She smiled, reminded of last Christmas, when she'd opened the gift box containing the scarf. "Two very special people gave it to me."

"Dad was the one who picked it out, so I really can't take much credit." Connor looked away. After a long pause, he said, "Look, I'm sorry about following you the other night."

"Sorry?" She smiled at him. "Connor, dear, you saved my life."

"I know, but I was just being nosy. I had no idea what he had planned for you. Or, what you had planned for him."

Emma took a sip of her tea. "I'm just sorry I put you in that position."

"You didn't. I put myself there."

"I used poor judgment. I do this sort of thing for a living, but this was personal. I was too close to it. I should have hired someone else to investigate."

"But you got what you needed. You recorded Lance on your phone admitting he killed Dad, and that he was going to kill you as well." Connor frowned. "He might've tried to kill me too, out of fear that someday my memory of the accident would come back."

Emma shuddered. She hadn't wanted to think about that possibility.

Now, she would never have to.

† † †

LAUREN BUCKINGHAM is a native of Ohio who has called Arizona home for the past fifteen years. An avid reader who has been writing as long as she can remember, she has several publishing credits for short stories as well as a one-act play. When not writing, she enjoys arts and crafts, cooking and spending time with family.

RULES OF SEPARATION
SUSAN BUDAVARI

DANA Garrett slipped out of bed and put her clothes back on.

"Do you have to go?" Frank Porter inched his head up the pillow.

"Gary will be home before six. It's his birthday and we're going to Casino Arizona for dinner."

"When are you going to tell him about us? Time is slipping away."

"We've been over this. I can't leave him." Dana frowned. "He loves me. He's been good to me, faithful and supportive. I can't just walk out on him."

"But you don't love him...anymore. And your kids are all grown and out of the house."

She padded to the side of the bed and caressed Frank's face. "I do love you. Our time will come, I promise."

Frank sighed. "Will I see you this weekend?"

She shook her head. "Sorry. I meant to tell you. Gary and I are going to Sedona. It's our twenty-fifth wedding anniversary."

Frank sat up. "And you're going to *celebrate*? What's wrong with this picture?"

"A lot. But until I figure a way out, that's how it is."

Frank got up and reached out with open arms. They held each other tightly for several moments. Dana eased away. "I gotta go. I'll miss you this weekend but please don't call me."

"I won't. I'll be thinking of you." He pouted. "I adore you. But I'm not sure how much more waiting I can take."

THAT evening Dana and her husband enjoyed a sumptuous steak dinner at the casino. She had been surprised at the friendly nods Gary received from the wait staff when they entered the restaurant. "People here seem to know you."

"We have our branch brokers' meeting here every month. I've told you that."

Dana didn't remember Gary mentioning the casino meetings, but she usually tuned out the talk about his insurance business.

After they finished dinner and were waiting for the check, Gary's cell phone pinged. He glanced at the screen and excused himself to go to the rest room. When he returned several minutes later, the carefree happy look on his face had disappeared.

DANA was only twenty and Gary twenty-one when they married. They had three kids: a boy and two girls. Their son, Gary, Jr., was twenty-two, Lonnie twenty and Clare nineteen. Their marriage had been what the world might describe as good…but far from perfect. Whose is?

They had agreed to celebrate their anniversary with a weekend in Sedona, splurging on a luxurious suite at a four star hotel. Dana felt recharged every time she was surrounded by the gorgeous red rocks. It helped refresh her soul.

They had always lived in Phoenix. Gary was a solid guy, a hard-working insurance broker, a family man who worked long hours to provide for his family. When you marry young, you grow together. But people change. You think you know them after so long together. Sometimes you don't.

Dana's mother had told her every couple experiences some sort of re-evaluation in their mid-forties. No longer young but certainly not old, lots of people change their lives in their forties. Set new goals. Take new jobs. Find new partners. Some stay put and prosper. Others suffer.

Dana didn't remember whose idea it was, but during their time in Sedona they decided to put everything on the table—to go forward with a clean slate. Gary wanted a no-holds barred dialogue. She preferred to keep some things secret. And she did have a big secret. His name was Frank and he was the divorced father of her son's best friend.

Dana and Gary had enjoyed decent communication during their marriage—or so she thought—but there were sensitive areas they didn't touch. Gary had teased her about her reluctance to be open. He suggested they bring along a couple of bottles of champagne to help loosen their tongues.

They checked in then had cocktails and dinner in the hotel's Mexican restaurant. Afterwards they returned to their suite, changed into comfortable clothes and sat on the living room sofa. Gary opened a bottle of champagne and they began to talk.

It started out pretty routinely. They reminisced about their youth, their regrets about things they'd meant to do but hadn't gotten around to, what each of them would do if they lost the other—through death, not divorce. Eventually, Gary wanted to talk about the question every married couple wonders about but doesn't ask. He reached for Dana's hand and kissed it lightly. "Honey, have you ever been unfaithful in mind or body during the twenty-five years we've been married?" He had a silly grin on his face. Probably too much bubbly. Neither of them was a big drinker. His phone rang in the bedroom. He held his hand up with his palm facing her. "Think about your answer. I've been expecting that call but I'll be right back." He winked at her and disappeared for more than five minutes.

When he came back he was no longer smiling.

"What's going on?" she asked.

"Nothing."

She didn't believe him.

Gary's mood had clearly changed. He said, "I've done a lot of thinking and concluded it's really important for us to clear the air and be honest with each other." He seemed to be struggling to regain his composure and appear relaxed. He added, "What's said in Sedona can stay in Sedona. A quarter century is too long a time for two people to be together, loving only each other, and not having any lapses. It's also ample time to build trust."

She wasn't quite sure where he was going. Her inner self warned her it might be a good idea to stop here. But she kept silent. Dana was usually reluctant to broach sensitive topics. She really didn't have a lot to say about herself that was in any way juicy. Other than the issue of Frank. And she wasn't going there.

Gary said, "Before I start, I want to be sure you haven't changed your mind about doing this. If you have, we can stop right here. To set your mind at ease, everything I'm going to tell you happened years ago. But I'd like to get it off my chest and we can go from there. Are you willing?"

Although apprehensive, Dana wondered what he could tell her

she didn't already know. That he enjoyed flirting with younger women at parties? That he over-complimented their friends' wives? That he went out of his way to do favors for neighborhood women, especially the young, single ones—and that he might expect favors in return? She knew all of that and it never really worried her. He was home every night sharing her bed. He never embarrassed her in public. "Go ahead. I'm a big girl. I can take it."

And then he started. He talked about some of their old friends—no longer friends—they hung out with when they were a lot younger. "You remember Carlos's wife, Isabella, and how we always kidded around? Well she had a habit of coming on to me and it went a bit too far once or twice."

Dana gulped. "*Once or twice?* Did Carlos know? I didn't."

"He sort of caught us."

"You're putting me on, right?"

He looked at her with moist eyes then looked away. "No, babe. I'm sorry. I was a little drunk when it happened. Carlos and I decided we'd avoid any further temptation and not get together anymore."

"Didn't Isabella and Carlos get divorced?"

"Yeah, but a while afterwards." He hesitated. "It wasn't because of that."

She remembered now how all of a sudden they had stopped seeing Carlos and Isabella. At the time, she figured they were having marriage problems but little did she imagine Gary was involved. Dana took a deep breath and stared at her *faithful* husband. She wasn't quite sure how she felt. "Anything else you have to get off your chest?"

He poured a little more champagne into his glass and took a swallow. "Well, you remember the time you went to visit your mother when she lived in Yuma. You were away for a full week and we had a babysitter for the kids. She was a really cute nineteen year old and one night we got a little too chummy after the kids went to sleep and…"

"Oh, Gary. That's disgusting." She couldn't believe what he was saying. Gary—her devoted, upstanding, ethical husband—was a sleaze. Her breath caught in her throat. She didn't know if she could take any more of this. She refilled her glass and chugged it down in one gulp. All these years she'd had complete faith in him and he was whoring around behind her back. She had always trusted him. Taken his fidelity for granted. What a fool she was. What a fool to torture herself about her own indiscretion.

His mumbling drew her from her thoughts. "Babe, there weren't too many other times. Really meaningless, not love affairs. Some of my buddies routinely had long-term girlfriends they thought they were in love with. I never did." He took a deep breath and let it out. "There's just one other woman I have to tell you about. Lonnie's seventh grade teacher."

"Miss Reeser? Lonnie's math teacher? The one with the long legs and big bottom?"

He nodded.

Lonnie had a rough time in her charter middle school, particularly with math. They had worried Miss Reeser would fail Lonnie. Gary had worked it out. Dana's mind raced when she thought of how he'd taken care of it. She stood and pressed a tender area in her midsection and burped up some bile. She had trouble getting the words out. "Gary, I'm beyond words." If she'd had something heavy in her hands, she might have hit him with it. Her rationalization button turned on. Was she going to let this bother her? Before she knew, it hadn't bothered her. Did she really care? She sure as hell did.

"Tell me you're glad this is all out in the open. Say you forgive me. After all, I'm just a man."

That last phrase did it. As if being a man afforded him special privileges? Dana couldn't contain her rage. What did he expect her to say? It wasn't okay with her. No matter how long ago any of it happened. No one likes to have been played for a fool and have it thrown in their face. It's demeaning. If he could do this, and more, he didn't value her as a person. And he wasn't worth any sacrifice. She bit her lip. She wasn't going to cry. What would that accomplish? She folded her hands in front of her and pressed so hard her knuckles turned white.

"Gary, how do you think all of this makes me feel?"

He looked at her, his lips puckered. "I'm sorry. I thought you'd want to know. Especially, since it's all in the past. I got it out of my system and haven't done any of that stuff for years. And I won't. Come here, babe, give me a hug. You know you love me."

He was right. In a certain way she did love him but not as much as she loved Frank. It became crystal clear to her at that very moment, she also loathed Gary. Her feelings confused her. Had she stopped caring, really caring—or was she in shock and not able to understand what was happening? She decided she would find a guilt-free way out of this marriage.

She stood and faced him. She folded her arms in front of her, staring at them. "Since it's confession time, is there anything else?"

His expression turned very serious. "You are very intuitive. Before I get to it. Is there something you want to tell me?"

She thought for a moment. *"No."* She had no intention of letting him off the hook by confessing her *meaningful* transgression.

He rubbed his forehead. "There is a money issue." He took a deep breath and put on a pitiful face. "I got myself into some really big trouble."

"What do you mean?"

"I needed money for the business. I gambled at the casino to raise it. I lost. Then I borrowed money from the wrong people. Now they want it all back. They gave me an ultimatum. That's what the call was about."

"What kind of ultimatum?"

"Pay off my entire debt by next Saturday or…they kill me. And maybe you, too."

"You can't be serious." Her voice trembled.

"I wish it weren't true."

She locked eyes with him. "How much money?"

"Sixty thousand dollars. Cash."

Dana folded herself into a chair. "Where on earth are you going to get that kind of money? Everything we had went into the kids' college expenses."

"I have some and I'm counting on your mother for most of it. She's loaded."

"What makes you think she'd give it to me for you?"

"She's on in years and you're her only child."

"I can't tell her I need money to pay your gambling debts."

"Tell her anything you'd like. Just figure out how to get the money from her in the next week. Or our lives as we know them are over. Think of the kids."

She jumped up. "Precisely when do you need to deliver this

money?"

"They told me to bring cash next Saturday at five PM to room Four at the DeLite Motel on 44th Street near Sky Harbor." He stood and bowed his head. "You have my word, if you do this for me, from here on I'll toe the line in every way. I'll be a model husband." He threw his arms around her and held on to her, as if his life depended on it.

"I can't guarantee I'll be able to get the money. But I'll try."

Gary's eyebrows shot up and his mouth opened wide. He sighed. Dana felt no pity for him. She knew he depended on her to come through for him. And she knew this was her way out of their marriage.

They went to bed in separate rooms and left for home at dawn.

ON Monday morning she called her mother. Dana was entirely truthful with her. Her mother had without fail been good at solving Dana's problems. The most she could give Dana was thirty thousand dollars and it would take several days to get it together. Dana informed Gary and he said he'd manage somehow to get the rest.

Meanwhile, when she told Frank, he insisted on hiring a PI to find out if Gary was telling the truth or using a ruse to get money from Dana for another purpose. The PI confirmed Gary owed big bucks to a Phoenix loan shark with a long rap sheet and a ruthless reputation. The man, Joey T, collected on debts one way or the other. He took no prisoners.

FRIDAY evening, Dana told a very nervous Gary she'd meet him in the motel parking lot at ten to five on Saturday evening. She'd bring thirty-thousand dollars in stacks of hundred-dollar bills.

As promised, Dana arrived at the seedy motel on time. She got into Gary's car and passed the money to him in a shopping bag. He added it to a heavy black satchel holding his share.

"There's been a slight change of plans," he said frowning. "The guys want you to deliver the cash."

"Why me?" She didn't like the sound of this.

"They think I'll pull something."

Dana reluctantly agreed once Gary assured her the thugs were only interested in getting paid.

He gave the satchel to her and said he'd wait in the car for her.

She got out and hurried to room Four on the ground floor of the motel, barely reaching the door by five o'clock.

† † †

MINUTES later Gary heard a noise. *A gun shot?* Then a black SUV backed up to the door of room Four. The driver went inside. Shortly thereafter two men got into the SUV and pulled away.

Gary figured Joey T's men had quickly discovered the money on top of the satchel was real, whereas, the thirty thousand underneath, merely photocopies. Dana deserved what she got. From the day he'd learned of her love affair with Frank Porter, he'd looked for a way to get even with her and to pay off his debt at the same time. Everything was now in place for him to leave town.

He pressed the ignition and was ready to head to the airport, when there was a knock on his car window. He flinched at the sound. Ralphie, Joey T's second in command, stood there.

Gary lowered the window. "What do you want? Is Dana okay?"

"She's still inside." Ralphie placed a gun with a silencer up to Gary's temple. "I have a message from Joey T. He doesn't like guys who try to cheat him and make their wives take the fall."

He pulled the trigger.

† † †

SUSAN BUDAVARI has always been an avid mystery reader. After years as a scientific writer/editor and encyclopedist in the pharmaceutical industry in New Jersey, she moved to Arizona and began writing fiction. She is the author of the Merano & Bell Novels featuring a small-town Arizona PI (and ex-NJ cop) and his physician wife. *Reason to Hide* is the latest book in the series. With Merle McCann, Susan co-authored *Beyond the Broken Door*, Winner of the Anthology/Fiction Award, 2020 New Mexico-Arizona Book Awards. She served as an advisor on the board of directors of Sisters in Crime Desert Sleuths Chapter. SusanBudavari.com

ASK ME TOMORROW
WILLIAM BUTLER

ALERTED by the crunch of footsteps on the gravel path, I pushed aside the curtains and looked out the window. It was Bill, my temporary boss while I recovered from some injuries, and ex-husband as of four years ago. Before he could knock, I pulled on my bathrobe and opened the door.

"Margo, you have a new mission. Throw something on and meet me by the fountain." He spoke softly, as if to a frightened animal, and pointed to a corner of the large backyard.

"I'll be there in a minute." The blue bruises on my face had faded to yellow blotches during the month I was in the guesthouse. In seven years of being a member of an agency's enforcement team, this was the first time I'd been injured. At least, the suspects who attacked me got the worst of it.

Without another word, Bill walked back along the path to his house.

Ten minutes later, I had dressed and rung Bill on the intercom that connected the guesthouse to the main house. He said he'd be right out.

I hung up the phone, eager to start a new mission. Sitting around waiting for a medical clearance was boring. I glanced in the mirror on the way out. Makeup covered my few remaining bruises. I stepped outside and closed the door. This was the nicest safe house I'd ever seen. A rambling Southwestern-style home with a two-bedroom guesthouse separated by a lush backyard crowded with trees and fragrant bushes. A pool and a hot tub stood in the center of the yard with a wood bench and bubbling stone fountain in the corner. Did he specify this spot because ambient noise covered conversation?

I had sat on the bench for only a moment when Bill approached carrying a green file folder, a gray box the size of a hardcover book, and nine pink tea roses. He took a seat at the end of the bench and handed me the green file folder. "The only reason the agency is letting us work together on this is it's a rush job. High priority." He pointed at the folder. "Take a look."

I opened the folder and glanced at a three-page dossier, then put it and the folder on the bench. "Sam Peterson? Isn't this the guy you arrested last year, but the charges didn't stick?"

Bill nodded. He took a paper from his jacket pocket and held it out for me to read. "Here's a signed authorization from the Disposition Committee. Peterson has to die today. We need custody of the body. It must look like natural causes." He spoke with no passion as if reading a recipe. "I'm to do planning and backup. You do the deed."

Apparently satisfied that I had read the kill authorization, he refolded it and slid it back into his pocket.

"Our troubled personal history aside, you're a good choice," he said. "The target doesn't know you. Also, he'll be less defensive when a female approaches.

Agents are not supposed to question assignments, but I couldn't help myself. "Why Peterson and why the rush?"

His eyes narrowed for a moment. Then he pointed at the green folder. "It's all in the dossier. Peterson was once a respected scientist. When his wife died, he became an odd recluse. Now he's leaving the country carrying sensitive information. We need to stop him without alarming his co-conspirators."

"Do you recognize this?" He opened the metal case. Inside were three thick, mottled brown pens lying in cushioned depressions. One pen was circumscribed with a yellow band imprinted with the word SIMULATOR. There also were two aluminum safety cases to carry pens, a bottle of blue softgels, a clear plastic bag of fabric-covered vials the size of cigarettes, and a pair of skin-colored cloth gloves.

"I've seen this type of weapon before. On one occasion, I assisted in its use."

He nodded once. "Normally, I would hit the target. As you mentioned, he knows me." He laid the gray box and the flowers between us on the bench.

I wondered about the flowers. It would be gross if he started giving me things like this. "So, I'm to write him off with one of these pens?"

Bill glanced at me and then at the metal box. "Right." He

picked a bluish-green sprig from a nearby rosemary bush, held it to his nose, and looked into the distance. "Peterson intends to board a private aircraft tomorrow. We must stop him."

I nodded. Bill seldom spoke. When he did, it paid to listen.

"We've never worked as a team, but you have a great reputation," he said.

Bill fixed his gaze on me as if trying to read my body language. It was not a good feeling.

He spoke more quickly. "This has to go well. No second chances." He handed me a photo. "Your target."

The photo was of a middle-aged man standing on a street corner, apparently waiting for a green light. Peterson was in sharp focus, the background blurred. There was no depth. They must have used a telephoto lens from a great distance. "I'll recognize him."

Bill pulled additional sprigs from the rosemary bush and crushed them in his hand. In the still air, the aroma encircled us. "I know where he'll be this afternoon."

A familiar feeling of dread rose from my stomach. "Not much preparation time."

"True, but it's not me who's asking. It's a matter of national security." Bill looked toward the driveway.

The pool man opened the gate, came into the backyard, took a sample of the water from the hot tub, and left. We said nothing until he was out of earshot.

"If I do the deed in less than four hours, the antidote pill won't protect me," I said.

"The system is improved," he said. "Coverage starts ten minutes after you swallow the blue pill. It will last for six hours, but you must sniff the ampoule of ammonia within a half-hour of expressing the pen."

Bill removed the simulator pen from the box and handed it to me. "The spray from this is inert. The other two pens are active. We haven't changed the weapon, except for the composition of the poison and the improved antidote. The poison degrades an hour after use. It will look as if Peterson had a heart attack."

I verified the word SIMULATOR on the brown pen and rotated the cap one hundred and eighty degrees. A small button clicked-up near the end. Holding the weapon with four curled fingers and my thumb on the button, I pointed the pen at the trunk of a tree about three feet away. The button snapped as it was pressed, followed by a sharp hiss. What looked like a small puff of steam sprayed out from the end of the weapon. Barely visible droplets on an area one foot in diameter glistened on the tree's bark.

Bill looked at his watch.

I dropped the pen back into the gray box. "How far away is the target?"

"A twenty-minute drive."

Bill's orange cat sauntered out of the bushes and rubbed against my leg.

"This is a summary execution of an American so that other Americans will be safer?" I asked. A sanctioned killing, yes. But to most people, this was murder.

"Exactly, Margo. If he leaves the country, we won't be able to touch him, and the material he's carrying will be in the wrong hands."

"Killing him is self-defense." It was a rationalization I used when they ordered me to do something horrible. But every time, days later, bad feelings came.

For a moment, I thought I saw his lips twist into a wry smile.

"That's true," he said. "We don't want Peterson's co-conspirators to panic and hide. If it looks like he died of heart failure, no one will suspect foul play. I'll arrange to transfer the body to an appropriate place for disposition."

I looked into Bill's eyes and saw no sign of deception. Still, how can you be sure with someone who was an intelligence officer for ten years?

"One spray in the face and Peterson will fall immediately," he said. He took a white piece of cloth from his pocket and unfolded it. Inside was an official-looking card bordered in red and blue, which read,

> I, Samuel Peterson, have a serious heart condition.
> In an emergency, please contact my nearest relative,
> Paul Bricks.

A phone number followed.

"Who is Bricks?" I asked.

His lips tightened for a moment. "It's an identity I use for certain jobs. If you can, slip the card into his wallet. It'll make it easier for us to gain access to the body. Peterson may be carrying a loaded flash drive, internally." He unfolded a map and pointed at a location. "If the target sticks to his routine, in an hour, he'll be at a cemetery in Phoenix, just north of McDowell, visiting his wife's niche in the mausoleum. Looks like a good place to do the deed."

I glanced at the map. "It's close." I pulled on the skin-colored cloth gloves then swallowed one of the blue softgels. Bill's eyes widened when I dropped several softgels and three of the ampoules of ammonia into my pocket.

"The improved formula in the antidote includes a sort of tranquilizer to reduce PTSD," he said. "The new stuff blocks parts of your memory. By tomorrow, you'll remember the facts, but little of the emotional experience."

Sounds like the relationship we had. I inserted an active pen into a safety case. The case looked like an aluminum cigar tube, inscribed with:

SULLY AGRICULTURE RESEARCH
CAUTION!
THE OBJECT INSIDE CONTAINS POWERFUL INSECTICIDES

The message included a reward notice and a toll-free telephone number. I dropped the pen into my pocket.

He handed me the bunch of pink roses. "Carry these as a prop when you walk into the mausoleum."

"One more thing. Embarrassing to ask. What if I get arrested?"

His eyebrows rose momentarily. "If local authorities become involved and you're in custody, it'll take time to clear you. We'll probably claim federal jurisdiction." Bill stood. "Take a minute. I'll wait for you in the car."

He turned away and walked to his white SUV parked in the driveway.

With her tail raised, the orange cat sauntered after the man who had just ordered an enemy's death.

I sat alone on the bench. It would be easy to linger for hours, breathing the sweet air and watching birds splashing in the noisy fountain.

This mission wouldn't be much different from the two I'd already completed. A tiny, brown-speckled gecko skittered off the bench then disappeared into the grass. Tomorrow, the lizard would be here, and Peterson would be dead. Carrying the little bunch of flowers, I walked toward the SUV. A familiar sense of detachment came over me as if I were watching a movie or acting in a play. Wiser heads had scripted my role.

Thirty minutes later, we drove through the cemetery gates. A burial was being held near the mausoleum. About twenty mourners stood, heads bowed, around an open grave.

Bill parked the SUV among ten cars lining the road. The age and condition of the vehicles varied considerably. As with past missions, a rising feeling of inevitability helped me move forward.

The gray granite mausoleum was about one hundred feet long, forty feet wide, and thirty feet tall with three entrances, one at the center and one at each end.

I pushed on the mausoleum's large oaken side door. It opened easily. Near the ceiling at each end of the building were stained-glass windows. To have both hands free, I stuck the flowers, stems first, into my back pocket.

Inside was a center arcade. Walls of smooth black marble spired to the vaulted ceiling. Names of the interred, each spaced several feet apart, were etched in stone from floor to ceiling, the length of the building. No security cameras were visible. With modern miniaturization, seeing none was not a guarantee there were none.

Colored light streamed through stained glass, painting blue and green patterns on the floor. The still air smelled like lilacs. Faint music broke the silence. No one else was in the building.

While waiting for Peterson to arrive, I removed the pen from the safety tube and put the tube in one pants pocket and the pen in another. I stared at the wall. The marble offered a distorted reflection. Even with gloves, the stone felt cool to my fingertips. I had touched a black wall like this before in D.C. The morning sun warmed that black wall, shining names carved on a dark memorial for men and women who would never know old age.

After a while, I became more aware of the music. It floated through the still air and into my head, gently caressing what was left of my emotions. The music seemed to say: Nothing to fear. This is a place of repose. All pain is gone, and yearnings quelled.

At the far end of the building, the oak door opened. The hinges made no sound. A shaft of daylight intruded. Moving my head slightly, I watched a man walk in my direction. He stopped twenty feet away and stared at a name close to the floor. I looked carefully at his profile. It was Sam Peterson. As always, the target's eyes were the first thing I saw and the last thing I forgot.

I grasped the weapon in my pocket with three fingers and turned the cap with a thumb and forefinger while being careful to avoid pressing the trigger. There was a rumor an operator died when he accidentally got the full dose even though he previously took the antidote. The trigger extended with a click, something felt, more than heard. I moved a little closer to the target.

Sam Peterson glanced at me, then stared at the smooth marble wall and whispered, "This young woman has learned too early that a common sorrow joins humankind." He touched the polished stone, behind which lay his wife's remains. "My life is cursed. I've lost my only love. Now there is no joy in life. Food tastes like cardboard. It hurts to live."

At first, I thought Peterson spoke to me, but his focus was on a name carved into the black marble wall.

"Emily, you must understand," he said. "The foreigner talked about how his countrymen lived as an extended family and how, when I emigrate, I will reside in a city filled with friends, a place with little crime and no drunkenness. A nation still ruled by The Creator. I could practice science in a place that acknowledged God as compassionate and merciful."

My footfalls echoed off marble as I walked toward Peterson. From a few paces away, I held up the brown pen and said, "Did you drop this?" A side shot would work, but a frontal facial spray was optimal.

Peterson turned toward me. His eyes widened as if surprised I was so near. He leaned forward as if to better see the object in my hand.

I stepped closer, holding the pen out.

His lips moved, but I heard no sound. Peterson took in a breath.

I fired the weapon at the center of his face. In the quiet room, the brief hiss was audible. The spray smelled like crescent-shaped almond cookies I had eaten during an assignment in Sao Paulo. The fragrance dissipated in moments.

A wide-eyed perplexed expression formed on Peterson's face.

He gasped as if breathing through a pillow. After three long seconds, he fell backward, hitting hard on the dark marble floor. The hollow sound of his head making a double bounce echoed in the room. It sounded like a dropped coconut.

No one else had entered the mausoleum, so I removed the handkerchief-wrapped, red and blue-bordered card from my pocket. With gloved hands, I pushed the card against Peterson's fingers several times making sure to get prints on both sides and then placed it in his wallet. There was a strange taste in my mouth, and my heart was pounding.

A bluish hue spread across Peterson's face. It would have been a nice color on a wall. A puddle of blood spread out from under his head.

With the pink flowers in hand, I quickly left the building. Bright sunlight and street noise startled me. There was no evidence anyone had observed what had just happened inside. People attending the funeral were leaving. Mourners' cars moved slowly away from the grave. Bill waited in his SUV, engine running. I climbed in and closed the door.

I dropped the now disheveled flowers on the floor. "It's done."

"The medical card?" Bill asked.

"I put it in Peterson's wallet. Paul Bricks should be getting a call soon."

Even from the side, I saw him roll his eyes.

As we drove away, I crushed the cloth-wrapped glass ammonia ampoule and snorted the fumes up both nostrils. For a few seconds, it was difficult to concentrate with my nose and eyes reacting to the second part of the antidote.

I'd done the job well. Peterson hadn't suffered needlessly. He probably didn't know what was happening. Anyway, an assassin has no responsibility when the activity is authorized. I felt proud of how smoothly it had gone and that a traitor received his due. Once the adrenaline rush went away, less-comfortable feelings would displace my bravado. Unless the emotion suppressant drug, in the softgel I swallowed, worked.

Stopped at a red light, I looked at Bill. "What's next?"

He turned his face toward me. "Your part of the mission is complete. How are you feeling?"

"Ask me tomorrow."

† † †

WILLIAM BUTLER Bill Butler was born and raised in NYC. In his freshman year, he quit high school to work on a midway in a fair. At age seventeen, Bill joined the army. Years later, he returned to Manhattan and worked as a private detective while earning a few degrees. He eventually settled in Scottsdale, Arizona. He managed a vocational rehabilitation office located in the Phoenix Good Samaritan Rehabilitation Institute in Phoenix prior to retiring. Nine of his short stories are published. One of his favorites is featured in the 2017 Desert Sleuths anthology, *SoWest: Killer Nights*.

NO GOOD DEED
PATRICIA CURREN

ANOTHER long day done. Heather exited her Nissan and walked from her condominium to the bank of locked mailboxes. Another postcard from her older brother Bobby had arrived. It was always fun to hear from him, not just because of the break from bills and ads, but because he included entertaining details about the places he visited.

A month ago, he had begun a tour of several countries. Every week, she'd received a card written in his tiny block print. She'd wait to read this one over dinner—to jazz up her pre-packaged meal.

A short time later, she read:

> HI SIS – BARCELONA WAS AMAZING. I CAN'T
> BELIEVE THE IDIOTS WHO RUN WITH THE BULLS
> HERE IN PAMPLONA. TALK ABOUT A DEATH WISH!
> DO YOU RECALL OUR PRETEND BULL FIGHTS WHEN
> WE WERE KIDS? CAN STILL SEE YOU WAVING
> MOM'S RED SILK SCARF AS A CAPE. WE GOT IN A
> LITTLE JAM OVER THAT, HUH? NEXT STOP:
> PURTUGAL.
> LOVE BOBBY

She flipped the card and studied the picture of the handsome matador. Maybe she should've accepted her brother's invite to travel with him. Vacation wasn't a problem—she hadn't taken any extended time off since her divorce five years ago. A workaholic, she knew the push was on at her Phoenix software firm for a new product rollout. Meeting that deadline had seemed more important than Bobby's invitation.

He had urged, *"Come on, you need to have some fun. With your looks, you'll have guys in every country falling at your feet."*

Staring at the colorful card, she regretted her decision. Her fourteen-hour work days were sucking the lifeblood out of her. She left for work in the darkness in the morning and returned home in the dark. She wouldn't recognize her neighbors in a crowd.

Heather carried her plate to the sink and refilled her wine glass. Moving to the living room, she opened her laptop and googled a popular dating website to submit her profile. Halfway through she slammed the computer shut. It was all so contrived. Besides, it could be dangerous. Better to meet men in a natural setting. But how? Bars weren't her thing. She didn't attend church anymore now that her parents were gone. No interests other than work. Sighing, she rose and prepared for bed.

† † †

HEATHER waited in the checkout lane at Safeway. She'd be glad when Bobby returned. There'd been no postcard from him since the one from Spain two weeks ago. *Should I be worried?* She'd heard nothing about his time in Portugal, and he still had Italy, Germany, and the Scandinavian countries to go.

Suddenly, the hair on the back of her neck prickled. Wheeling around, she was greeted by an elderly woman. "Hello, dear, how are you?"

Relieved, Heather said, "Fine, and you?" That sparked an uncomfortable conversation, which lasted until time to unload her cart. As she left the market, she scolded herself. *Don't be ridiculous. You're just nervous because Bobby's not here – he's always been your protector. You hardly need to fear little old ladies!*

Her brother's next two cards waited in the mailbox when she returned home, one from Lisbon, the other postmarked Rome. Another of the post office's anomalies at work. Happy to hear from him at last, she devoured his missives immediately.

> HEY SIS – HERE'S THE OCEANARIUM IN LISBON. THE
> LARGEST INDOOR AQUARIUM IN EUROPE
> STRADLES A MAJOR RIVER. THE HIGHLIGHT IS A 23-
> FOOT-DEEP OCEAN TANK THAT HOUSES EELS,
> BARRACUDAS, SHARKS, ETC. IT REMINDED ME OF
> MY COAST GUARD DAYS.
> LOVE, BOBBY

On the other side of the card, a beautiful building was backlit against the night sky. The light reflected off the river below it.

Disappointed with the shortness of his note, she read the next.

> SIS – HERE'S THE SISTINE CHAPEL. COULDN'T BRING
> MYSELF TO TOUR THE VATICAN MUSEUMS – TOO
> MUCH WEALTH AT THE PEOPLE'S EXPENSE. I KNOW
> YOU AGREE. REMEMBER THE TIME WE SNUCK INTO
> ST. BRIDGET'S AND STUCK ALL THE OFFERING
> PLATES TOGETHER WITH SUPER GLUE? WELL
> WORTH THE HUNDRED HAIL MARY'S AND
> CLEANING THE VESTIBULE FOR A MONTH. HAR,
> HAR! ANYWAY, YOU'D ADORE THE ART.
> LOVE, BOBBY

As she turned over the card and admired the shot of the most famous chapel in the world, the same eeriness she'd felt at Safeway, passed over her. Heather peered into the gathering twilight. Nothing stirred. Again, she chastised herself for letting her imagination run unchecked and returned to the condo.

† † †

WORK hadn't let up and stress had begun to take its toll. She found her usual two glasses of wine had turned into four, and tonight proved no exception.

Maybe her tipsiness was why she answered the call from an unknown number. Normally, she'd let those go to voicemail. "Hello?" Heather hoped she wasn't slurring.

The voice at the other end said, "Hi. You don't know me, but I'm a friend of your brother's. I've moved here from Massachusetts. Since Bobby was going to be out of the country, he gave me your name and number. He said you'd be willing to help me get the lay of the land."

She cringed inside. *Bobby's setting me up again.*

The caller continued, "I served in the Coast Guard with your brother and he encouraged me to make the change to a snow-free climate. I know absolutely nothing about Arizona, other than the Grand Canyon's supposed to be fantastic. Shoot, I even need help finding a laundromat." He laughed. "My name's Josh, by the way."

His rumbly laughter stirred something deep within her. She went mute.

"Hey, I get it if you'd rather not. I am a stranger after all."

Bobby had written in one of his earlier cards that his phone had been stolen and he didn't want to replace it until he returned home. So she couldn't call him to check on Josh. It would've been nice to find out more about this guy. But if her brother vouched for him, he must be okay. She'd play the Good Samaritan. She drew a breath. "No, it's fine. I can meet you at the Mesa Starbucks on Power and Broadway this Saturday at ten. Know where that is?"

"Nope, but I'll find out. That's terrific. See you then."

Heather stared at the phone's dark screen and it hit home how lonely she'd been. Suddenly, she hoped this guy wouldn't fit the pattern of Bobby's other dorky friends.

† † †

SATURDAY morning, Heather spent more time on her makeup than usual. She walked to her closet and retrieved a pair of chocolate brown leggings and a flowing apricot top.

She arrived at Starbucks fifteen minutes early. When she entered, a sturdy looking fellow in khaki shorts and a sage green T-shirt gazed at her. He covered the few feet to the door. "You're Heather."

"How'd you know?"

"You're a much more attractive version of your brother." He grinned, stuck out his hand and she felt her own hand being swallowed up in his massive paw. "How 'bout I get our drinks—the least I can do for your trouble."

"Sure, I'll have a short mocha." She sat at the table he'd vacated and looked him over as he joined the line. He wasn't tall, but was well-muscled, his calves as sinewy as an ultra-marathoner. An attractive tan revealed time in the outdoors.

A few minutes later, he sat across from her and she took a sip of her coffee. "You've known Bobby since the service, huh? I don't remember him mentioning you."

He chuckled. "That's funny. He's told me plenty about you—mostly regarding the trouble you two scared up as kids."

Heather grimaced. "Like what?"

"Like the time you broke into the home rooms at your middle school and hid all the felt-tip markers and the teachers' lesson plans." He stirred a packet of sugar into his Americano. "When do you expect him back?"

"Not sure, exactly. Probably the end of next month. So, do you want to get started?"

"Yeah. I brought my iPad and can check the locations of local businesses while we talk."

After Heather detailed the markets, malls, and other places he inquired about, he said, "This is great. What about fun things to do and see?"

She told him about the local sports teams, the Riparian Preserve, Canyon de Chelly, and the Petrified Forest, until his eyes lost focus.

"What do you recommend?"

"Besh-Ba-Gowah's really cool."

"Besh-Ba what?"

The way he wrinkled up his face made her laugh. "It's a prehistoric Indian pueblo an hour away. Some of the buildings are restored to what they must've looked like hundreds of years ago."

"How about we check it out?"

"We?"

"Yeah, we—like right now."

She considered his offer. He wasn't a Leonardo DiCaprio. More like a Joaquin Phoenix, he had an air of mystery. An unexpected effervescence formed in her belly as she raised her cup to her lips. "Sure, but not today. I've got laundry to do and grocery shopping after working all week."

"Ten tomorrow morning, okay? Give me your address and I'll swing by for you." She didn't hesitate. After all, he was Bobby's friend.

† † †

THE next morning Josh was right on time. He escorted her to his SUV and held the passenger door open. She couldn't remember the last time a man had done that for her.

Heather directed him toward US 60 and as they drove east, she talked about their destination. "We're headed a little outside of Globe, an old mining town. There's a museum and a small park at the pueblo. It's believed it was built by the Salado tribe, and there's speculation about what caused their extinction. Some believe they were attacked by a warring tribe. Others think it may've been a natural calamity, like illness or drought."

Josh turned from the steering wheel. "Fascinating. Tell me more."

"I don't want to take all the surprise out of it, but there'll be excavated artifacts, like pottery and woven objects. The last time I toured it was during the blazing August heat and the refreshing coolness of one of the reconstructed homes blew me away. I can't fathom how people who lived eight-hundred-years ago figured out how to do that."

When they arrived, Josh paid the nominal entrance fee and they spent hours there—he was enthralled with the creativity of the ancient tribe. Finally, back in the SUV, he scrolled through the photos he'd taken with his phone and leaned in to show her his favorites. The smell of sun and cologne emanating from his body sent a pleasant buzz through her.

On the way home, they stopped for a late lunch in Apache Junction. She offered to pay since he'd driven, but he refused. "Look, I can't tell you what a great time I've had today. Can we get together again? I want to see more of Arizona—and you, too, of course."

She looked into those mysterious eyes and wilted. "I told you how crazy my job is, but how about next weekend? We can hit the Riparian Preserve."

† † †

HEATHER could scarcely believe she and Josh had only been an item for three weeks. It seemed like many months. When, after a few dates, she'd learned he was staying in a motel until he could find a place, she insisted he move into her spare bedroom. That didn't last long. She had fallen, and fallen hard.

Always attentive to her every need, the only thing he complained about was the many hours she spent at work. He'd found a job with long hours, too, at an architectural firm. He biked to and from his office in Tempe. Yet he still arrived home before she did.

On the weekends, they'd catch up. Josh loved repeating the stories Bobby had told him about her. Sometimes, if the tale didn't make her look too goofy, she'd enjoy it, too.

† † †

ONE Friday, Heather arrived home early. They'd finished the new product rollout ahead of schedule and her ecstatic boss had shooed them away for a head start on the weekend. Inside the door, she eased out of her shoes and padded down the hallway to change clothes. A rustling noise greeted her—Josh must be home, too.

From the bedroom doorway, she saw him with his back turned, going through papers in the file cabinet where she kept her financial information. He was so engrossed he hadn't heard her enter.

Stunned, she stared for a moment, then backed away and tiptoed to the front door. "Hey, I'm home!" This time she thumped one of her shoes against the wall then walked into the kitchen for a glass of water. "Where are you?"

The toilet flushed. *Nice cover, Josh.*

He appeared in the kitchen doorway. "You're early—that's great—wanna go out to eat?" He swept her into his arms for a kiss.

She mustered the wherewithal to pretend everything was fine. "Sure," she said, all the while processing what she'd seen.

Over the next few days, Heather contemplated what to do. Snooping wasn't breaking the law so calling the police was pointless. She told herself she was overreacting, but deep down, she knew she should have gotten to know Josh better before letting him move in.

Bobby sent another card from Sweden saying he'd be home in two days. She'd read it at the mailbox and relief surged through her. She tucked the missive into her work bag.

The next day, she arrived home from work to find Josh sprawled in front of the TV holding a beer.

"Hey, babe." He rose and hugged her tightly. His breath smelled strongly of hops and there were three empties on the end table. Taking her elbow, he steered her to the sofa. "Just watching the news—that virus in China is crazy, huh?"

She settled an old floppy throw pillow behind her tired back and leaned into it. "Yeah, I hope Bobby can get home before they close down the borders."

"Shouldn't be a problem. He's already on his way."

Heather froze.

"You okay, babe?"

She stared at him. "How do you know he's on his way?"

A cunning look passed over his face. "You told me."

"No I didn't." She started to get up, but he pulled her back. Despite the warm room, she felt cold inside. "Who are you, really? I saw you going through my financials the other day."

Josh rubbed his chin and looked around the room as if an answer would appear from nowhere. Finally, he said, "Guess I'm busted." He chuckled. "If you really wanna know, I'm your mail carrier."

"What?"

"Yeah, you were the perfect mark. I found out all I needed to know from your idiot brother's postcards. I began watching you and saw the long hours you worked and that you lived alone. That meant you probably had few friends and plenty of dough."

"You don't even know Bobby?" She was stating the obvious, but still couldn't grasp it. "But how did you get my phone number?"

"I guess stupidity runs in your family. Ever heard of something called the Internet?" He clutched her arm and guided her to the dining room table, shoving her into a chair. "When I read the card that Bobby was on his way home, I knew I'd have to act soon." Josh reached under a stack of papers and retrieved two documents. He jammed a pen into her hand. "I've got a friend who will notarize these later."

Through blurry eyes, she saw one paper changing the beneficiary on her 401K from Bobby to Josh. The other was the deed to her condo. "Sign these, dammit!" He squeezed the back of her neck so hard she cried out.

He'll get control of everything I've worked my whole life for. The thought sent shock waves through her. Heather gauged the distance to the front door. Bolting up, she sprinted toward safety, but his arms grabbed her around the knees and the floor came up to meet her. The wind knocked out of her, Josh pulled her upright and propelled her back to the table. Again, he forced the pen between her trembling fingers.

Her signature looked like nothing more than a scribble. "There," she whispered.

Josh yanked her up and dragged her toward the sofa where he hooked his leg around her ankles and she went down on her back.

He grabbed the floppy throw pillow.

"I can't tell you how grateful I am for your rescuing me from that mind-numbing job at the post office. Now I can travel—have some adventures of my own." He straddled her and jammed the pillow over her face. "Goodbye, Heather."

She kicked and fought like a lioness, once gaining purchase in an eye socket, but he knocked her hand away and increased the pressure on the pillow. Her lungs screamed for air. There were only seconds left to stop him. Her head was near the end table with Josh's beer bottles. She flailed her arms.

He laughed. "What the hell are you doing? Give up, slut."

A thrill coursed down her spine as her hand closed around one of the bottles. She raised it and blindly aimed for his head. The impact jolted up her arm.

It wasn't enough.

IT is said when one dies, their life flashes before their eyes, but not with Heather. Instead, she saw her brother's face and LOVE, BOBBY written in his tiny block print on so many postcards.

As the final darkness closed in, she regretted all she'd left undone.

† † †

PATRICIA CURREN is the author of the young adult Kendra Morgan mystery trilogy. She is currently working on an adult mystery set in Seattle, featuring a female detective, who despite major character flaws, continues to close cases, and consequently, keep her job. In addition to whodunits, she has penned stories about felines and fitness for magazines and newspapers. Patricia attributes much of her writing success to her membership in the Sisters in Crime Desert Sleuths Chapter. She's also a member of the Society of Southwestern Authors, Valley of the Sun chapter. Patricia facilitates the Scottsdale Scribes critique group. Facebook.com/TrishCurren

SEASONS OF DEATH
MEG E. DOBSON

MOMMA'S garden.

Two steps in, I returned to the battered bucket on the wood utility table by the house, picked out her garden shears and covered my head with her straw hat, worn soft from years of use. I went to her flowers.

Out here in the rocky, cactus-strewn desert this place was an oasis. A gulch shaded by its massive rock walls and given life by the stream running through it. I set a fast pace, inspected the plants, scuffing the soil beneath them. Breathed deep the scent of imported peat and blooming flowers. Yanked a stray weed. Clipped off the dying flowers.

Deadheading. A labor of tough love Momma and I enjoyed together. In this yard, the sole place we found peace with each other.

The tulips were past their prime, but the calla lilies, my namesake, shot up to the sun, ready to open in their glory. The buds dotted the beds in pastel simplicity. Coral-bells, bobbing daisies, and wild-seeded blue and purple bachelor buttons. My emotions flat-lined with the hard labor. When I felt ready, I followed my nose to Momma's favorite—her bed of roses.

Low to the ground in late spring, their delicate flowers sent out a cloying scent, overwhelming, entrapping. The roses flourished throughout their overlapped stages of life. Tight yellow buds, the first shy blush that revealed the interior's soft peach. In their prime the petals curled back to bursting, showcasing the soft white center. Finally, the hardened rosehips, fruit of the seedhead. Once the plant reaches that last stage, it produces no new buds until the next season. As in all life, you must cut them off.

Rosehips now covered Momma's pride. Untouched, unattended, unloved.

Her illness far more disabling than she'd let on in her weekly e-mails and our occasional phone calls, her garden revealed her weakness. Only Momma touched her roses, and now me. The sun was setting, but I couldn't leave them. Not like this.

By the time I finished it was dark. Spotlights flipped on, their artful light and shadow exposed the garden for night viewing. I heard Gary at Momma's French doors. His voice had aged. I'd aged. With sadness, I accepted I'd never hear his teenage laugh again. But it was good. Familiar. It was home.

"Calla. I heard you were back."

I stood and stretched, not caring that my jeans and shirt were dirty, that they smelled of sweat. Native red clay and expensive black dirt—hauled in annually for decades—caked beneath my nails. A sign of honest labor. Gary would like that.

He stepped into the garden, his face in shadow, his expression obscured. Still holding the hand clippers, I approached him, then hesitated, unsure how best to greet him. A heartbeat later, I shrugged, held out my arms, and let him choose.

He let out a short laugh and pulled me into his arms, unmindful of my soiled clothes against his starch-scented uniform, still crisp although I suspected he'd worn it all day. I'd once caught him cleaning his dorm room mini-fridge with a toothbrush. I grinned back at him when he didn't let my waist go after the hug. So I encircled his, dragged him with me as I put away Momma's garden shears, returned her battered straw hat to its peg. I flipped on the overhead fan to ward off the stillness of late spring heat, and we sat on the old swing. It still creaked.

"The hours we spent on this thing," he said.

"And if it stopped squeaking, Momma hollered out the window, remember?"

"Heck yeah. I bet she heard every word, every moan we made out here."

I laughed. It felt good—the sound of it full of good memories. A childhood full. Two young lovers full. The later ones, the painful ones, the ones where I'd hurt him, present between us, but unspoken.

"Will you be heading back to Chicago?" he asked. His real question, *Will you be staying here, taking over your momma's business interests?* But that was too close to those hurtful memories.

"I thought so, but now that I'm back..." I couldn't say the

words. I didn't want to get his hopes up if he held hopes. I'd never entered a permanent relationship. The social media rumor mill said Gary hadn't either—a fling here or there, but nothing permanent for either of us. I didn't have the right to hurt him again, didn't even know if I *could* hurt him. We, us, were ancient history now— twenty years since our high school loves.

He stood up as the security light inside snapped on, set by Momma long before her surgery forced her to leave and stay gone. The soft glow landed on Gary. His uniform implied stability which mirrored his dedication, his honor. His responsibility for his community, his people. I ordered myself to ignore the scab I picked with such thoughts. Gary could live anywhere, but his home was his uniform, his role as sheriff, the protector of Pinal County and Rose Arbor, its county seat. An incongruous name in the desert but Momma's momma, and hers before that had each ruled with an iron fist. The right bribe and the town's name became official. What the wealth of a mining enterprise couldn't buy in that century of robber barons.

Gary's hand closed on mine. His fingers stroked with gentleness. "Rose Arbor needs you. Things went downhill long before your momma got sick. The town council got away from her. They voted down a new outlet mall that would have brought in jobs, money. Downtown is dying and both factories shut down."

"Momma wanted an outlet mall?" Shocked didn't describe my feelings.

"Yeah. She changed these last few years, mellowed I guess."

Mellowed, like Momma's roses with their soft white centers in old age. The thought softened me as much as it troubled. Momma took care of things. Made sure that everything remained Andy Griffith, Mayberry pure in Rose Arbor.

Maintaining that purity cost money and the Manelli family—*my family*—funneled vast amounts of it into the community. But that money didn't just buy Mayberry. It also bought silence. A deep well of it that shielded us from scrutiny. Raised us above the law. So far above it that it tore a rift straight through the middle of Gary and me. He planted his strong, honorable feet here in the dirt of Rose Arbor while I let mine carry me away to Chicago.

I ran far physically, but not so far in reality. I worked as a CPA at the Manelli headquarters located on the Golden Mile, auditing the legitimate side of our interests. It was the other side of our money that Gary hated. I was more ambivalent. There were always bad guys somewhere in the world. Sometimes, those bad guys sat at our table for Sunday supper.

Rose Arbor was meant to shelter the next generation. Give them roots before they left the black and white behind and entered the family's world of ever shifting gray. Momma never allowed changes. I lied to myself now that I didn't care. Imagine that. Momma changed.

Gary's fingers formed an unbinding tendril around my hand. "Would you like a ride tomorrow?"

His touch, the gentle vine, was perfect. Familiar. I could be gone for years, and the connection would always be there between us. "I'd like that."

After he left, I sat on the patio while the scent of Momma's roses drifted on the breeze. I thought about her, our fight. The anger when I left. The hurt I'd caused her. Caused Gary. The scent of her roses was always heaviest at night.

FOR a small community, the hospital was large. It served the entire county, but anyone who needed real care shuttled off to larger facilities elsewhere. Momma hadn't been shuttled. Rose Arbor was hers. She'd die here with her people. If she died—when she died—they would be mine.

I took a deep breath. Rose Arbor was a feudal society within a democracy—an aberration. People who were born here, who lived here, and who died here—knew it for what it was. A planned community—before the term existed—thanks to generations of Manelli women and our family wealth. Rose Arbor was our garden and we tended it well.

Max, the man who had entered her life after my father died decades ago, stood in the cafeteria surrounded by his ranch buddies. Heads bowed, voices hushed, hats held in worrying hands. I nodded at Gary and he went to join them, while I slipped by and headed to the top floor. Momma would be in the large corner room with two windows, the same room where Grandma and Grandpa died. Our spot for meeting the maker. Only my Dad had broken the cycle, having died in the Gulf War. The first of us.

Machines on either side of the bed beeped. Tubes pulsed with liquids, and Momma was its failing heart. The machines kept her alive now, the rosehips hardening, stealing life from the rose. I'd come to sever the connection, to allow new growth a healthy beginning, as Momma would have wanted. With Max's permission. He held the life directive. Not me, her only heir. I'd left in anger and Momma'd never changed it back when our emotions cooled. It hadn't seemed important. Then.

A crystal vase filled with Momma's pastel roses rested on the windowsill. Even their heavy scent couldn't disguise the thick antiseptic odors of pending death.

I imagined myself in the bed, my face wrinkled with age like hers. I rested my own hands on her delicate, long fingers. With age my hands, my face, would look like hers. We were twins separated by a generation. We'd been too close in temperament. The same sharp anger. The impatience for incompetence, intolerance for weakness. Manelli women had backbone.

I leaned down and kissed her cheek. My own cheek years from now.

"Calla," from the doorway. Max's voice was tentative, hesitant, so unlike the man himself. A crotchety bastard, but he was Momma's crotchety bastard. I would inherit him, too.

In the hallway behind him, Gary stood, hands stuffed in his pockets, mirroring Max.

"Max," I said. An arrogant man, yet he shuffled his feet, the sixty-plus-year-old student caught in the wrong. "It's over, Max."

There were tears in his eyes, in his voice, "I can't, Calla."

"It's over, Max." His shoulders fell, and I reached out for him. Momma would have wanted it that way. Gary filled the empty spot on my other side. I flipped the switch to the machine. Shut it down.

My eyes met Gary's. I was the new Rose Arbor. And I was staying.

† † †

73

MEG E. DOBSON's short stories have appeared in national anthologies like Malice Domestic, Poisoned Pen Press, and SinC Desert Sleuths. Additional award-winning shorts were honored twice by the Tempe Community Writing Forum. Her flash fiction placed top-five three times at Writers' Police Academy. Her young adult crime fiction novel, *Chaos Theory*, a Kami Files Mystery, was published by the Poisoned Pen's imprint press. MegEDobson.com

CHANGING WOMAN
BEVERLY FORSYTH

CHANA liked the Phoenix city park when it was near empty like this. She counted the entrance columns, tall and statuesque. The Romans, an ancient people, invented concrete. The detail cemented itself in her memory. They reminded her of totem poles. Seven. Eight. Nine. Walk to the arboretum center. Dizzying lines of up, down, and across. The air smelled of popcorn and pizza. She yearned for hot fry bread. This land once belonged to her father, his father, and his father before him. Then the city claimed eminent domain. Of course, the city paid. But it wasn't the money her father wanted. His soul grieved.

Chana had helped her father lay the foundation of her childhood home—the hogan, he'd built after the land was sold. *"Brush the wet concrete,"* her father had instructed, *"until it is smooth and free of marks."* Her brothers, her father, and she worked side by side. The memories were sweet.

When his time was close, he did not call his sons. The death watchers, four from his clan, waited in the next room. The father had taught his sons to follow the traditions of the Diné—the laws, the stories, the traditions of old. His sons were noble men on the rez, who would be torn between love of their father and the love for the Navajo way. What he wanted was forbidden. Walking Bear yearned to go home, to walk among the living, to remain for all time.

Near death, he summoned his beloved daughter. This would be the last time she gazed upon his face. His eyes locked with hers, and she felt unable to move. She noticed a small piece of ash on her sleeve, the ash the death watchers used to protect themselves from evil spirits.

"You are more White than Indian," he said.

Chana knew he spoke the truth. Her blood was pure, but her heart was torn. She believed one must go out into the world and make their way—to live and work and love beyond the *Diné* way. *"Why must I be one or the other?"* she had once argued vehemently with the tribal elders. *"I can be both. I want to see the world."*

"I want to go home," her father spoke in a voice wracked with pain. "What I ask is unforgivable, yet I ask."

Chana, his only daughter, shut her eyes. Could she do this? Her heart wept inside her chest. She was afraid, more afraid than she had ever been in her life. She nodded. Evil spirits can smell the dying. The unspeakable waited outside the door.

Chana brushed and braided her father's long white hair—his crown of wisdom. With scissors, she cut the braid from his head. From hands and feet, she clipped each nail. From his frail finger, she slipped the animal-shaped turquoise, mounted in silver and made by his own hands. Eyes barely alive watched her remove his medicine bag from around his neck.

Without looking, she gently placed his braid, nail shavings, and ring, the essence of him, into his leather medicine bag.

"Father, are you sure?" Chana asked. Her heart beat so fast that she could feel it trying to break free of her chest. Could the medicine man in the next room hear the *thump, thump, thump* thudding in her ears? Every instinct warned her to say no to her beloved father. To not gaze upon the dying. To run. To grieve from afar. To be safe.

"Be strong, my daughter," were the words she thought she heard. The moan shuttered along her skin. Her hair stood on end. If he died while she was here, would the evil spirits haunt her? The four death watchers were in the next room and wondered why the great elder had called for his daughter. It was so risky. Perhaps, she had sinned and needed to receive her father's forgiveness. Yet, it was dangerous for her to stand so close to death, to look death in the face. If the dead are not buried properly, the spirit will return. The death watchers must have thought her sin was great to break the taboo.

With his silver blade, she sliced her father's palm. The White man's knife was purchased from a White man's store with a handle of intricate silver scrolling. When she and Walking Bear passed this store, the owner always waved and Walking Bear waved back. The clerk looked at the dollars in her small hand and the knife she prized. The clerk had said, *"Hmmm... This store doesn't carry anything in your price range. You need to go to a dollar store a few blocks over."* The owner, who she had seen on the TV sometime speaking, stepped up and the clerk moved aside.

As Chana explained her need for the knife, the White man listened. With a key, he unlocked the felt lined display and removed the knife. He told a story of a sixteen-year boy who had been to a party and then sped along the rez dirt road. The car had hit a large hole and the car rolled and then rolled again. Walking Bear pulled him from the car in the black, black night with not a single house light in sight and drove him to the hospital. Walking Bear sat with him until his parents arrived, at first concerned and then angry.

"What happened to the boy?" Chana had asked. She'd never heard this story.

The White man laughed out loud, free of guilt. *"He grew up to be a lawyer and then a judge and bought a gun and knife store and sometimes negotiates with a savvy ten year old."* His laughter was an open door.

"I think there are too many zeros on this price tag," the White man said. Chana eyes lit from within. The White man reached out and with a single finger touched her forehead, and Chana felt her grandmother, once again, anoint her cheeks, her palms with white paint, the final blessing that marked her *Kinaaldá* ceremony from child to woman. Chana was changed and changing. She closed her eyes and felt *Changing Woman* embrace her.

Walking Bear's blood flowed freely into the open pouch. His hand caressed the contents, known only to him, one last time. She pressed the knife to her chest, her father's blood marking her skin.

"How can I leave you?" Chana asked.

Her father could no longer answer. He closed his eyes and breathed his last breath.

The next day, her father's body was buried in the Navajo cemetery. No one spoke Walking Bear's name. From afar, hot flames consumed the timber hogan and her father's possessions. She watched. No one knew her crime, but she had sinned against all Navajos. Her father's spirit walked with her. To look upon the dead, to call their name, to take their possessions stirred the *chindi*, the spirit of the dead one. The spirit did not travel to the next world but lingered in the land of the living. When the dead hear their name, the yearning comes upon them and the spirit reaches out and grabs hold. They see their things and don't let go. It was tradition that his possessions be buried with her father or burned in his hogan. The elders did not know that she had taken his essence and the pouch which he cherished. The guilt weighted her soul.

The elders burned everything so that her father would not linger in this world but journey to the next. It is forbidden that the dead remain among the living. Ghost sickness could touch her brothers, their families, her clan, and with ghost sickness, death is never far away.

† † †

THE night breeze felt good on her face. Tourists passed without thinking of what or who possessed the land before it was now, before it was sold, raped, cement poured. The park was a commercial success and visitors poured in daily. Chic shops lined the streets all around. However, rumors now surfaced of a great silver grizzly that roamed the public park at night.

For nearly 100 years, Arizona had been bereft of the giant land walker, but now newspapers were ablaze with news of a lone grizzly and fiercely speculated from where it could have possibly come. There were too many sightings to be ignored. Videos caught flashes of movement and vague outlines. Environmentalists were excited about the possibility and what this could mean for the future.

Park Rangers were criticized because they could not seem to trap the giant bear. The bear came and went and from where and to whence they knew not. Tourists were afraid to be in the park after dark. Some were excited.

An expanse of concrete flowed in all directions. The city workers, who had grid the land, poured multiple sections. It was confusing to locate, but Chana found the site where once stood her family home and a pasture for sheep. She paid a city worker to use his saw to break through the concrete. He did not ask why she wanted the hole. Instead, he took the money and left her with a small bucket of wet concrete.

She poured water into the hole to soften the soil. With her

hands she clawed, breaking her fingernails on the hardened earth below. She clenched and unclenched her bruised and scratched fingers. Deep in the freshly scraped earth, she placed her father's leather pouch, the essence of him, along with his silver ring. With smooth even strokes, she repaired the concrete as she had been taught in her youth. *Hanííbááz*, the full moon, stood as a silent witness.

When she stood straight, her back ached as she gazed into the face of *Hanííbááz* and raised her arms in an open embrace. The *Diné* say: *Do not look at a full moon or she will follow you.* Chana gazed.

† † †

HER phone indicated the exact coordinates from her midnight journey four seasons ago. As the sky deepened, people hurried toward the park's exits, fearing the giant silverback grizzly might appear. The noise of people moving, voices, tall grasses, a hint of wind, and the smell of a far off distance rain assailed her senses.

The tips of branches, thick with bud, and a sense of spring quickened her step. Chana knelt before the midnight vault of the slumbering bear. Here was her father's tomb, his home, his land. Could she confess? She did not know. How could she speak of her crime? Would her people forgive her? If her brothers knew, would they even speak to her again? Or would she become an outcast among her people, her family. Only a Navajo would understand her sin, and her sin was great, perhaps too great, in the eyes of the *Diné*. For now, this was her secret, one which she dare not confess. Maybe, in time, she would tell the children, her children yet unborn, of how Walking Bear's spirit awoke to reclaim his home, and now the Great Grizzly walks the Arizona land.

Chana spread her thick-weave, geometric design blanket to pad the concrete. She placed her outspread hands over the sepulcher, still warm from the afternoon sun. She had many things to tell Walking Bear. The moon followed her to New York and London and Rome and arched tunnels in Venice. People looked but she did not notice.

"Hello, Walking Bear," Chana greeted her father. She waited for the great grizzly and Mother Moon. She closed her eyes and breathed home. Of course, she would confess to Walking Bear,

79

although she was sure he already knew it was she who kept his knife. "Your Navajo daughter has returned."

† † †

BEVERLY FORSYTH, who resides in Odessa, Texas, earned her Ph.D. in American Literature. Her writing has appeared in a variety of scholarly, literary, and commercial publications including *American Women Writers: 1900-1945* (Greenwood Press), *English in Texas, The South Carolina Review, Studies in the Novel, Research and Reflections, Cosmopolitan, USA Today, The Dallas Morning News, Texas Business,* and *The Texas Monthly Guidebook to Texas* (3rd edition). Her short fiction has appeared in *New Texas.* Forsyth is currently working on a crime novel about two detectives, White and Navajo, who team up to solve an abduction set in West Texas. BKForsyth.wordpress.com

DOUBLE OR NOTHING
DENISE GANLEY

GWEN'S phone blew up in the back pocket of her jeans. She set the griddle spatula down and dug it out, still vibrating from multiple texts.

CODE BURGUNDY
CROW ALLEY

"Shit."

Code Burgundy meant her brother needed life or death help.

Gwen unwrapped her apron and threw it on the counter. She abandoned the flattop grill, didn't wait for Love Life Kitchen's sous-chef to respond, and ran out the door thumbing back:

OMW, 15 MIN ETA.

Two minutes later, Gwen floored the twenty-year-old Honda to its limit.

Crow alley meant the crow graffiti in a Tempe alley where they had walked Dillon's cocker mutt a week ago. In hindsight, the little shit had probably taken her on some kind of recon mission. She didn't remember which alley it'd been, and now that it was dark…well, shit.

She tried not to worry that Dillon hadn't responded. Or about what he'd gotten himself into now that he was a licensed private idiot. He'd perfectly timed his latest dumb move for when she returned to civilian life.

Dillon had sworn on a stack of vintage *Teen Beat* magazines that he would not, under any circumstances, drag her into his detecting business. Barely holding on to her frayed mental health after her recent discharge from service, she needed the calm life her therapist prescribed. This had better be an actual emergency. No, she didn't want that either.

Gwen forced herself to bottleneck the what-ifs and only think about her next few steps. She slid back into her army training. Get there. Find Dillon.

She darted through traffic, glad she hadn't risked driving on fumes until payday.

Gwen skirted around ASU and downtown Tempe, finally turning into the housing tract where they had started their walk, and tried to remember the weaving route they had taken.

Adrenaline already high, it kicked up a notch.

She texted:

NEARBY. CANT REMEMBER ALLEY

Identical alleys ran between the main streets. Gwen picked one and dodged garbage bins waiting for tomorrow's pickup as she crawled through the narrow passage.

There! The crow on the wall. She hit the headlights, spelling out *d-i-c-k* in Morse code. When she hit "c", her passenger door opened and Dillon scooted inside.

The sight of her brother, safe, slowed her heart to a relieved canter. She took a deep breath to slow it further.

"Okay?"

"Duck Dodgers. But we have a situation."

He threw on his seatbelt, then flipped through the photos on his camera.

"Where'd you get that behemoth?" Gwen waved a hand at the large lens. "It's not exactly subtle."

"Mom bought it for me."

Gwen snorted. "Mom would not give you anything to support your 'filthy job'."

"I swapped out the Kitchen Aid mixer she bought me." He clicked through more photos.

"Nice knowing ya."

"She won't find out. Unless my evil twin tells her."

"This evil twin is saving your sorry butt."

"Here. The view wasn't great, but I think this a-hole was building a couple Molotovs." Dillon angled the camera to her. "He just left the house with a buddy and my guess is he's heading toward my client."

"Okay. Where to?"

"Take Hardy south to Thirteenth Street, then head towards Gammage."

Gwen frowned, speeding her way through the streets. "What

happened to Javier?"

Dillon sighed. "Vegas."

"Stop fucking your employees."

"Contractors."

"You need permanent backup. Someone you're not sleeping with."

Dillon turned on his charm. "You're the best backup around, Sarge."

"No. Where's your car?"

"I Ubered."

"You Ubered. To a stakeout. Without backup."

Silence.

Dillon finally muttered. "Javier slashed my tires, and I didn't have a chance to replace them. It was supposed to be a cake night."

Gwen chortled, then sobered. "What's going on?"

"Stalker ex." Dillon pulled out his phone and showed her a photo of a guy with deep set eyes and a narrow nose.

Gwen took a quick glance and turned back to driving.

"Jeremy Sanders. I'm digging up dirt. Client is Alex Jimenez, a friend of a friend. I removed a GPS tracker on his car, scrubbed his phone and laptop of spyware, and relocated him to Joe-lo's house while they're in Rocky Point. I'm guessing Sanders didn't like that."

"Does Alex have an order of protection?"

"Yeah, but we know how well that works."

Gwen sidestepped that landmine. "What's your plan?"

"I texted him to hide at a neighbor's house for a few hours until it was clear. He left the lights and TV on. The cars are there, so it looks like they're home, but there's no one in the house. I was thinking, let this guy throw his Molotovs at an empty house and catch him in the act. Then the police have a better chance of charging and locking him up."

"That's a terrible idea. Someone could still get hurt, not to mention the property damage. You know, all they have to do is catch him with Molotovs in his possession. Why aren't we calling the police now?"

"If I'm wrong, it'll be harder to protect Alex. Sanders'll know we're on to him. For all I know, he's heading to the desert to throw his babies for fun. Or they weren't explosives at all. He's dangerous. I don't want to overplay our hand."

"Our?"

"I'm deputizing you, Sis," Dillon said, squeezing her shoulder. "You're on the case now."

"PI's can't deputize, dumbass. And what you mean is, 'Gwen, I know I promised I wouldn't drag you into my shit, but can you pretty please help me out this one time only?'" Gwen gave him the side eye.

"Oh, you've been practicing Mom's look. It's getting better. Probably because you're old now."

"You can't use age jokes effectively when Mom shat you out two minutes before me."

"But, little sister, no one would guess that when looking at us. Bet you're regretting not moisturizing enough."

Gwen knuckle-punched his arm.

"Ow." Dillon sat forward. "Okay, slow through here. Joe-lo's house is five up on the left. Park a couple houses back so we can watch but not so they can see us."

Gwen eased the Civic to the curb in front of a dark house.

"I don't see his car. Red Chevy Malibu." Dillon looked through the telephoto lens. "There's no way we beat him here. Maybe I was wrong."

The street was quiet.

A flash of lights behind them had Gwen looking in the rearview. "Or maybe he just took a drive-by to scout, then circled back."

They ducked down below the windows as the car slowly passed.

"That's him." Dillon repeatedly clicked the camera. He hopped out and crept behind the car, taking more photos as he did so.

The red car slinked forward toward the house and stopped.

"Call the police already!" she whisper-yelled.

Gwen grabbed the expandable tactical baton she hid under her driver's seat. She tucked it into the back pocket of her jeans as she slid out of the car and crouched beside it in the street.

Dillon placed the camera on the car's hood, still aimed, clicking with one hand as he dialed 911 with the other.

The red car stopped, two men jumped out. The driver wore a ball cap low over his face. He held two bottles. The passenger, a squat guy, reached into his pants and pulled something out.

Not a gun, please not a gun.

He flicked his wrist, a flame sparked. Before Gwen got more than a step toward him, he held it to the rags in his buddy's bottles.

"Hey!" Gwen shouted, trotted towards them, too far and too late to stop the Molotovs.

The bottles were lit, flaming, and hurled in seconds. One exploded against the front door and the other against a car parked in the driveway.

Both men hustled into their car and peeled out.

Gwen dove back into the Civic, unlatched the fire extinguisher below the front passenger seat, and raced to the burning car. Thank god she insisted on keeping some Army preparedness protocols.

Gwen yanked her shirt up over her nose against the caustic fumes of burning gasoline, but it wouldn't stay put. She did her best to avoid breathing in deeply. The stench hurt her chest and triggered terrible memories, but she couldn't deal with any of that now.

Focus on your hands.

Her hands sprayed almost the entire cannister on and around the gas tank, extinguishing the fire. Glass crunched under her feet.

Dillon had the garden hose on full blast, but the water pressure was a joke, and he struggled to get enough water to smother the fire.

Flames still broiled the door, burning the red paint off and charring the wood surface. Whatever plants had grown in the narrow garden against the house facade had been incinerated.

Gwen hustled over and used what remained in the cannister to douse the persistent flames.

She should have made her brother call the police sooner.

Dillon leaned over, turned the hose on the top of his head. He scrubbed his face, then shook out his wet hair.

He huffed out a breath. "I bet I qualify for one of those hottie firefighter calendars now."

"Joe-lo is going to kill you for this."

Dillon squinted at the damage and sighed.

The sound of sirens relaxed Gwen's shoulders.

With one last glance to make sure the fires were truly out, she slumped to the curb several feet away. Her left hand shook. Not again. She rubbed it against her jeans and tried to breathe deeply, but that stench was still in her nose.

Everyone was safe. Everyone was fine. She repeated it to herself.

Dillon sat down next to her, bumped her shoulder with his. "Dibs on any hot first responders."

Despite herself, Gwen snorted.

† † †

GWEN had given her brief statement to a Tempe police officer and fire investigator, and returned to her piece of curb to wait. Dillon had been surprisingly steady and businesslike while working with the investigators. He'd even handed over his photo disc for evidence. Hopefully, he had nothing on there that could get him into trouble.

Dillon's client, Alex Jimenez, was a slight man, dwarfed by the police officer who spoke to him. He cradled his arms against his chest and kept staring at the crispy front door. Gwen knew that look, half relieved he survived the violence and half terrified about what could happen next. The man's ex was clearly a violent and controlling bully. And Gwen loathed bullies.

Alex finished his statement, wandered over.

Dillon hugged the man. "I'm sorry."

Alex clung tighter.

"How did he find me again?"

Gwen stood, waited for them to break apart before asking, "Is there a chance someone gave up your location? Perhaps not intentionally?"

Alex shook his head. "I've not told anyone nor been on social."

"My sister, Gwen."

Alex nodded.

"You should stay with us tonight." Gwen had not planned to say that, but once the words were out, she didn't regret them.

Dillon nodded. "My sister is former Army. You're safer with us. Leave all your tech here. Just grab a change of clothes."

"Okay," Alex said.

"We just need some sleep, then we'll regroup at breakfast," Dillon said.

† † †

GWEN did not sleep.

The events of the evening had jabbed at some old shit that she thought she had worked through. After the first nightmare, she knew better than to go back to sleep. Normally, she'd get up and go for a run, but she had people under her watch.

Gwen was mid-push-up in the wee hours when she heard something.

Rustling. Outside.

She grabbed her phone and the baton from under her pillow and darted to the living room. Alex was sound asleep on the couch. She nudged him awake.

He grumbled.

"Quiet. Someone's outside," Gwen whispered.

Alex's eyes widened, fear sparking.

"It's okay, I'm gonna handle it."

Gwen handed him her phone. "Wake up Dillon and call the police. Lock yourself in the guest bathroom. Don't open the door until I say."

She edged over to the front door, peeked through the peep hole. Someone was trying to pick the lock. Sanders. How did this guy keep finding Alex?

And what did he want exactly?

The cheap dead bolt would be no match for anyone who wanted to get inside.

Dillon appeared beside her before she could make a move. She motioned him away from the door.

"I'm going out the patio, will circle around. Lock the door behind me," she whispered.

"We should take him on together."

Gwen shook her head.

"What? I'm an orange belt in Taekwondo now."

Gwen rolled her eyes. "Stay here and look after Alex."

"What if he has backup?"

"I'll take care of that too." She did not want her brother getting hurt.

Dillon frowned.

Gwen slid open the patio door. She breathed in relief when she heard Dillon lock it behind her.

The backyard was tiny, with nothing but a bistro table and chair on the cement square. There was no way anyone could hide.

She padded to the gate, lifted the latch carefully, and was through it, walking across the front yard in moments.

Sanders crouched over the welcome mat, fussing with the door lock, a baseball bat on the ground.

There was zero cover.

If this guy had found a gun in the last few hours, she was screwed.

"You need to leave." Her voice was in full Sergeant mode. Clear. Measured. Steel. "Now."

The man startled, clutched the bat with both hands, squared his shoulders. He glared at her, then stood, kicked the door. A couple more of his kicks and that door would break open.

"Stop." Gwen walked towards him. "Alex is not here. Leave."

He kicked again. The door groaned but held.

There was little likelihood she'd be able to talk him down, but she'd try.

"We're just storing his belongings. He's not here." She hazarded a guess that this guy had tagged something else with a GPS device they had not yet discovered.

Sanders stepped away from the porch, bat in his hands, fury in his shoulders. "Who the hell are you?"

Gwen stood her ground outside the porch with enough room to move. "The police are on their way, and this is your last chance for peace."

His laugh was hateful and choked. "Fuck you." He held the bat up, pushed towards her.

In one smooth movement, Gwen shook out the expandable baton parallel to her leg and held it up by her head.

The man's eyes bugged. He tried to say something but couldn't form words.

The idiot swung the bat like he was hitting a grand slam, with a long follow through, leaving his flank wide open for a pummel. A tempting target, but she was better off dismantling his weapon hand. He swung again.

Gwen dodged back from his wild swing, the end of the bat catching her rib. Shit.

She ignored the pain to get close enough. Her baton arm coiled and ready to attack. She struck the baton on his right hand and then whipped back and struck his left hand. Like two rattlesnake bites in rapid succession. But far more painful and bone breaking.

A scream. The thud of the bat falling to the grass.

Gwen kicked him behind the knees to make him kneel, pushed him all the way over, and shoved the bat away with her foot. "Face down on the ground. Hands on your head."

Sanders whimpered. His hands lay limp, not quite making it to the back of his head. He lifted his head to shout, "Alex, I just want to talk. I love you! You mean everything to me!"

Gwen patted him down, pulled a switchblade out of his boot and tossed it to the bat.

"I'm suing your ass," he hissed.

"Be my fucking guest."

Lord have mercy, that had felt amazing! The adrenaline nearly covered up the aching of her rib. Bruised, hopefully not broken.

A car horn blared. Gwen jumped. Heart racing. Glanced down the street.

Dillon shouted in triumph by a sedan several condos down. He jogged over, arms above his head, imitating Rocky Balboa.

Gwen put a foot on Sanders' back to remind him she was there.

"I took out his backup," Dillon said, and held up a stun gun and some car keys. "He's not going anywhere before the police get here."

"Be sure. Get your ass back over there."

Dillon laughed. "Dude's out."

He held out a fist. Gwen sighed, bumped it.

Dillon jogged back to the car.

Police lights flashed.

† † †

THE three of them gave their second statements to the police within 24 hours. Gwen smiled when she saw an officer shove Sanders into the back of the police cruiser instead of the ambulance. Bastard deserved to stew in the pain of his broken hands.

Dillon sauntered over. He gave her his twin smile. The one he only used for her. Right before he talked her into something she didn't want to do.

"Come work with me instead of slinging veggie burgers all day."

"Don't want the drama."

"You work in the service industry, there's always drama."

"I hide in the kitchen. It's drama lite."

"We make a great team, Gwennie. Together we're unstoppable."

The last of whatever resistance she had withered away. The fact was, Gwen's veins buzzed. She'd been in her element. No illusions, she relished taking shitheads down. She almost even liked doing it with her brother.

Dillon grinned like he had just beat her to the cereal box prize. Like her joining him had been inevitable.

Maybe it had been.

Gwen checked herself for shaking hands. Minimal, but there. She'd figure out another way to deal with her nerves.

"Trial basis," Gwen said, trying not to grin back. "Part time."

† † †

DENISE GANLEY earned creative writing certificates from Arizona State University's Virginia G. Piper Center for Creative Writing and Phoenix College. She writes crime, the fantastical, and relationships steeped in witty banter. Denise lives in the Sonoran desert with her high maintenance kitties and her fat tire bike (which she needs to start riding to warrant its purchase.) If you want to know when Denise's next story will come out, please visit her website at DeniseGanley.com, where you can sign up to receive an email when she has her next release. She'll never spam you because she takes her karma seriously. DeniseGanley.com

FINE LINES
ROBERTA GIBSON

THE lap desk tipped as her trembling knees knocked, sending the papers sliding across the bamboo surface.

Maybe she should have let her psychiatrist write a prescription, instead of trying to work through the anxiety on her own. Too late now.

That corner of the master bedroom was the coolest place in the house during the intense Arizona summer and most days it was the quietest. Her light-brown hair cascaded into her face as she looked down at the pages in front of her. She sighed and reached into the pocket of her shorts for a hair band. Slipping the loose strands into a ponytail, she pulled her bare feet up onto the ottoman and adjusted the lap desk.

In an effort to suppress the quakes of fear, she began to edit the manuscript again.

> They had saved for months for this trip to Barbados.
> It was going to be the trip of a lifetime.

She drew a red line through the last sentence. *Cliché.*

Over the top of her glasses, she watched as her husband brought another pair of pants to the suitcase lying open on the bed. When he adjusted the contents, the T-shirt he wore rose up, exposing the inviting curve of his lower abdomen, shadowed with dark swirls of hair. In the past she would run her fingers along the elastic band of his running pants, perhaps even... But lately he didn't like her to make the first move. She shook her head and resumed reading.

> The trip was supposed to save their marriage.

Using the noun trip again? What about vacation? Or cruise?

> He had traveled the world before he met her, but she had
> never been outside the country. Perhaps having a shared

experience would improve things.
It hadn't helped so far. They had argued violently three
times in the last three days.

She crossed off the last part and changed it to *in as many days*.
She nibbled the tip of her pen before she wrote, *Try to show, not
tell*.

Most people edited on their computers these days, but she
enjoyed the feel of paper. Running the pen over the textured
surface soothed her.

"What're you doing?" he asked, as he slipped another crisply
folded shirt into the suitcase and reached for matching slacks.

"Thought I'd finish up the manuscript I found on your
desktop."

He dropped the pants onto the bed and advanced across the
room. "From my computer? Which one? Let me see."

He grabbed a few pages and stood rubbing his left hand
through his black curls as he read them. "This needs a lot of work."
He dropped the pages on the bed. "More work than you have time
for right now."

"It's no prob—"

"Let me put it back in the office for you." He lunged for the
rest of the pile.

She blocked him. "I'm nervous about the trip. You know
editing calms me. Gives me something else to think about."

He stood over her, his voice getting louder. "You shouldn't be
doing that right now."

"Hey. Chill." She gathered the papers close to her chest. "It's
no big deal."

"You'll make us miss the plane. Leave it."

She forced a smile. "I'm all packed. I'll read a few pages, then
get ready."

Instead of easing the tension between them, her attempt at
smoothing things over only seemed to intensify the strain and she
couldn't understand why. She hoped it was because he was also
nervous about the trip.

"Fine." He strode into his closet. She heard the hangers
banging against one another.

He was disappointed in her and it made him angry. So

angry he wanted to lash out. He felt like a volcano about
to explode.

She put a line through *He felt like*, and changed it to *He was*. She
wrote, "An exploding volcano is cliché. How about something
unusual, such as an egg in a microwave?"

He appeared in front of her again. "Are you sure you're
packed? We've got to be in the airport in three hours."

"Of course. I finished yesterday."

He reminded her of a saguaro cactus when he towered over
her like this, prickly and unmoving. She glanced out the window
where real saguaros dry-roasted in the sun.

"Did you bring a winter coat?" he asked. "It's going to be cold
in New Zealand. South Island especially. He said we'd go skiing."

"Yep." She curled up tighter, shifting her shoulders to block
him if he made another grab for the pages. "But I'd probably be
happier nestled by the fire in the lodge with a good book while you
and your brother hit the slopes." The idea of speeding down the
side of a mountain on skis gave her the chills.

He hovered. "Come on—put that down and take your shower.
We need to leave soon."

"You always want to get to the airport too early. We've got
time. I'd like to be as fresh as possible when we start out." Besides,
the pounding water on her tense body would be the opposite of
relaxing.

Giving up, he strode to the bed and began to count out pairs
of folded socks. Argyles one pile, athletic socks another.

After a moment of silence, he asked her, "How's the manuscript?"

She pondered the page in front of her, then looked up at him.
"The wife's pretty dull. Most of her dialogue is bland."

He turned his back, making a noncommittal sound.

"It's going to take a lot of work to give her a more realistic
voice." Was that sweat on his neck or was he still damp from the
shower?

He held up two socks. "Brown or black?"

She pointed to the brown.

He added the black pair to the open suitcase. "What're you
going to…?"

"I don't know," she said. Editing soothed her because it

reminded her of their old, familiar rhythm, their closeness. Talking through a manuscript's rough spots with her husband used to be one of her favorite things about the job. Lately, however, they'd done nothing but argue. Everything she suggested was "absurd" or "unnecessary." She straightened her shoulders. She didn't want to give up on what they'd had. "Maybe inject some conflicting goals. Some quirks to give her a unique personality."

True to form, his eyes moved upward in annoyance. "We're only editors. Don't try to be the writer."

She stared at him for a moment. "Who sent this to you, anyway?"

"There's no name on the cover page?" He began pawing through the laundry hamper. He pulled out a tee and sniffed it.

She turned over the stack of papers and shook her head. "No cover sheet."

"Why do you want to know?"

Even though it sounded like an innocent question, she suspected it wasn't. She readjusted the pages, pondering the safest response. "Curious about the author."

"You know, I think Thomas sent it. One of his clients who wants to self-publish." He knocked his running shoes together over the wastebasket and slipped them into a cloth bag.

Thomas was his old college buddy, the one who seemed to think they worked for him. His friend was a con artist and scammer, but her husband didn't seem to care. "I wish you'd quit taking work from him. He never has anything good."

"That's why. His clients need a quality editor more than most. Plus, we need the money." He looked at her pointedly.

"Don't start that again." She was tired of their fights over bills but slipped into the same old argument anyway. "If we're having money problems, we shouldn't be going on this trip."

"Why don't you want to visit my brother? It's been three years."

Another argument they had had before. "It's not about visiting your brother."

"It'll be good to get away from the heat." His voice softened seductively. "Spend some down time together."

At one time, that tone would have been enough to fill her with longing. Expectation. Instead, her stomach clenched.

Apprehension.

She said, "You keep saying we don't have enough money. You're sending me mixed messages."

He mumbled as he walked into the bathroom.

"What did you say?" she asked.

"Nothing," he said over his shoulder before slamming the door between them.

> That's when he met the vixen. She was alive, fresh, and sexy. So different from his stodgy wife who stuffed herself with sweets and never got dressed up anymore. He was literally a stallion around a mare in heat.

She removed *and* after fresh. She grimaced, crossed out *literally*. She gave up on the rest.

A few minutes later the doorbell rang. She sprang up to answer, knowing he would ignore it. After peeping through the hole, she unlocked the door and swung it open.

"Margie!"

Looking cool as an ice sculpture in spite of the heat, her best friend swept through the door, a gift bag swinging in her grip.

After their hug, Margie stepped back and surveyed her. "You're not dressed yet? Aren't you leaving today?"

As always, she felt rumpled and in disarray compared to her friend. "In a couple of hours."

"Here." Margie pushed the bag at her. "For the flight."

She peeked inside to see an assortment of magazines and paperback books. "You know me too well. Thanks," she said, smiling. "You want to come in for a minute?"

Margie nodded. After they settled in the kitchen, Margie leaned in and asked, "Have you told him yet? The D word?"

Although Margie had been her best friend since they could talk, she had noticed a change in their relationship. In the past Margie had always been the one who monopolized the conversation. Once she told her confidante she was considering a divorce, however, Margie wanted to hear all about it.

"I'm waiting. We're going on this vacation to try to reconnect."

Margie bit her lip. "But I thought—"

"Things have been better since we decided to go."

She tugged on her ear lobe. It was true. Things *had* been better since she'd said yes to the trip. Almost as good as they'd been in the beginning...until that blowup about the manuscript this morning. But that was stress, wasn't it?

Margie tilted her head and asked, "Are you sure you're not in denial?"

"No. But it's not an easy decision to walk away. Plus, there are practical considerations. One of us would have to buy out the other's share of the business. Neither of us has the money to do that right now."

"But you're the one who does the real work. He can't even spell. Can't he find another job?"

"We complement each other. He's the customer interface." He was more than that. Her husband was attractive. Irresistible to woman. Even beautiful, vivacious Margie wasn't immune to his charms. She tended to laugh a little too loud at his jokes. Hold his gaze a little too long. Just last weekend at her birthday party, one of Margie's work friends—who'd obviously had too much to drink—made the comment that her best friend and her husband looked like a couple. Like they belonged together.

Margie stared out the window for a moment, her features still. "So, you've changed your mind?"

"I'm hopeful."

They talked for a few more minutes before Margie made an excuse to leave.

AFTER she took a quick shower and changed into an outfit the salesperson had guaranteed would make her travels worry free, she sat down and started to rifle through the manuscript again.

> He bearly could contain his contempt for her. It was time to act.

She crossed out bearly and wrote *barely*. Reading it again, she drew a line through barely, too. She added *n't* after could. "He couldn't contain his contempt for her."

He stood over her again. "Who was at the door?"

"Margie."

"She's been around a lot lately."

"I think she has a bit of a crush on you." She held her breath, wanting to gauge his reaction, but also not wanting to see it.

"It's annoying." He laid his hand on hers, reminding her again of last weekend. The way he kept finding reasons to touch her best friend. He hadn't seemed annoyed by Margie then.

He removed his hand as if he had touched something hot. "Time for lunch."

"I'm too nervous to eat."

"That's ridiculous. Besides, you don't know when your next good meal will be."

She shrugged, set the papers aside, and followed him to the kitchen.

She warmed up some leftover pozole, ladled it into two bowls and tipped some hot sauce into his. She toyed with the hominy, then tried a spoonful of the broth. Her stomach roiled. When he finished his and left for his office, she dumped her bowl and did the dishes.

She piled her suitcase and bag in the hallway by the door. They still had an hour before their ride was due to arrive. She scooped up the manuscript and settled at the dining room table.

> He wanted to make it look like an accident. The kind
> an unsuspecting tourist might get themselves into.

She put a line through *the kind*, and changed it to *something*. She changed her mind and instead added a comma after accident, combining the two sentences into one. She pondered how to fix the mix of singular and plural. Finally, she struck a line through the last two words and changed them to *involved in*.

He pulled his suitcase into the hallway, too. After looking at his watch, he sat down across from her.

"Hey," she said, waving to the pile of papers. "Got a second? This is tough to edit and I'd like to ask your opinion."

"I guess." He pulled out his phone and began scrolling. "What's it about anyway?"

"A man is planning to murder his wife during their second honeymoon." She closed her eyes and rubbed the middle of her forehead where her anxiety had planted a headache. Not what she needed on top of her queasy stomach.

He set the phone down, but avoided eye contact. "So?"

"It's...weird. I'm not sure about the genre."

"You've finished it? Already?" he asked.

"Well, I skimmed through." She had done more than skim. She'd chewed through the manuscript in the last two hours, simultaneously engrossed and confused by what she was reading. "I was trying to see where it was going. It isn't set up like a typical mystery."

He still wouldn't meet her gaze. He glanced at his watch. "Explain."

She searched for the right words. The tension was taking a toll. "Instead of finding the body at the beginning and someone investigating, it's written in chronological order. He kills her at the end."

"So what? If the central question is whether the crime will happen…" He glanced at his watch again.

"It's a suspense novel. Or a thriller. Except no one is working to stop the murder." Her tone sharpened along with her anxiety. "It reads like a how-to manual."

His phone rang. Their ride had arrived.

As they pulled their suitcases down the front walkway, he asked over his shoulder, "Does he get away with it?"

"As it's written." She stumbled, her knees knocking as she followed him to the car. "But I may change the ending."

† † †

ROBERTA GIBSON came to writing after a career as a scientist. Her flash creative nonfiction was published in *Hippocampus Magazine* and her nonfiction short story, "The Punch Line," received a Commendation from the Society of Southwest Authors 2017 Writing Contest. She lives in Phoenix, Arizona with her husband and son. In her spare time she gardens and takes nature photographs. She also writes for multiple blogs, some of which you can find at her website: RobertaGibsonwrites.com

HE HAD IT COMING
KATHERINE ATWELL HERBERT

IT happened to me again. A death. Another death. And again, I'm sitting here in the same soulless interrogation room. But the death wasn't my fault. I swear to you, it wasn't my fault. I know, you're wondering what the hell I'm talking about. Sorry, sometimes, I get ahead of myself. This time it started with Willie. That's Wilhelmina my BFF. Jeez, I don't know why I used that abbreviation. Isn't it pretty passé by this time?

Let's go back to the beginning in case you were busy deleting the selfies you took with a guy you now despise. You'll love this. I met a gorgeous—well he was—guy at an outdoor, afternoon jazz concert in Scottsdale. Despite warning myself—I've got an overactive id, ego, superego thing going on—I spiraled into a sexy romance. Although I tend to resist romance that comes along too easily, I was a goner.

Then I discovered he was playing me. Not because he couldn't keep out of other women's beds, but because his scheme was to relieve me of several thousand *dineros* from my trust fund (it's pretty big), after which he and his *wife* planned to return to Missouri—if you can imagine anyone wanting to actually return there once they've left.

Jarrod was a genuine asshole. But more than that, he actually planned to push me off a roof, twenty-some stories up. In my fight to save my life it was Jarrod who took the swan dive and wound up splattered on the asphalt. End of my romance. And one criminal less in the world. Long story short—too late, I know—I got off with self-defense, but I never got together with the cute deputy who initially interviewed me.

And please, don't start in with 'did I really need to push him off? Did I try and save him at the last minute?' It's too much like some kind of serious existential question to me. Besides, I've waited too long now to tell you the calamitous tale of my friend

Willie. I'll just hint that the family that preys together (yes, I said prey) apparently are the most screwed up lot of humans currently slithering across the country.

† † †

OF course, I won't tell whatever officer comes in to question me that "he had it coming." That would be too honest. But he did. Brian Small deserved what he got—like all the men in that song and dance from the musical *Chicago*. You did know that's where the song came from, didn't you? Well, now you do.

I hope this officer is the same guy as last time. That one never had the follow-up I hoped for, but this could be a second chance.

Anyway, Willie and I celebrated with total abandon after I got cleared in my first go around with the forces of the law. And then, WTF, it happened again.

It started, like the last one, on a Sunday afternoon at a concert/art show in Scottsdale. What's with Scottsdale anyway? I thought all they cared about were ancient tourists from the Midwest, like Missouri, who come with cash hanging out of their handbags. Are they also harboring con men? You already know that answer. Even now I really can't believe that although I'm neither a black ops guy nor a CIA agent, twice in my life I've been marked for murder. Either I have a target on my back or Willie and I ought to stop attending arty afternoons in Scottsdale.

But there we were. Besides too much marginal art sold out of pop-up tents and mediocre music from bands a far pace from prime time, there's a load of food and about a zillion members of the under-twelve set careening through the crowds. I don't mind them. You've got to admire their pure energy.

After a bit of strolling around, Willie and I decided it was time for some refreshment.

She chose to battle the crowd at the beer table, "I know you're not much up for an IPA, so what can I get you?"

"A pilsner is good."

She nodded, "Find something actually edible for us, huh?"

"Why try," I told her, "Isn't eating junk why we go to these things? Aren't they an excuse to eat food that your digestive system considers a bio-hazard?"

She shrugged me off and disappeared into the crowd.

After we got our liquid fortification and gastro delights, Willie spotted an empty table and zoomed toward it.

A kid racing to an unknown destination crashed into her. The food on her plate lifted off like a pop-up fly but she aced the catch and regained her balance. The kid looked stunned, mumbled a "Sorry," and dashed off.

"The little bastard gave me a whack in the ankle," Willie said and limped toward the empty table.

"At least he said he was sorry," I said.

"B.F.D."

She was right, but let's face it, trying to corral a kid's spirit is mostly hope over experience. I looked down the walkway separating the vendors and saw the boy still racing through the crowd. He came to an abrupt stop next to a man, or woman, who handed him a couple of bills. The figure forking over the bucks was in profile. What was that, giving him a bonus for every ankle he winged? Oh, who cares. Doesn't matter. But it turned out to matter a lot.

† † †

THAT day became one of physical assaults for Willie. When she went off to get us a refill, a hunk of a guy with a smile that shouted seduction accidentally bumped into her—he was looking in the opposite direction at a kid, yeah another one, or the same one that attacked Willie's ankle and had been trampling over civilized life as we know it. The man, his name was Brian, apologized and then asked her out for a drink. She suggested they meet later on, after the festival closed. When I asked her later, she said she wanted to check him out on Facebook first.

The next day Willie told me she thought it was either odd or charming that when she introduced herself, he said, "Oh, I know you already and I can't wait to get to know you better."

What with Willie's hormones bursting to express themselves, she didn't worry about it. "He was," she said, "not the little engine that could. He was the turbo that powered a long freight train." Willie found her bliss, at least for that night. Maybe it could be more. It happens. But wait.

A few days later I got a freaky call from Willie. It was late for a work night, after 11 p.m. I had drunk too much at a meeting that went on too long. But she was half screaming, half crying and shouted. "I'm scared to hell they'll come back."

"Who?"

"They, they came into my house, barged their way in!"

"Who are they?"

"Them, Brian and the rest of them!"

"Right. I'll be right there. Did you call the cops?"

"Yeah."

"I'm coming pronto or sooner." Just then I heard her doorbell and she hung up. *Oh My God.* I hoped whoever they were hadn't come back. Tipsy and tired or not, a friend's emergency always comes first.

I threw on Levis, a jacket, and my favorite Vera Wang scarf. Yes, we occasionally wear jackets in this part of Arizona. We're not all desert and heat. If you think that, you're way too unsophisticated to live in America. Willie's place is about fifteen minutes from mine in good traffic, twenty or so when it sucks. I might have to double park. Her condo is close to a community college and I swear half the world attends them. At night. So I slide into the Audi and played beat-the-lights all the way there.

When I reached her townhouse, patrol cars nosed in around Willie's place and cops and neighbors littered the sidewalks. I made my way through them to the front door. An officer just a few inches shorter than King Kong blocked it, his back to the door.

"Hi…," I said, and checked his name tag. "Keith. I need to go inside. Wilhelmina called me and asked me to come."

He mumbled a "This is a crime scene. No one's allowed in." and turned to look over the crowd.

Really? I could give him a hard push but that would be like me trying to push the Rock of Gibraltar into the Atlantic. I put on my sweet-little-girl smile and tapped him on the shoulder. He looked down at me like "what now?"

"You need proof? I'm her best friend, you know her bestie. I can describe everything in her living room."

"You can't now," he said and stepped inside then closed the door on me. How rude was that? How could he possibly play it this way? To me! Okay, just so you know, I usually don't do this, but, occasionally it's required. I pounded on the door. He opened it slowly and stared at me. Blank as a small appliance.

"Listen Keith, I'm on the Governor's staff and if you don't let me in, you'll regret it." I flipped out my I.D. (for my dad's office staff BTW) and thrust it close to his beady eyes. I figured he couldn't read. As if each step brought him closer to his own death, he slowly let me in.

When I got a few feet by him I heard him snicker. You know, the-through-the-nose laugh that sounds as disgusting as mud wrestlers fornicating. Not that I've ever seen that, but you know the Internet. It's got pictures of everything you never wanted to see.

Officer Keith was right. I couldn't name everything in Willie's living room. It could qualify for FEMA funds. I made my way through the broken lamps, toppled-over chairs and throw pillows that were now just free-floating stuffing. The worst was the shattered large-screen TV. It looked ominous, a little like those glasses on the billboard in *The Great Gatsby*.

When I opened the door to Willie's bedroom, I found her sitting on the bed shaking with bruises tarnishing her face and upper arms plus a couple of shallow cuts and a whale of a black eye. What kind of donnybrook had she refereed?

The officer standing next to the bed looked my way when I came in. I nodded.

"I'm Ramon," he said.

I said hello and introduced myself.

Ramon looked back down at Willie. "Are you sure you don't want go to the emergency room?"

She shook her head.

"It would reassure you that you're okay. There's a lot of bruising..."

"I'm okay." Willie trembled a little as she said it.

He nodded and squeezed his lips together like a dad whose advice wasn't being taken, but he didn't press her. "Well, your descriptions will be a big help in finding these guys. And when we do, we'll find something to charge them with, there are plenty of options."

I sat down next to her. She curled into my arms and caught her breath between jerky sobs. I hugged her like a mom and told her the lies we all repeat in those situations, "It'll be all right. You'll be all right." Okay, they're not really lies, they're more like trying to will the future. Ramon continued to look at Willie. I swear I saw tenderness. I think he wanted to get to know her.

After the cops got the info they needed, and an officer was left to guard the house for the night—I may have had something to do with that—the others left. As soon as everyone was gone I made Willie a cup of chamomile tea. I thought I'd get her into bed and stay the night on what was left of the couch. She wanted to talk. And out it came, the whole story of Mr. Brian Turbo Train. After a couple of deep swallows of tea she began her horror story.

"We came back here after our drink," she said and took another sip of tea. "And he was, it was, well you know, great. In the morning he left and said he would be back as soon as I got home from work. I didn't believe him. I was sure it was probably a one-nighter when he didn't show up the next day. Well, I told you all that already, didn't I?" Willie was silent again. I wondered if she wanted to go on. I was about to ask when she began again.

"When I got home two nights later, Brian was waiting for me. He apologized and we went inside. He was nervous and paced around. I thought he was worried that I wouldn't let him stay again so I asked him 'what's up?' He told me he thought I wasn't who I told him I was. I laughed and said, 'Who do you think I am?' At that moment, a woman and a kid came crashing through the front door."

Willie stopped again. This time she looked up at me and pursed her lips like she didn't want to say what she was about to. "Know who it was?" she finally asked and without waiting for a reply added, "It was Crystal, Jarrod's wife. Remember the little innocent cutie that claimed she knew nothing of Jarrod's scheme to get your money?"

"Oh my god! No way!" I said.

"Way!

"So?"

"And the kid? The same brat that ran into me at the art show! They called him Georgie."

"What in hell?"

"At this point Brian stood up, threatening like and said, 'Are you or are you not Nora Judson, Senator Judson's daughter?'

"Jarrod's wife screamed at him, 'You're both so stupid you

make stupid people seem like geniuses,' and she bats the kid in the head with her purse. He screeches and moves out of her range. The poor kid already had some bruises on his arms and face, so I figured he'd already gotten one beating.

"Brian grabbed the kid by the arm and flung him on the couch, 'Georgie told me this girl,' and he pointed at me, 'was Nora. How the hell could I know she wasn't the target? I wouldn't know Nora from *Dora the Explorer*.'

"Georgie popped up then and said, 'I heard her name when she was getting food at that counter. The guy called her Nora. That's why I ran into her so you would know which one was Nora.' Brian told him to shut up. And Jarrod's wife screamed something about me not looking anything like you."

"No kidding." Just to catch you up at bit, you ought to know that while I'm a straight-haired blonde without enough bumps in the right places, Willie is a…lover's delight. Dark flowing curly hair and a va-va-voom shape.

"From there," Willie said, "I guess Brian decided that he may as well knock me off because what would happen to him otherwise? Crystal stepped in and tried to stop him.

"She looked at me and said she had planned to kill you because you murdered Jarrod… Then she lunged at Brian telling him to calm down. He was the only brother she had and though he was dumb as a computer bot, she needed him. He shoved her away. She fell on top of Georgie. The kid pushed her off. She thudded onto the floor and that really got the action going. Brian pinned me against the wall, Crystal started throwing things at him and me, and kid got into a shoving match with her."

I guess my jaw dropped to the floor. This scene was too surreal though I'll never admit that to anyone that I wasn't perfectly calm.

Willie told me she got a little leverage and kicked Brian right where it really hurts—I guess it's a good idea to take a few self-defense classes, as she had. She watched him fall back and then the wife pushed him all the way to the floor and struggled to pin him there. The kid jumped on top of them. They finished off whatever furniture was left after the earlier skirmish and that's when the television gave up its life. She finished her story with, "I rushed into the bedroom, locked the door, and dialed nine-one-one."

"And?"

"When things quieted on the other side of my bedroom door I could hear voices but couldn't tell what they were saying until I caught the words, 'We'll get her yet.' Then I heard the front door close. I opened the bedroom door. They were gone. But there's something else, Nora."

Oh, I thought. That's a very bad way to begin a story. You never want a good friend to say it and you really don't want to hear your doctor say it. "Something else" just means "trouble ahead." But I've cultivated the image of being in control so I had to swallow my misgivings. "And that would be?" I asked casually.

"They found your address and they may be on their way over there now."

I just stood there for a few seconds. "Damn Crystal and damn Brian. I'm gone." I told her.

"Be careful," she called as I grabbed my car keys.

"I'll leave you in the hands of the officer out front." Then I flew to my car and returned home as fast as I left. I hoped I could get there and get safely in if they came knocking or worse were already there.

All was quiet when I got home. My tension fell a few points when the garage door ground its way to the floor. I entered the building with my code and did the same with the elevator then breathed a sigh of relief as the doors popped closed. The fourteenth-floor hallway was empty. I entered my place. Still and quiet. I'd be all right I thought. The building was secure.

I put the key in to set the door's deadbolt when it burst open. Brian barged through and shoved me to the floor. Before I could get up, he grabbed my hair and dragged me to toward the balcony. Believe me, you never want that to happen to you. It hurts like hell and think of all the time you'll spend with your stylist trying to repair it all later.

Behind us Crystal's nasal bray harmonized with her screams of "Let me do her" as she rushed toward us. On the balcony Brian forced me to my feet and slammed me at the railing but as he did, Crystal reached out to grab me. Brian's shock allowed me to slip from his hands and I slid to the floor. The harridan couldn't stop in time and crashed into him. He fell backwards and before he could catch himself went over the railing. She almost followed but grabbed hold of the railing and collapsed on the balcony huffing and puffing.

I got to my feet, looked over the balcony and was ready to give Brian the two-fingered salute I had given Jarrod but Crystal rose and lunged at me. I held my ground and gave her a shove. She grabbed at me trying to stay upright but got only my scarf as she fell backwards. I pinned her so fast you would have thought I was on WWE's A-list. I slapped her hard across the cheek. I know today women slug. Slapping is so retro. But, apologies, it was an automatic move. I rolled her over, wrapped my Vera Wang tightly around her wrists, dragged her to the railing and tied her to it. If I was lucky, it would last until the police arrived. I looked up. Georgie stood in the open doorway. I took a step toward him. He disappeared. I hope he found a better place.

So here I am again, in this windowless cell waiting for an officer. The wife is down the hall. I'm sure Daddy will be here soon. I hope the same dreamy officer I had before shows up. Indeed I do. I hear some noise on the other side of the door. Sayonara, my phone's about dead.

Officer Edna, wearing a scowl, came through the door.

† † †

KATHERINE (Kate) ATWELL HERBERT is the author of four books on screenwriting: *Writing Scripts Hollywood Will Love* (2 editions), *Selling Scripts to Hollywood*, *The Perfect Screenplay*, *Writing It and Selling It*, which are based on her experience in Hollywood as a screenwriter, analyst, and development director. She's also written for national, regional, and local publications as well for newspapers here and in Los Angeles. As a live theater publicist, journalist, and poet she won several local and national awards. Kate chaired the Film Program at Scottsdale Community College for 11 years and is currently focused on short mystery stories and recently finished her first mystery novel.

COOPED UP
TOM LEVEEN

BRIAN built the cage in a day. The chickens needed a bigger coop, and he was thrilled to be able to build one for his father.

His dad, Bill, sat on the back porch of his out-of-the-way single-bedroom home outside Sierra Vista. Brian had only known about the place for a week, ever since his dad reached out after three decades of separation.

"There's some things I need to say," Bill had told him over the phone. He sounded frail. "Will you come, son?"

And of course Brian said yes, because obeying one's father was just what one did.

He didn't want to disappoint.

He took a day off work and drove down from Phoenix in the relentless July heat. That morning, at dawn, the temperature clocked in at 90. That meant 115 or more by afternoon.

So be it. His curiosity was too piqued to be put off by heat. He'd spent a lot of time under that Sonoran sun as a kid. It wouldn't bother him.

The little house wasn't a shack, but it wasn't much more, either. A dusty Chevy pickup sat parked on the gravel driveway—same model, different year as Brian's own. The echo unnerved him; he'd somehow bought the same damn car as his dad. *Christ.*

The property had no fence; it sat at the bottom of a steep dirt hill on its own small, flat plot. Creosote, mesquite, and saguaro surrounded the house at irregular intervals. There was no garage, no carport, not even a pavement slab, just tan gravel spread around the house to a distance of about ten feet. Brian saw a long, low chicken coop on the west side of the little house, and the sight of it made his heart twist. Dad had raised chickens as far back as he could remember. At a glance, Brian figured about five Cochins and three Gold Sex Link hens, scratching in the dirt. The coop was simple: two-by-fours and hexagonal wire mesh, four feet tall by ten or so feet long.

"Still at it," Brian muttered, and parked the truck next to his dad's.

When the front door opened, Brian wasn't sure he'd concealed his shock at Dad's appearance. The man was *old*—shockingly old. His feet were enormous and swathed in Ace bandages. His forearms and biceps had withered, and he required a walker.

Dad blinked at him and seemed to search for a smile to put on a face that hadn't smiled for as long as Brian had been alive.

"You came."

"You called."

"Well." Dad turned and shuffled into the house, so Brian followed, closing the door.

He took note of things as Dad went into the living room. Bedroom off the entry hall, dark and crowded with bookshelves and boxes. What might be in those boxes, Brian could only imagine. The entry spilled into a living space and open-floorplan kitchen, with Spartan appointments. A big TV was set up in one corner in front of a blue recliner and side table, on which sat a plate of crumbs. A wheelchair was folded up and resting against the wall nearest the recliner. A sliding glass door showed a covered tile patio and small patch of dead grass beyond.

Past the tiny yard, desert landscape extended to the horizon, broken only by distant bruise-colored mountains. No other houses, no buildings, no electrical poles. Thinking back, Brian guessed it had been five minutes or more between the last house he'd seen and arriving here.

Dad was totally isolated.

There was a stout round table shoved gracelessly into the corner near the glass door, and Dad sat on one of its two chairs. Brian wondered, but didn't care, who in the hell would ever sit in the other one. He stayed on his feet, hands in the pockets of his cargo shorts.

"I, uh…just wanted you to know that I…I maybe coulda done things differently, is all." Dad coughed a little bit and sounded like he swallowed whatever came up.

Brian fought a disgusted sneer. "That's all, huh?"

"That's all."

"Is that an apology?"

"Well, it's what I got, son."

"Why? Because you're old and dying?"

"Well…that might have something to do with it."

Simultaneously uncomfortable with the closest thing to affection he'd ever experienced and swelling anger at the past coming back to haunt him, Brian paced to the sliding glass door, looking past the patio and yard to the distant mountains.

"You must not get a lot a visitors down this way," he said, folding his arms.

"No, not many."

"You look like you could use some help, to be honest."

"I get by."

Brian's gaze drifted to the chicken coop. The hens poked around in the dirt and sipped from a tin waterer.

"How do you feed the chickens?"

"Toss the feed in through the wire. It's easy. Getting out there and back is a chore these days, but."

"But you don't get to go inside the coop. You know, like the old days."

Dad sighed. "No. That's true."

Brian faced him. "I don't have to be home any time soon. Let me put up a new coop for you. So you could go inside."

"Oh, for heaven's sake, Brian, you can't—"

"Sure I can. Hell, you'd be amazed at what I can do." He jingled his keys. "There's not much more to really say, is there, Dad? It's early, and I passed a Home Depot on the way in, about, what, twenty minutes from here? I know how much you love those old girls. Look, I'll be right back."

"Son—"

"Back in an hour."

He was out the door before Dad could say anything else.

Not a handy person but not unfamiliar with tools, Brian ran mental calculations as he drove to the big box hardware store. Just in case Dad didn't have tools at the house, he'd have to invest a little there, but no big deal. Lumber, a screw gun, some fasteners, tacks, chicken wire, hinges…no problem. It didn't have to be perfect. Just big enough for Dad to get inside and be with the chickens.

The heat punished him as he loaded his haul from a big orange cart into the bed of the Chevy. God damn, it was not going to be a good time out in Dad's back yard as the sun rose higher. But what the hell. It was the least he could do.

Brian backed the truck alongside the west side of the house. He unloaded the materials to the center of the patch of dead grass, carelessly piling everything up. The bed of the Chevy was half empty when Dad wheeled himself onto the patio and watched.

"You don't have to," he called.

"Too late, already done," Brian called back, and dumped the last load.

He got to work on the image in his head, laying out wood as the new DeWalt charged up. He expected Dad to call out instructions or corrections, but the old man was still, not even sipping water in the heat. For his own part, Brian let himself into and out of the house for frequent water breaks, not wanting to end up passed out from heat exhaustion. Who knew if the old man would bother calling for help. He certainly didn't have the strength to pull Brian into the shade or get him more water; he'd barely managed to maneuver himself out to the patio in the wheelchair.

The coop took shape more readily than Brian had expected. But then, by mid-day, he was motivated to wrap up and get home. He kept himself cooled off with a hose coiled near the extant chicken coop, and by lunchtime stepped back to take in his creation.

"I think that'll work," he announced.

Dad may have nodded a little, Brian couldn't tell. The chickens by then had retreated to the relatively cool darkness of their covered nesting boxes.

The new coop stood eight feet tall and sixteen feet long. The fresh chicken screen sparkled, shiny and strong. Brian tested the simple door he'd constructed on thick metal hinges. It swung easily and silently. The hasp-and-staple style latch clanged.

"So," Brian said. "Let's give it a try."

He remembered how to do the next part from Dad.

The nesting boxes had a rear door that could be lowered to gather eggs. There weren't but a few eggs when Brian opened it. The girls had gone into hiding from the terrible sun, so it was an easy if dusty experience moving each hen to their new home.

"There's no nesting box in yours," Dad called.

Brian got the last chicken in and shut the gate, slapping the latch closed. He dusted his hands together. "Yeah, I just realized that. That's okay."

"It's not okay. They'll burn up. Be like some KFC out here in the yard in this heat."

"Huh. You think so?"

Dad nodded.

Brian gazed at the structure for a long time, debating. Then he shrugged and went to go get behind Dad's wheelchair.

"Let's try it out," he said, and wheeled Dad off the patio. "Make sure you can get in okay."

The chair rocked and bobbled over the rutted landscape.

"There's no ramp," Dad said, hands dangling limp off the sides of the wheelchair.

"Oh, that's okay. I'll just help you over the threshold."

"How am I supposed to do it myself?"

They reached the coop. Brian stepped on the little footrests at the rear of the chair and leaned his dad back. "Not sure. I hadn't thought that far ahead."

"Son..."

Brian opened the gate, shoved the wheels up and over the two-by-four at its base, and got his dad into the coop. The girls clucked and fluttered but none tried to get out. They knew Bill well.

Brian sighed satisfactorily.

He remembered how to do the next part from Dad, too.

Brian stepped out of the coop and closed the gate. He brandished a new padlock from one pocket and snapped it closed over the latch.

Dad still faced away from the gate in his chair. "What was that? What did you do?"

Brian stepped into his view and half-hunkered, his hands on his knees, staring into his father's eyes. "Let me know if this starts ringing any bells, Dad."

It did. Brian could see it did. Terror rose up in the old man's eyes like a spider climbing a thread. "You...you can't leave me out here."

"Yes I can."

"The heat. I got no water. I got no shade..."

"Nope."

"Dammit, boy, get me out of here!"

Brian shook his head. "You shouldn't have called me. You shouldn't have moved to a place where no one can hear you and where no one cares. *You shouldn't have locked me up in a fucking chicken coop.*"

The old man's voice trembled. "Only when you were bad…just once or twice…"

"For *years*. Till I got strong enough and had the balls enough to kick my way out of it. You remember that day? You left me and mom a week later. Three, four, five times a week, for hours at a time you put me in there. What, you thought I'd forget, is that it? Because I didn't, Dad. I didn't. Not even after thirty-whatever years. You should have just moved out here and died. Oh, well."

"You were bad," Dad pleaded, as if this would make everything all right. "You had to learn…"

Brian stood straight.

"Looks like I did. I'm leaving now. Although, wait. I do have to wonder…without any feed, what do you think the girls will eat?"

His father cast a comically worried glance at the chickens clucking around him.

"You can't do this!"

"You were bad. So you'll stay in there as long as I say you stay in there."

"*Brian!*"

Brian ignored him. He walked quickly to the Chevy, slapped the tailgate shut, and climbed in.

He watched in the rearview mirror as Dad pushed against the wire with both hands, his fingers like chicken's claws. Brian watched, and waited.

The screen held. He'd tripled up on the U-shaped tacks and Dad was far too scrawny in his upper body to push it loose.

Brian glanced at the digital thermometer readout on his dashboard.

One hundred sixteen.

"Thanks for the call, Dad," he said, and drove the truck over the gravel and on to the dirt road.

† † †

TOM LEVEEN is an award-winning novelist and Bram Stoker Award finalist, with nine novels published by imprints of Penguin Random House, Simon & Schuster, and others. He has also written for the comic book series SPAWN. He is the former artistic director of two different theatre companies in the Phoenix metro area, where he has lived his entire life. TomLeveen.com

FADE TO BLACK
SUSAN CUMMINS MILLER

TUESDAY night. First full moon of winter. The Time When the Crazies Come Out of the Woodwork on the seasonal calendar of Pima County Sheriff's detective Toni Navarro.

Toni and her partner, Scott Munger, had drawn the short straws at roll call. Desk duty. The first few hours were unseasonably quiet. A power outage a few blocks away drew all available deputies to work traffic control at the intersections. Toni had nearly brought her case files up to date when the phone buzzed in Munger's cubicle across the aisle.

"Got a live one, Navarro. Lady at the front desk says she can identify Ben Riggs' killer." He resumed typing.

"Who's Ben Riggs?" Toni asked.

"Damned if I know. Not one of our cases anyway—I just checked."

"I'll take it."

Toni negotiated the narrow corridor between overcrowded cubicles and opened the door to their inner sanctum. She could see no one waiting in the reception area beyond the glass screen. She said, "Karin?"

"You ready?" said the uniformed officer on duty. The two words held an undertone of humor. But Karin rarely smiled, much less laughed.

Toni looked at her.

"Meet Delilah Barrie," Karin said. "She screened okay, and we double-checked with the wand." She punched the buzzer.

Toni opened the door to reception. An Ewok slid off a chair. Four-foot-nothing. Eyes the color of chocolate diamonds gleamed above at least three striped scarves wrapped around the woman's head and neck. The stripes and colors clashed with a bubblegum-pink wool cape and pea-green leggings. It was only fifty-five degrees outside.

"I have trouble thermo-regulating." The Ewok's high-pitched voice was muffled, but the diction was so pure Toni caught every syllable. One small mittened hand held a penlight. The other clutched a woven satchel worked with yellow camels.

"I see," Toni said, though she didn't.

"Interview room, or back at your desk?" Karin said.

"Desk." She held out her hand. "Detective Toni Navarro."

"A woman detective, fancy that. Can't have been easy."

When Toni responded with a noncommittal grunt, the Ewok slipped the flashlight into her satchel, took off her right mitten, and waved her hand as if testing the air temperature. Nodding, she brushed Toni's hand with a feather-light touch. "Delilah Barrie. Barrie with an i-e, not a y."

"As in *Peter Pan*."

"Exactly. But no relation."

Toni smiled. "This way, Ms. Barrie."

"It's doctor. Theater and Film. USC. Class of '62."

Toni led the way through the silent rabbit warren. Outside, a north wind slid down the face of the Santa Catalinas to collide with air currents venting through Redington Pass. This unseen river followed Tanque Verde Road, whipping the flags on the pole in the parking lot, moaning through the branches of the palo verde and mesquite trees. The temperature would drop rapidly.

"You have someplace to sleep tonight?" she asked Dr. Barrie as they passed Munger's desk. "If not, I'm sure Detective Munger would be happy to call around and find a bed for you." She grinned at him over Barrie's head. Munger rolled his eyes and discreetly flipped her off.

"No worries. I'm set," Barrie said.

Delilah began divesting herself of her layers, piling them on the extra chair. Toni grabbed Munger's second chair.

"Thank you, dear." Delilah plopped her tiny, yellow-leotard-clad body in the chair. She shivered in the warm room, retrieved her pink wool cape from the pile, and draped it over her lap.

"Coffee?" Toni said.

"Tea would be nice. Decaf Earl Grey, if you have it. I do love my oil of bergamot, but caffeine keeps me up."

"Er, yes. Munger?"

"Coming up," he said.

Toni set her phone to record the interview, took out her notebook and pen, and said, "I know you showed your ID to Karin when your arrived, but would you mind showing it again?"

Barrie rummaged in the satchel. Her feet, in Argyle socks and child-size sneakers, swung back and forth inches above the floor. "I don't have a driver's license, of course. I'll be ninety-six soon. The eyes are still good, but people drive so fast nowadays. And the streets are so crowded—I nearly hit a jaywalker the last time I was behind the wheel. Not that it wouldn't have served the urchin right. He was playing with his cell phone and not watching where he was going. That was five years ago." With a triumphant expression, Barrie produced a Medicare card.

Toni jotted down the number and handed back the card. "This is helpful. But do you have something with your address and picture? A passport, perhaps?"

"Haven't left the country since nineteen-eighty-two. Visited Oxford, where my mother was born, and played Titania in *A Midsummer Night's Dream*. It was delicious. But that seemed to put my travel bug to rest. All I need or want is right here."

"And what would that be?"

"A big screen TV…a grocery store, restaurant, and pharmacy within walking distance…and interesting people to talk to. Like you and Detective Munger."

Toni's partner had returned from the break room with a ceramic mug of steaming water and a tea bag. Where he'd gotten the Earl Grey, Toni didn't know. He set the tea down on Toni's desk, then pulled his own chair over to join them. There wasn't enough space in the cubicle, so he blocked the opening.

"You don't mind if Detective Munger sits in, do you?" Toni said, as if Barrie had any say in the matter. Their desks were only eight feet apart. He'd hear every word whether he was in Toni's cubicle or not.

"The more the merrier, dear."

"Now, could you tell me about—" Toni looked at Munger.

"Ben Riggs," Munger supplied.

"Right. Ben Riggs." She opened her notebook and picked up a pen. "We don't have any case under that name, I'm afraid."

"Understandable," Barrie said. "He's used so many names.

Sometimes even I can't keep them straight."

"Could you give us some of his aliases?"

"I wasn't expecting a pop quiz, but…" Dr. Barrie pushed up her confetti-colored knit hat to scratch thinning silver hair. "Well, here are a couple of my favorites: Todd Hunter and…oh, yes, T. J. Memphis. Will that do for a start?"

"Yes, thanks," Toni said, and tipped her head at Munger. He scooted his chair back to his cubicle and began typing.

Toni turned her gaze back to Barrie. "And you witnessed an attack on Mr. Riggs?"

Barrie looked at Toni as if she were one Allen wrench short of a full set. "Ben was murdered. I thought I made that clear to the gatekeeper."

Toni sat up straighter. For someone who'd witnessed a homicide, Barrie seemed remarkably relaxed—sanguine even. Munger stopped typing. He stood and shook his head. No calls had come in. Was Barrie making it up?

Toni said, "You witnessed a homicide? Where? When?"

"It happened about an hour ago, dear. Maybe two. Anyway, just before the power went out. At the liquor store. Ben stopped there on his way home from work—to buy a bottle of champagne. He was celebrating his promotion to partner."

"Partner?"

"Yes. In Riggs, Bonsall and Partridge." More key-tapping from Munger's cubicle. "It's a law firm," Barrie said. "You must have heard of it."

"Can't say that I have," said Toni. "You speak of Ben Riggs as if he's a friend. Do you know him well?"

Barrie's tinkling laugh sounded oddly familiar. "Since he was in short pants, dear. The first Riggs is Ben's father, Jamison. Oh, has anyone called Ben's parents to tell them the news? They'll be destroyed. Ben was Jamison's son by his first wife…Christina…no, that's not right." The wrinkles on her wizened face screwed tight as she concentrated.

"That's okay—"

"Brittany." Barrie beamed. The wrinkles eased. "Brittany Riggs. 'Rule, Britannia!' How could I forget?" She hummed a few bars.

Toni leaned back. It was going to be a long night. "We'll make sure the Riggses are—"

"Parents worry so, even when their children are grown. My parents were Munchkins—met on the set of *The Wizard of Oz.*"

Which explained why Barrie's laugh sounded familiar. "Yes, well, we'll make sure that the Riggses are notified. But could you tell me where you were and what you saw?"

"Ah," Barrie nodded. "'The facts, ma'am, just the facts.' I did love *Dragnet*, didn't you?"

"Absolutely," Toni said, though the show had been on before her time. "To get back to what happened to Ben Riggs...?"

"Right. You're just so easy to talk to, that I do go on." Barrie straightened up, moved the cape from her knees to the pile on the chair, and got down to business. "There was a man at the back of the store. He was holding a gun on the manager, a man from Pakistan, I believe...or maybe India? Or Bangladesh—I always forget to include Bangladesh. I suppose that's because it wasn't a country when I studied geography." Her voice trailed off.

"A man was holding a gun on the manager?" Toni prompted.

"Yes. The gunman was backlit. It was like a scene out of *The Thin Man*, one of my all-time favorite films, so I couldn't see his face. But I'll swear in court it was Clint Jones—Ben's half-brother, you know, from Brittany's first marriage. I recognized the way Clint kind of shrugged and hunched his shoulders to make his coat fit better. And he had that little jerk of the head, like Jesús Alou when he was getting set at the plate."

"Jesús Alou?" Munger's keystrokes paused.

"Played for the Giants back in the Sixties." Toni's grandfather, *abuelo* Navarro, had been a baseball fanatic. In his later years, his mind retreated to the Dodgers-Giants contests of his youth. Toni could still reel off the starting lineups from back in the day.

"You didn't see Clint Jones clearly?" Toni said.

Barrie shook her head. "Just his shadow. When Ben came in, Clint turned away from the manager and pulled the trigger—shot Ben just as he was reaching for the champagne." Barrie paused, considering. "It all happened so quickly. And then the lights went out."

"What happened to the manager?"

"He skedaddled out the rear door while Clint was distracted. I guess he—the manager, I mean—turned out the lights." Barrie smiled. "Smart move. Reminded me of the early gangster films—you know, *Little Caesar* or *Public Enemy*."

Tony heard Munger sigh. Interviewing Barrie was like herding hamsters. The good doctor's thoughts tended to scatter and clump, scatter and clump. So far Toni's notes consisted of four statements:

Victim: Ben Riggs
Parents: Jamison and Brittany Riggs; divorced (presumably—need to check)
Offender: Clint Jones (neck twitch); half-brother of victim
Scene: liquor store

"And Clint—what did he do next?" Toni said.

Barrie's brow furrowed. "I'm not sure."

"That's okay," Toni said. "It's been a traumatic evening for you. Let's move on to the liquor store. Where is it, exactly?"

"The scene of the crime? On Main Street. I don't know the address."

Toni wrote that down, her mind reviewing all the businesses on Main Street, which cut through Tucson's Downtown district. Much of Main had been eaten up by street widening and the building of the convention center years ago. More importantly, the area was within Tucson City limits. She'd turn the case and Dr. Barrie over to the Tucson Police Department once the interview ended.

"Munger?" Toni called.

"Still checking," he said. Scott prided himself on being able to multitask.

"Could I get a skosh more hot water, please?" Barrie asked.

Toni took Barrie's mug and went to the break room. Delilah's voice followed after her with yet another non sequitur, or perhaps a continuation of a previously interrupted thought. "I was always small, you know—how could I not be with Munchkin parents? So they used me to play children. I had dark eyes and the blackest hair you ever did see—black as Liz Taylor's. They got around the child labor laws and the education requirements by casting me as a child. Spanish, Mexican, or Indian—American Indian, that is. From a distance you couldn't tell, as long as they bound my breasts.

"Worked with Duke and Holden and Hudson. Damn, Rock

Hudson was handsome. Face made for film. Too bad he was gay. *The Magnificent Seven* was my favorite part. But then the Westerns died out, so I went back to school. Height doesn't matter when you're teaching college."

Main Street was at least fifteen miles from the eastern substation, Toni thought, removing the mug full of water from the microwave. How had Barrie gotten there? Did she have a driver waiting outside?

Toni set the mug down on the corner of her desk. "Incoming," Munger called, and tossed her another teabag. Toni handed the foil-wrapped packet to Barrie, saying, "Do you mind if I backtrack a little?"

"Not at all. Fire away."

"What took you to Main Street? It's miles from here."

"Oh, that's no problem. I was with my friends, Ada, Ruthie, and Leroy. We're kind of like the Four Musketeers. Leroy is d'Artagnan, because he's the youngest."

"Could you give me Leroy, Ruthie, and Ada's last names—just for the record?"

Delilah rattled off three full names. Toni heard Munger attack the keyboard.

"Did any of your friends witness the shooting?"

"Well, Ada might have dozed off. She's narcoleptic, so you can't always tell."

"But the others?"

"We discussed it, of course. So exciting. But I was the only one who recognized Clint Jones, so I was elected to come in."

"You didn't call nine-one-one?"

"I don't have a phone," Barrie said. "They've gotten so expensive. And all my friends and relatives are gone, so who would I call? Besides, we all expected the manager to phone it in from the back room."

"Where were you standing when Mr. Jones shot his brother?"

"Outside. But I could see it all very clearly through the glass."

"Did Mr. Jones pass you as he ran out? Did he see you?"

Barrie laughed. The notes, high and bright, cascaded like the song of a canyon wren. "If he had, he'd have thought I was a decked-out fire hydrant. Most people don't notice me. Their eyes just don't travel down that far, especially the geezers in Tucson who wear bifocals. I'm in the fuzzy area."

Scott rolled his chair over to join them. He looked at Toni. Grinned. Held up a sheet of paper. "I looked you up on the Internet Movie Database," he said to Barrie. "You were in forty films."

"Fifty-three, actually. But I wasn't credited in the earlier ones."

He made a note on his sheet. "Where do you live now?"

"Up the street at Desert Winds. Very convenient, except for the traffic. But I always cross at the light."

"Winds damaged power lines near there this evening."

The birdlike head bobbed up and down. "My friends and I were worried that the manager's emergency call might have been interrupted before the police got all the information. And I thought maybe Ben Riggs was still alive—though he wasn't even twitching when everything faded to black...No, that's not quite right. There was no 'fading' about it."

"And you're sure Ben Riggs was shot at a liquor store on Main Street?" Munger said.

"That's what I've been trying to tell you." She turned to Toni and said in a stage whisper, "He's a little slow, isn't he?"

"He'll get there," Toni whispered back.

Scott glared at her, and then turned back to Barrie. "By any chance did the shooting take place in, er, a town called Bishop's Run?"

"Well, of course," Barrie said. "I think it's not far from Cabot Cove...or maybe Knot's Landing." And to Toni, "Detective Munger's catching up nicely."

The phone on Toni's desk buzzed. "An attendant from Desert Winds is here, searching for Delilah Barrie," Karin said.

"We'll bring her out."

Barrie downed the last of the decaf Earl Grey. Standing, she said, "Did they say if the power was back on?"

Munger walked over to the window and looked northeast, as Toni helped Barrie don the multiple layers of sweater, coat, cape, scarves and mittens. "Not yet," he said.

"Can't be helped." Barrie wrapped the last scarf around her head. Her muffled voice said, "You won't forget to put out a BOLO for Clint Jones?"

Toni looked at Scott over Barrie's head. "Well, Dr. Barrie,

that'll be up to the Bishop's Run Police Department. But don't worry, I'm sure they'll do everything in their power to, um, solve the case."

"They always do. It's very reassuring." Barrie accepted Munger's arm to escort her down the corridor. "Good night, Detective Navarro."

"It's been a pleasure, Dr. Barrie."

"Stay tuned," said Munger to no one in particular.

Munger had just returned to his warm keyboard when the phone rang on Toni's desk. The mobile unit officer identified himself, then said, "Homicide at the new discount liquor store across the street from you. Looks like it happened while the power was out."

"Be there in two." Hanging up, Toni said, "Munger, you're not going to believe this."

† † †

Tucson writer **SUSAN CUMMINS MILLER**, a former field geologist and college instructor, pens the Frankie MacFarlane, Geologist, mysteries and compiled and edited *A Sweet, Separate Intimacy: Women Writers of the American Frontier, 1800-1922*. Her poems, short stories, and essays have appeared in, or are forthcoming in, numerous journals and anthologies, including *And All Our Yesterdays, What We Talk About When We Talk About It: I, II, The Write Launch, Tempered Runes Press: Bluing the Blade, Impermanent Earth,* and *So West: So Deadly*. A poetry chapbook, *Making Silent Stones Sing*, will be released later this year. SusanCumminsMiller.com

CREATURES OF HABIT
CHARLOTTE MORGANTI

SOME habits die hard. Like my tendency toward cynicism. When Alice Ross from *Dying to Travel* magazine offered to review Four Sisters Resort, the five-star hotel my sister Chelsea and I own outside Sedona, I suspected her real goal was a week of luxury. *Gratis*. But we'd experienced a dip in bookings over the summer, so I silenced my inner cynic and agreed.

She arrived on a Thursday morning in September. In our first interview, I outlined Four Sisters' history—my parents built the resort and when they died twenty years ago, my sisters and I inherited it. "Thanks for the snapshot, Ms. Morris," Alice said.

"Suzanne's fine."

"Okay." Alice grinned and leaned forward. "From the resort's name, I assume there are four sisters. I could never own anything with my siblings. We fight over everything."

Oh, the stories I could tell her about our screaming matches—all instigated by Chelsea's desire to "have a life." However, Mom didn't raise an idiot, so I ignored Alice's leading comment. "Four originally. Unfortunately, Rebecca and Jeanie died recently, so that leaves Chelsea and me."

Alice gasped. "How awful! You lost two sisters at once?"

"No, not together. They died in separate accidents, but recently." I bit my bottom lip to stop it quivering.

"My condolences."

"Thanks. Let's continue?"

She smoothed her notebook page. "Your website mentions horses. Do you offer lessons?"

"Absolutely. Our wrangler, Trevor Agorasto, has expanded our programs since he joined us a year ago. Lessons, trail rides. His latest plan is therapy horses."

"Ooh, good idea," she said. "I noticed the resort is a ways from

127

Sedona. Any problems keeping staff in such a remote location?"

Another dodge-me topic. Chelsea thought I didn't know she and Trevor had been an item since Christmas. I was thankful because, before Trevor, she'd had innumerable romances with employees. When she inevitably dumped her flavor-of-the-day, the fellow would quit and I had to find another chef, trainer, or masseur. If Chelsea wasn't family, I'd have fired her long ago.

Best not have these juicy tidbits appear in a travel magazine, so I said, "No problem keeping staff. We pay well to compensate for the commute."

AFTER lunch Chelsea came to my office. "Buy me out. I have a life to live."

I sighed. "Rebecca said no. Jeanie said no. It's my turn now, is it?"

"Exactly."

"Why? You have everything here—a suite, fabulous amenities, all free."

"Argh, that old song. I'm young. I want to travel, enjoy life. You're...whatever. You like your rut."

She'd almost called me old. Chelsea was thirty-five, Mom's bonus baby. Twenty years younger than me. "Use your monthly draw to travel."

"It's a pittance! Doesn't even keep me in shoes."

"Oh Chels, such drama. Buy fewer shoes."

Chelsea glared. "That's bitchy." She slammed the door as she left.

THAT evening, as usual, I carried my glass of California red into the garden. Completely screened, the gazebo was my private bug-and critter-free refuge. On my way across the lawn I phoned my friend Kate and suggested El Rincon for our weekly Friday lunch. I had barely clicked off when someone screamed.

Dropping everything, I rushed around the corner of the hotel. As Alice Ross raced past me, she pointed at the gazebo and screeched. "Snake! Big one. Omigod."

The gazebo door was ajar. Coiled near my favorite rattan chair was a twitchy rattler. I wanted to follow Alice in retreat but fought down the panic and stood guard until Trevor arrived and bagged the snake.

I found Alice shivering in a chair in our lobby. "All's well," I said. "Please don't think this is a usual occurrence."

She raised an eyebrow. "I researched your sisters' accidents. Rebecca fell from a horse in February and Jeanie fell in a hot tub in June. No witnesses either time? Weird. Now a snake? You'd think someone has a mega grudge against the resort." She paused. "Or against the owners."

Alice sounded almost as paranoid as Jeanie. "You're shaken," I said. "Imagining things."

† † †

FRIDAY I was running late, but my standard shortcut—a lonely, dusty track through the hills only a few of us knew about—helped me arrive at El Rincon in Tlaquepaque Village just as a taxi deposited Kate outside the restaurant. She studied my face. "You look frazzled."

I told her about the snake episode. "Beats me how either Alice or that snake got into the gazebo, because we keep it locked. And to top it off, I dropped my cell phone when Alice screamed and now it's MIA."

Kate patted my arm. "What's worse? Losing a phone or exposing a travel writer to a rattler?"

I laughed. "The latter. Definitely."

After lunch I bought a painting of a horse and cowhand posed beneath a starlit sky. "Come and help me decide where to hang this," I said to Kate. "Then I'll drive you home."

It was a fair hike to my car. I always parked away from others to avoid nicks. The painting gained weight with each step and when we finally reached the vehicle I said, "I'm buying miniatures from now on."

Kate looked past me, squinting. "Is that Chelsea?" She shook her head. "No—probably someone with a similar build."

The car sputtered when I started it, but then righted itself. As we drove along the shortcut, I told Kate about my argument with Chelsea. "She doesn't care the resort is our parents' legacy. Says it's time to let go. What should I do?"

"Are you asking me as a friend or as the resort's attorney?"

"Both."

129

Kate surprised me by saying, "Why not buy her share? Let her live her life."

"I can't afford to."

"Hmmm, okay. Suppose she found another buyer?"

"Mom and Dad wanted to keep the resort in the family. Isn't that why they created a joint tenancy with survivorship for us girls? The old 'last one wins' scenario?"

"Oof, that's blunt," Kate said.

"But that's how it works, correct?"

Kate nodded. "Yes. They set it up so when one of you dies, her share automatically goes to the others. But no matter what your parents wanted, legally Chelsea could sell her interest, with your consent."

The engine missed. I depressed the accelerator. The engine sputtered. "What's going on?"

Kate glanced at the gauges. "Is the tank low?"

"Half-full."

As if to spite me, the engine quit. The car glided to a stop. I stared at the empty expanse surrounding the roadway. We were a long twenty-five miles from home. I tried the ignition. When the engine turned over and died again, Kate grabbed her phone. "Time for the cavalry." She called AAA first and then Don, her husband.

The car's interior was sweltering so we stood outside and hoped for a breeze. I dug two bottles of water from the trunk and handed one to Kate. "What's the ETA for help?"

"Tow guy says fifteen minutes. Don needs a bit longer."

I opened my water, drank a third, and splashed some on my hands and face. "Back to Chelsea selling. Her buyer and I would be joint owners?"

Kate swallowed some water. "Yes, but without survivorship. You'd be more like independent partners."

"And if I die?"

Kate said, "Your half goes to whomever you direct in your last will."

I spotted a dark vehicle in the distance behind us. "That was quick."

Kate squinted at it. "Not Triple A. Their trucks are white."

I shivered. I remembered Alice's comments and Jeanie's paranoia. "Get in the car. Lock the doors."

"What?"

"Alice Ross thinks someone's targeting the resort." Then I took a deep breath and blurted, "Jeanie believed Chelsea arranged Rebecca's accident, because Rebecca refused to buy her out. At the time, I called it paranoia. Then Jeanie died. Now the snake."

Kate's eyes went wide. "Right, better paranoid and alive, than blasé and dead."

We hustled into the car and locked the doors. I held my breath and watched the approaching vehicle in the mirror.

As the truck closed the distance I realized it was a pickup. Orange and brown. "Pretty sure that's Trevor, our wrangler." Still channeling Jeanie's paranoia, I said, "Perfect timing. Serendipity or design?"

Once Trevor stopped behind us and exited his truck I got out of my car.

He approached, shading his eyes against the sun. "Need help, Ms. Morris?"

"No, we're okay."

When Kate opened her door and climbed out, Trevor jerked in response. "Ah, didn't see your passenger. I was worried you were stranded."

"I would have been, but Kate called Triple A."

Kate pointed behind Trevor. "That's our tow now. My husband won't be far behind."

Trevor glanced over his shoulder and then turned back to me. "You should stick to main roads. Breaking down on a lonely track like this could be fatal." He waved, returned to his truck, and pulled away.

By the time my car was loaded onto the tow truck's bed, I'd decided Trevor's timing was happenstance. When Don arrived, he and Kate waited while I finalized the paperwork and asked the tow truck driver to take my car to my mechanic.

About five miles from the resort, when we negotiated a turn, I noticed Chelsea's black SUV some distance behind us. "There's Chelsea."

"Hmmm," Kate said.

I caught the note of suspicion in Kate's voice. My stomach clenched. "Uh-huh. No traffic on this road for ages, and now it's like LA."

SHORTLY after we found a table in the poolside lounge Chelsea appeared, carrying shopping bags. "Hi everyone," she said, joining us. "I saw you on the shortcut. Where's your car, Suzanne?"

I filled her in before asking, "Were you at Tlaquepaque?"

She shook her head. "No—Hillside. Bought some cool sandals at A Step Up." She grinned at me. "Yeah, yeah, I should buy fewer shoes."

"Sorry for that crack." I hesitated and then said, "About your half of the resort—Kate says you can sell to someone other than me with my consent. Should we try to find a buyer I could partner with?"

Chelsea swatted the question away. "I've changed my mind."

I stared at her, my mouth agape. "But yesterday—"

She hugged herself and grinned. "Yesterday I didn't have a good reason to stay." She giggled. "Today I do. I'm engaged. To Trevor."

"Engaged?"

"Isn't it great? He proposed last night. He said he'd rather wrangle horses in the desert with me than sit by himself in a courtroom defending horse thieves."

Kate asked, "Trevor's an attorney?"

Chelsea shook her head. "No. He did go to law school but says indoor jobs aren't for him."

"So you don't want out?" I said.

"Not anymore. When I mentioned selling my share, Trevor suggested keeping it as an investment."

At that moment, Alice Ross and our security chief, Edgar, approached the table. Edgar waved my cell phone. "We found it."

"Hallelujah!"

He gestured at Alice. "This lady found it in the spa."

"I more or less sat on it in the spa foyer," Alice said. "It was wedged between cushions."

Kate and I exchanged looks. How did the phone get from the lawn last night to the spa today?

"Join us, Alice." I introduced everyone. I waved a server over and ordered Prosecco. "We have two things to toast now—my prodigal phone and Chelsea and Trevor's engagement."

Alice plunked into a chair and leaned toward Chelsea.

"Engaged! How wonderful! Have you known each other long?"

"More than a year, but the romance bloomed around Christmas."

The waiter arrived and poured our Prosecco. I raised my glass. "To Chelsea. A long, happy marriage." Before I could take a sip, my phone rang. It was my mechanic with news that floored me.

"Sand," I said, when the call ended. "That's why the engine quit. Sand clogged the line."

"Weird," Alice said. "How would sand get into your tank?"

"Vandalism, he said."

Chelsea downed her Prosecco and stood up. "People never cease to amaze me. Gotta run. Special dinner tonight." She tapped me on the shoulder. "Brunch tomorrow?"

Jeanie must have been sitting on my shoulder because I had a wild, paranoid idea. "I can't. I'm going to hike Rebecca's favorite trail in the morning and picnic at the spot where she died."

"Alone?"

I shrugged. "I'd ask you to join me but I'm craving solitude."

I pulled Kate and Don aside before they left. "I hate to think Chelsea could be behind these accidents. But I have to know, so I gave her a prime opening. Can you watch my back?"

† † †

SATURDAY morning I hiked the trail, opened my picnic basket in the shade of junipers and ate my muffin. I tried not to stare at the spot where Kate and Don hid out. If I wanted solitude, I got it. Nothing happened. Not even a snake bothered me.

When I returned to the resort I discovered Chelsea had spent the morning in our spa. She looked fabulous. I looked like I'd hiked miles in the heat.

That evening, to soothe my conscience for suspecting Chelsea, I invited her and Trevor to join me for dinner. During dessert I asked Trevor if he still wanted to do the therapy riding program.

"For sure. Most of our horses are feisty though, and not the best for therapy."

I promised to think about buying more horses and said goodnight.

Later, as I readied for bed, I received a text message from an unknown number. Above a link, it said:

SHE WAS MY COUSIN.

I clicked the link and read the article from the *Vallejo Times-Herald*. Then I forwarded it to Kate and spent an hour on the phone with her before replying to the text.

† † †

SUNDAY morning Kate phoned me. "All's ready."

I put the phone on speaker before stashing it in my pocket. I grabbed my printout of the article and walked to the stables. I found Trevor sorting tack.

"Hey," he said. "Come to talk horses?"

"More like horseshit." I waved the article at him. "Interesting piece in your hometown newspaper about Monica Agorasto. You told us you were single."

"Yeah, so?"

"Monica was your wife. You're widowed."

He fingered a halter. "True. Which qualifies me as single. I wanted to avoid pity."

"Or avoid questions about how she died?" I read from the printout: "Fell, hitting her head on the pool surround."

He grimaced. "A stupid accident. She'd been drinking. Probably slipped on the wet tiles. Our neighbor found her, but it was too late."

"You weren't there. Of course."

"I'd gone to get ice cream. She wanted Ben & Jerry's Chubby Hubby. I drove to five stores before I found it."

"You inherited millions. Enough to quit your law practice."

His head jerked. I said, "Oh, that's right! You told Chelsea you never worked as an attorney. But you did. In fact, you were a real estate specialist. Did you tell Chelsea about Monica?"

Trevor stared at me without expression. He moved to Lightning's stall and opened the gate.

I followed him. "Of course not. Too risky. Chelsea would see similarities with Jeanie's death—a fall and head injury. Or perhaps she'd wonder about Rebecca's accident—another fall and head injury. And if Chelsea learned you were a real estate attorney, she'd realize you understand exactly how joint tenancy with survivorship

134

works, and that if all her sisters died, Chelsea would own everything."

Rage made my voice shake. "That's what you wanted, isn't it? If anyone agreed to buy Chelsea's interest you would have talked her out of it, just like you did the other night."

He snorted. "You're delusional."

"You wish. The other thing Chelsea would figure out? That if she married you, she'd soon be like Monica. Dead."

He said, "Hogwash."

"Hardly. Your habit of making murder look like an accident will be your undoing."

Trevor grabbed my arm and pulled me close. My heart rate jumped.

He sneered. "We're all creatures of habit, Suzanne. Rebecca riding the same trail, at the same time. Jeanie getting soused in the hot tub every evening. You and your gazebo and shortcut to Sedona."

I struggled to pry his hand from my arm. "Let go of me."

"Careful, now. Even Lightning has habits. Like one I taught him—to rear up when I wave my arm. That's what threw Rebecca from her saddle. Unfortunately, the fall didn't quite finish her off, so I had to. As for you? Well, you'll startle Lightning and he'll kick you. Stomp on you. I'll console Chelsea. We'll get married and—"

Chelsea and Kate appeared in the stable entrance, followed by three police officers.

Kate waved her cell phone. "Heard it all."

"Wedding's off, Bucko," Chelsea said.

Trevor glanced at them. As I wrenched from Trevor's grasp, his arm jerked upward. Lightning reared, one hoof smacked Trevor's head, and Trevor collapsed in a heap.

"Gee, Trevor," I said. "What an unfortunate habit Lightning has."

THAT evening I sat with Kate, Chelsea, and Alice over cocktails. "Kate, thanks for convincing the police and Chelsea to take me seriously."

"Piece-o-cake," she said. "Unlike the trouble Trevor will have convincing a jury he's innocent."

I laughed and then said to Alice, "Initially I thought your goal was a free week at the resort. Instead, you wanted to save a life or two. Thank you."

"Thank my cousin Monica. After she died three years ago, I kept track of Trevor. When I read about Jeanie's death, the similarities unsettled me. So I came here. I apologize for the subterfuge."

In a perfect world my inner cynic would have died right then, right there. But habits are tenacious and don't go down without a fight.

"I'm tough," I said. "You can tell me. Your review was a ruse, right?"

"Wrong. The magazine wants the article." Alice smiled. "But I'll omit the rattler."

† † †

CHARLOTTE MORGANTI has been a burger flipper, beer slinger and a corporate finance/mining lawyer. In addition to her law degree, she holds a Master of Fine Arts in creative writing. Now retired from legal practice, she focuses on writing crime fiction—novels and short stories, ranging from gritty investigations to lighter capers. Charlotte and her husband live on the Sunshine Coast of British Columbia, Canada, where it's mostly sunny, except when it's raining. CharlotteMorganti.com

IRIS
JULIE MORRISON

MOST kids only like animals when they're small. I read early–at four–my mother helping me learn names of not just animals but plants too. One of my first books was about flowers.

If I read it with my mom, I'd point out each one, "Lily pad!" "Orchid!" "Passionflower!"

If the relatives were around, they'd point to a spotted feline stalking the rainforest floor, then say something like, *"Wow, Flora! Look at the cat!"*

"Jaguar," I'd correct.

I guess I wasn't their favorite, and maybe Mom never was either. It's why we call them "the relatives" instead of "family."

If I drew it, our family tree would look like a lightning-struck pine. Mom and me barely hang on to one side by her broken marriage, while aunts and uncles and cousins stick out from my Great Uncle Doug's side in branches brushy but brittle.

Maybe I'd even add holes, like blight, to our side of the pine. Grandpa Dan died before my dad was even born, Grandma died last year, and Dad left. Mom says he flew off. I like to picture him as one of the ravens who visits us at the ranch, pecking and strutting and flapping, making noises like water gurgling out of the tap. When I hear that noise I know it's a raven, because the only place water runs on our ranch is away.

Mom says Newman has been like that as long as she's known it.

Mom does that—talks about the ranch like it's a person, calling it Newman, which is short for Newman Park.

I wonder if the ranch would like us better if we called it Park.

It looks like a park from a distance: waving green in the summer, yellow in the fall, white in the winter with snow. It doesn't feel like a park up close. Underneath those flowering weeds there are lots of rocks and not much grass. Mom says it's because the snowmelt races through every spring, and the weeds have learned to hold on to Newman because it's not going to work the other way around.

Mom and I must be a couple of weeds at heart.

I guess before Dad became a raven, he was a crook. It makes sense—ravens steal things. Mom says that Great Uncle Doug got mad when dad stole "from him and everybody" and didn't want Mom and me "looking like homeless bums," so he let us live in Newman's cabin, a whole desert and mountain range away from anything else having to do with him.

I don't remember a lot about when we moved—it wasn't long after the flower book. I was really young then. Now I'm seven.

I do remember the mud. Patches of snow on the ridge above Newman leaking like they were crying for the end of winter, making car-sized puddles on the dirt road.

Mom says water only stays long enough here to make a mess.

The water we drink comes from a plastic tank on the high corner of the park where the cabin backs up against Ponderosas standing twice as tall as the roof. It's like the cabin is trying to hide the supply from the rest of the ranch, wedging it between itself and the trees for protection. The trees, at least, are nice to us. They give us shade and lots and lots of pinecones to sell.

We gather the pinecones, then Mom dips them in kitchen-cleaner pine-smelling green wax. We rotate through different towns' weekend markets to sell them as gifts. We do the same thing with our iris, but without the wax.

We found iris that very first day we moved to Newman. We made exploring an adventure, putting on puffy coats and rubber boots to go sloshing. First over to the three-sided rusty tin barn—bare except for a floor of moldy hay. Then over to the crumbling tack room, a cinderblock building with wires running through the top, abandoned nests in the corners, and dusty bits of leather straps hanging from wooden pegs.

"Looks like a rat trapeze act," Mom said.

Next we walked a maze of metal piping and panels Mom said were corrals built for cows. I guess it wouldn't be bad to be a cow there. Ponderosas grow in every direction, and mountains peep over their tops looking out past the cabin.

After the corrals the mud got shallower, less slick. Mom said water must run north. She pointed toward the mountains when she said that, the opposite direction of the desert and the relatives, but the same direction of the stock pond. I don't know which is scarier. The relatives that remind me of predators, or the stock pond crouching like a hungry ogre beside Newman's cabin, brown dirt cheeks mounded at the sides around an empty mouth, just waiting for something to fall in.

I've seen a mound like that before. On a grave.

We had tried to bury our cat after a coyote got her. Newman's so rocky, we couldn't dig down deep enough, even for a cat, but I won't forget how the too-shallow grave looked like a miniature stock pond, and how I wondered what Newman must want in its pond more than water.

Mom says the only thing that stock pond has ever held are Wilson relatives' regrets.

Newman Park is almost a mile long, so by the time we got to the rocky gulch on its southern end, I would have sat down in the mud, but I told you the trees are nice to us, even providing stumps to rest on. Except Mom didn't. She scampered into the gulch like a squirrel, all bunched and quick and flowing with focus.

"Iris!" she called back to me like I should be excited. I would have been if she'd said "cocoa with marshmallows" but all I could see were spear-shaped leaves growing at the base and sides of that cut in the park like a consolation prize for the gulch with canyon-sized dreams that had never gotten water to believe in them.

"Easter's late this year," Mom said next. When I think of Easter I think of eggs, and by that time I was hungry so this statement was a little more interesting. "This iris could make for some beautiful baskets."

I didn't like the sound of that. Baskets meant carrying, which meant more walking.

Sure enough, that spring we walked Newman's length enough times to circle the earth, gathering bulbs to plant in baskets that Mom lined up in the old hay barn, then the back seat of the car, then in a line in front of a poster I drew of Easter eggs that we propped up in front of a folding table at a Flagstaff farmer's market.

"Don't see many farmers at these markets anymore," our first customer had said to Mom. "You're local?"

His voice reminded me of Newman's gulch, pebbly and rooted in something wearing further away each year.

"Susan Wilson," Mom told him, then that we'd just moved to Newman Park.

"First blue-eyed Susan I've ever seen," our customer said. He looked like a policeman: official, serious, expecting people to listen, but not surprised when they don't. He wore jeans and polished brown boots, a belt of the same color with a tooled silver buckle, a tan long sleeved shirt, and a black felt cowboy hat. He had a dark mustache, short dark hair and sunglasses.

Mom looked at him like she wasn't sure if he was the kind of mushroom that could make her sick.

A passer-by clapped our customer on the arm. "What are you—working undercover? No badge today, Waters?"

"You're not gonna make me need it, right?" our customer called back before removing his hat to Mom. "Owen Waters."

Mom offered a handshake after wiping soil from her fingers on the tail of her blouse, a blue T-shirt the color of robin's eggs that matched both of our eyes. We both have dark blonde hair too, except Mom let me streak mine with pink and purple like the eggs on my poster.

"Related to Doug?" Owen Waters asked, his tone as careful as a parent trying not to wake a baby.

"By marriage," Mom said in the tone she uses when I ask if I can have a candy bar at the grocery store checkout.

"In-laws or outlaws?" Owen Waters joked.

"Oh, just shirttail relatives," Mom said, pointing at her dirty blouse hem. "Of a kind."

Owen Waters laughed and I went back to my drawing. I'd started with a clover pasture, but I added the old hay barn. Something about Owen Waters made me think of it: tough and weathered. Doing all it can to keep off the rain.

He knelt down next to me after a few minutes, knees cracking like seed packets. "You're going to be an artist when you grow up?"

I shrugged.

"That old barn's still standing, is it?" he asked Mom. "A rancher I know used the place for shipping his herd a few years back. You still hauling water in? I know a guy…," which set them off talking some more.

A lady selling lanolin lotion made a sale across the way, laughing too loudly as she bagged a jar. Mom says lanolin comes from sheep. I added a sheep to my picture.

Owen Waters pointed to it. "Do you know, your grandfather wanted you to ride a sheep?"

Mom drew breath like when I tried to move one of the pallets in the hay barn on my own, without checking for snakes. Now she was looking at Owen Waters like he might be a rattler. I stopped coloring, and went very still.

"My dad met your grandpa," Owen Waters told me. "At the Monte Vista Hotel in Flagstaff one night."

He glanced at Mom, tipping his right hand in a drinking motion.

She crossed her arms like she does when I argue back.

"Doug had a guest up in the room—" Mr. Waters cleared his throat with another glance at Mom. "Dan was giving them some time, waiting down at the bar, just smiling to himself. My dad's chatty and got Dan to explain he and his brother had just sold some cattle, and he'd used his share of the money to buy the most gorgeous land he'd ever seen called Newman Park. Dan said he couldn't wait to move his pregnant wife to that beautiful land where their kids would get to run and ride and grow up happy."

Mom half-smiled, arms relaxing a bit.

"Now, my dad likes his jokes, so he says to your grandpa, 'Gonna teach the baby to ride, huh? Better be a short horse.'"

Mom's smile widened.

"And right back, despite a few too many, your grandpa says, 'we'll start 'em on a sheep.'"

Mom grinned then—her face like a butterfly opening its wings.

"Well, that made my dad laugh and he never forgot it. Did anybody ever tell you that story?"

I shook my head no.

Mom sighed, rubbing the tops of her arms like she didn't want to shiver. "Dan Wilson never made it back to Texas after that trip. All anyone knew from Doug was that there was a horrible accident when the brothers came to buy the land, and Doug had to sign by himself."

"Is that right?" Owen Waters blew out a breath and adjusted his hat, avoiding our eyes. "Horrible accident for Dan, but not so much for Doug?"

Mom's face closed like a trap as she held out a hand to me. I stood to take it, hugging her legs with my other arm.

Owen Waters stood next, hooking his thumbs through his belt loops before bending to retrieve my drawing, fitting it securely under our toolbox bank on the table. "Well. I'm sorry you never met your grandfather."

I hugged Mom harder, feeling like we'd just been in our own accident. Something had crashed, but I didn't know what.

Owen Waters cleared his throat again. "Maybe it'll come as better news that I know a shepherd looking for some pasture this spring. Goats, unfortunately, not sheep, but he'll pay. And they'll eat your weeds."

"That is better news." Mom's face softened like butter in a sunny window. "Why don't you take one of Flora's cards?"

Proudly, I selected one of the paper squares I had colored and cut out that morning. Owen Waters buttoned it into his top left shirt pocket.

"I think I better buy a couple of them baskets, too."

OWEN Waters knew a lot more than a shepherd. He knew a cattleman who wanted to use Newman's corrals for branding, a horse hauler who could use them for layovers, and a beekeeper who just needed quiet pasture, which is how we eventually got the beeswax we use for pinecone dip. The beekeeper's wife knew more than anyone, even plumbing, and taught Mom how to fix most of Newman's leaks herself.

IN our second year, Owen Waters knew a guy who would pay us to let him put up a roping arena beyond the corrals. Cowboys pulled their trailers in to ride there each weekend, and the horse hauler stayed over weekdays. Owen Waters came anytime animals did, badge on his belt, inspecting with his clipboard.

The day he drove a trailer to Newman I didn't recognize him, because he was smiling like a border collie, telling me to come see my surprise. I scrambled up onto the wheel well of his parked trailer, looked inside and saw a dozen sheep.

He grinned. "For mutton bustin' this weekend."

The next Saturday morning I mounted that curly bouncer bareback, holding on the best I could, but wool is slick with oil. When I fell off, Owen Waters came running to pick me up. When I told him falling hadn't hurt too much, he gave me his cowboy hat.

BEGINNING our third summer, a huge grand-daddy truck hauled in a machine to bore holes in the ground. Mom took me to go talk to the iris when it came, telling me about the actual Iris, goddess of the rainbow, who shows us our true colors. She said the iris flowers must be named for her because, unlike others, they don't change color depending on the soil they're in. Then she said something else.

"Flora, honey, we might have to move."

"Because of the digging machine?" I asked, already afraid of that hard, hungry snout.

"Newman still belongs to the relatives. If they find water on it for a well, they'll want to develop it for sale."

"To someone else, right?" I didn't know what land costs but I knew Newman had more land than we had money.

"I've made offers," Mom said. "But the relatives want it commercial or industrial. I'd keep it agricultural."

I pictured a little boy having to get dressed up in a suit instead of being allowed to run around in his play jeans and sneakers.

"But didn't you say nothing holds water here?" I asked.

"That's been the joke," she chuckled. "Every sale here has fallen through, which is why we've been here so long."

Now I understood why the cabin cowered under the trees in the corner. Like so many of the cattle I'd seen, it hadn't wanted to be tied up and sold.

That evening, Owen Waters brought a new box of crayons for me. I drew stretched out on Newman's porch as he talked to Mom on its steps.

She told him about the relatives sending the monster machine to find Newman's water.

"Sick with greed," Owen Waters muttered.

I drew people in yellow and green, infected-looking, around the stock pond.

"Susan, there's more to that Monte Vista story," Owen Waters said, adjusting his hat. "It's none of my business, but that night Dan confessed that Doug got their investment money by selling cattle that wandered onto the brothers' lease back in Texas. Doug claimed they were entitled to them as leaseholders, but Dan caught him once sabotaging their neighbor's tanks, and figured out the only reason the cattle wandered was because they were thirsty. Dan joked to my dad that being a reformed cattle thief was bad enough, but that, he knew in these parts, no one will forgive stealing water."

Mom went as still as hardened wax.

"Now, this might sound crazy to you, but I think this ranch stopped holding water the day Doug bought it out of its own sense of justice."

He adjusted his hat, then glanced at me, still and staring back with the puke green crayon in my hand. "And, you know, it may just be holding, and hiding, something else."

A few weeks later the cattleman dropped off a load of mamas and calves.

Owen Waters was there too, eyeing the herd and his clipboard.

Mom and I were busy filling troughs and spreading alfalfa when the enemy digger rolled up again, hungry for a new hole to grind.

Mom pointed it to the stock pond.

Just a few minutes after the machine started, men yelled for it to stop. It lifted its snout from the dirt like they were scolding it.

Told to keep to the fence lines, I watched as Owen Waters walked Mom over to the drillers. A sheriff arrived soon, then a white van. After a lot of loud pointing, the van people carried a zipped black sack from the pond.

The snout machine never came back.

† † †

A couple months later, a fat yellow envelope came in the mail. Mom handled it like the key to Heaven's gates, but it was just papers.

"We're home," she said, smiling. "Newman's ours!"

That day Newman really did feel like a park as Mom and I

skipped and laughed all the way to where the iris bloomed, the same blue as the smiling sky.

† † †

JULIE MORRISON is a native Arizonan, Flagstaff resident, horsewoman, dog person, and award-winning writer of both poetry and prose to celebrate all the aforementioned. She is also living proof that crime pays: after her short story was among those selected for *SoWest: Ladykillers*, a Flagstaff publisher expressed interest in one of her prize-winning manuscripts. Julie is just enough of a sleuth to deduce that this was no accident. That manuscript, *Barbed*, will find its way to bookstores in Fall of 2021. JulieMorrisonWriter.com

THE BACKPACK
CLAIRE MURRAY

I woke in a sweat in the pitch black of a moonless night in Henry's cabin. My ears worked just fine, however. Low, raspy voices chanted my name, sending a chill up my spine and ending at the base of my neck, my hairs bristling like a dog's. I knew Henry had gotten into witchcraft and other stuff I didn't believe in. But suddenly, ice crept from my fingers to my arms, then to my neck. My toes, feet, and legs came next, like ice filling my veins instead of blood. I couldn't stop shivering. Was that eyes peeking at me through the walls? I shook my head and the vision passed. The voices remained.

Hands shaking, I lit a match, successful after the first four ended up on the floor. The voices receded into the depths of the walls. Match flickered out; the voices resumed. I groaned, got up, and lit the lantern. Ahhh…silence. Opening the trap door in the floor, I couldn't resist one last taunt. "Henry, you're a real killjoy, little brother."

I sat in the wooden chair by the ramshackle table, head in my hands. Was I sweating or had the ice in my veins turned to water? We shoulda been celebrating. But no, by the time we'd left the sleepy town of Gila Bend in our dust and made it to his cabin in the Sonoran Desert, Henry'd growed a conscience.

We got to the cabin and counted the money, but Henry was still moaning over me using a loaded gun. No one was supposed to get hurt, he said. Yeah, like ya know, it doesn't always work out that way. But Henry kept on about it and I finally had enough.

"So what if I shot that teller?" I said. "Damned idiot was about to press the alarm button. Then where'd we be?"

"Bad juju, brother. Our Karma's gonna be all messed up," Henry restuffed all the money into his backpack. "We gotta give this back, set things right."

"Seems to me you're already messed up. That's what comes from foolin' with that witchy stuff." I tried to take the pack from him, but he clung to it like it was all his.

"Don't say stuff like that." Head hunched into his shoulders, his squinted eyes darted around the cabin. He lowered his voice. "They'll hear, take revenge."

I let go of the pack. "Who'll hear, Henry? What're you talking about?"

"Shssh." He seized a purple bottle off the shelf over the stove and cradled it and the backpack in his arms. "Bad Karma will come back on us. We took a man's life. Gotta do the right thing now…"

Hoo boy, was he messed up. I guess I'd missed too many of his growin' up years and he'd imagined friends with these spirit things. Poor kid. Just had me after Mom and Pop died and I hadn't been around much, exceptin' when I'd needed a driver for a heist. Henry was a good driver. Usually.

I ran my hands through my hair and said, "Don't know what happened to you while I was in prison, but you done gone plain crazy." I snatched the bottle out of his arms.

Henry shouted some weird mumbo jumbo and dropped the backpack. Then he came after me, eyes fixed on the bottle. How could that bottle be more important than the money?

He'd never told me why he wanted the money, and I'd never asked, but I could tell it was important to him when he'd laid out the plan on a prison visit. He just needed me for backup. Hey, give me my cut and I'm happy. So I'd said yes.

I didn't think a bottle off the head would've kilt him like that. But there he was, laying on the floor like a sack o' flour and me standin' there with that heavy purple bottle. Only now it was purply-red.

I got tired of walking around his body in that one-room cabin filled with special candles and masks for his crazy ceremonies, so I dumped him and all of that crap into the crawl space below the floor. Prob'ly made durin' prospectin' days. Good place to hide if you weren't sure whether someone coming across the desert was gonna visit or steal. I can use it if I ever need a hidey-hole after a job. Henry'd said the cabin was paid off, so I guess by rights it belongs to me now.

I went to bed, figurin' I'd hightail it out in the morning and spend a few months south, maybe Mexico. Let the heat of the robbery die down.

Then them voices had started. I wasn't gonna get any sleep now. I sat in the kitchen, lookin' at the trap door, and drunk what was left of the tequila I'd bought in town, hopin' to warm my bones. Them demon voices still had me shiverin'. I must've dozed 'cause I woke up in the chair with a stiff neck and the empty bottle on the floor beside me.

I couldn't leave Henry's body in the crawl space. Wouldn't be right, him bein' kin. It'd be like I'd run away without sayin' goodbye. So I drug his body outside and set it beside a tree. Birds were chirping. Sun was comin' up. I buried him right quick, the rotting tree giving me no trouble about roots. I was finally warm, what with the digging and the sun. I tossed all the mumbo jumbo stuff beside him and put that purply-red bottle in his hands. I didn't want nothin' to do with it, but it was important to Henry.

I covered him up, but you could tell the ground's been dug. I went back into the cabin and grabbed the plants Henry had all over. Mostly different types of cactus and a few bromeliads like the ones Mom used to keep in the house. I never had no use for plants, 'specially in the desert. They just use up water.

I planted them, pots and all, over Henry's grave, hoping no one would notice they don't take up as much space as I'd dug. Maybe. If I was lucky. Don't feel lucky right now.

I searched around and found some large rocks behind the cabin. Carried them over to the grave and set them in the bare spots. It looked better. I drug an old chair from the back and set it between the new garden and tree. Didn't know I had it in me to make somethin' like that.

Clouds were gathering when I finished, a needed break from the sun's heat. I had to hit the road, in case anyone's checkin' out desert cabins for two bank robbers. I said a few words first. "It's fittin' I'm leaving you here, Henry. We'd a parted ways pretty soon if you was alive. Your mumbo jumbo don't fit in my life. I sure don't fit in yours."

I grabbed his backpack. Along with the bank money, it held a baloney-and-cheese sandwich—his favorite—and a book—*Tales of the Revenged.* Huh. Crazy mumbo jumbo. But it hid the money, so I left it there and closed the pack. That's when I seen it. HENRY—

stitched in bright colors on the outside flap. Hadn't seen that when we was in the bank and prayed no one else had either. Hoisting it onto my shoulder, I left Henry's car behind and walked south into a thunderstorm.

Henry'd always been following me around growin' up. Mom would've whupped me good for leavin' him behind, so I'd learned him how to drive and be my getaway guy. It'd worked out okay 'ceptin' for that last time. I should've offed him for takin' off in the car and leavin' me behind in the bank just 'cause a cop had driven by. Come to think of it, he'd just been gettin' into that mumbo jumbo back then.

My footsteps, crashing thunder, and pelting rain were the only sounds as I walked for miles. The rain felt good, like it was washing my skin and sins clean. Maybe I am lucky.

Mexico here I come. I kept to the edge of the road so's to hide behind them big cactus if I heard a car. None came.

Soggy and downtrodden, even after the storm rolled out, I camped a ways off the road, with only Henry's sandwich for dinner. I'd take a cold steak and cheese sub any day over baloney, but Henry had his ways. Every day he'd eat the same thing. I'd take him out for lunch and, like a little kid, he'd ask for baloney and cheese. Momma had said he was special, whatever that means.

I bedded down under the stars with the backpack as a pillow, cursing Henry. I'd spent eight years in the pen to protect him, while he bought into crazy witchcraft and Karma and that garbage. I'd-a got out in four if I'd given up his name. Instead 'a bein' grateful, he wanted to return the loot. Never should have listened to him. His sudden conscience made it go bad. Worse for Henry, though. Life was funny like that.

"Well, Henry, looks like your Karma got run down or just plain up and left you." I rolled onto my side, the hard earth digging into my hip. At least I had the money.

Voices woke me. Different from the raspy demons in Henry's cabin, these were loud, clear, and accompanied by the *chuck-chak* of a rifle bein' cocked. I opened one eye and wished I hadn't, seeing as the barrel of a shotgun was pointed in my face. No, these weren't the mumbo jumbo voices from the cabin. Them spirits wouldn't be arresting me for robbery and Henry's murder.

I fessed up, hours and many cups of lukewarm coffee later,

after I learnt that lightning had set fire to the tree outside Henry's cabin. By the time the police stopped there, the tree had toppled, and deep roots had upheaved his body. It hadn't taken long for teams searching the road in both directions to find me, with Henry's name stitched on the backpack. I swear his name was glowing and pulsing when they pulled me to my feet, but none of 'em had seemed to notice.

Should've buried it with Henry.

† † †

CLAIRE A. MURRAY writes mystery, fantasy, and science fiction short stories, novellas, and novels. "The Backpack" will be her 9th published short story, following 2020s "Lucky Seven" and "Spirit in the Sky." Claire is a member of Sisters in Crime and its Guppy, New England, Desert Sleuths, and LA chapters, and the Short Mystery Fiction Society. A lifelong New Englander, she moved in mid-2020 to Arizona where she writes full time. There's more about her and links to her works at Cam-Writes.com, Where Character, Crime, and Mystery Collide, and On Facebook: facebook.com/clairemurraywrites.

NOTORIOUS IN SEDONA
KRIS NERI

"MOTHER, you've booked us into the most notorious spa in Sedona." I stared askance at the familiar pueblo resort, surrounded by towering red rocks, which I'd once loved. But a good friend of ours had been murdered there.

When Mother first suggested we take a Sedona spa vacation, I'd jumped at the chance—until I discovered where we'd be staying. Granted, we had enjoyed many Sedona jaunts at the *Cielo Azul* Spa & Resort, which had been owned by our dear friend, Lorna Rafferty. But Lorna had died there five months earlier, and her killer was still at large.

I thought maybe my mom booked us there to mourn our friend. But it seemed she had an agenda—to put someone in the hoosegow for Lorna's murder. I now realize she'd brought me along to figure out how.

Lorna Rafferty had been the famed beauty consultant who'd owned this resort and had developed a line of skincare products called Sedona Magic. While Lorna had profited from pampering wealthy women, she'd spread the bucks around to others who needed it, providing no-cost plastic surgery for victims of disfiguring violent crimes and makeovers for moms returning to the workforce.

"Beauty should be for everyone," Lorna had once told me.

She'd died from a massive dose of digoxin. Since their marriage was rocky, the police suspected Lorna's husband, Harry, of the dirty deed. But Harry was being interviewed on TV in Phoenix about the spa's charitable work, more than a hundred miles away, when the medical examiner maintained the poison must have been administered. Stymied, the Sedona PD had turned the case over to the Arizona Department of Public Safety, the state cops. They weren't making any more progress.

"Tracy, darling, places can't be notorious, only people." Mother tugged down the brim of her rugged desert fedora, her symbol of being a star amateur sleuth, and practiced the cold stare she would direct at any bad guys we might come across. "But if someone here is the notorious person responsible for killing Lorna, they're going to be sorry they crossed paths with me."

I expect that drama from my mother. She's Martha Collins, the movie star and someone who draws trouble like lights attract moths. Right, I'm Tracy Eaton, celebrity offspring, tasked from birth with protecting Mother from her worst impulses. And sometimes, my own.

The voluminous lobby, with its sandy pueblo walls and Native American weavings, resembled a humble tribal kiva, apart from being about a thousand times larger and a million times more expensive. A Native flautist set the mood.

Harry Rafferty came around the front desk and enveloped us in a group hug. "Martha, I'm so grateful for your support during this awful time."

There was a wickedly handsome quality to Harry's engaging grin and sparkling brown eyes. He'd always maintained he'd been Lorna's partner, when he was only an employee. Now, I guessed, the dazzling showman, whose nonstop performance could charm the pants off a nun, had won the prize.

Mother gave Harry's arm a gentle pat. "Of course, dear man."

His arctic-white smile widened.

"But I must tell you, darling Harry, Tracy is determined to prove you killed Lorna."

Huh? I can't always stop her from jumping off a cliff. Or pushing me.

Harry flashed me a phony smile. "Tracy, honey. I remember when you were a frisky little rug rat, tearing our gracious spa apart."

A gross exaggeration. Slight anyway.

He ran a shaky hand through his well-cut graying hair. "But, Martha, we both know our Tracy is no dimwit. She realizes the police cleared me."

Harry had nothing to fear from Mother, who wouldn't recognize the real world if it bit her on the fanny. All she ever did was act out movie scenes. She could never solve a crime that had frustrated two police forces. I hadn't considered him guilty before, but now, I wondered…

WHILE following the bellman to our suite, I whispered, "Mother, did you *want* to be childless? You didn't have to try to get me killed."

"Stop being dramatic, young lady."

Hilarious, coming from her.

"I wanted to light a fire under Harry."

I sighed. "So why am I the one getting burned?"

"You, Tracy? By taking action, I put myself in danger. Why is everything always about you?"

Yeah, I hate it when I do that.

A messy-looking security guard greeted us at our suite door. His rumpled uniform had to be a size too big, and while his hair seemed clean, he could not have combed it lately.

"Officer Roddy here." He pointed to the name stitched over the uniform's breast pocket. "The boss tells me you're threatening him."

Before I could answer, Mother jumped in with, "Officer Roddy, are we supposed to take you seriously, considering…" She wiggled her fingers before his messy form. "…this? No offense."

"None taken."

He squinted at me. "You, though, I'm gonna be watching."

"I'm shivering down to my bones," I said.

After what Mother had pulled with Harry, I actually was.

THE suite was expensively decorated in Southwestern style. Oddly, I could hear that tranquil flute music in here, too. That it was piped in made me uneasy. Could Harry listen in on us?

Mother stretched out on a tan chaise lounge, while I unpacked. "Tracy, hurry up. We need to work out a plan to take Harry down."

What? I thought she already had a plan. Besides, like the police, I didn't know how he could have killed Lorna.

I yanked something from her suitcase. "What is this?" It looked like the wireless clip microphone and receiver they'd used at the TV station in Scottsdale, where she'd made an appearance to promote her next movie. "Did you steal this?"

Mother shrugged. "I never know when I'm going to be interviewed. That mic worked so well. I figured they wouldn't mind if I borrowed it…forever."

She needed to be prepared for an impromptu speaking gig? Real world, my ass. Still, I actually wasn't too miffed that my mother had flirted with committing a felony. That gizmo gave me an idea.

WE'D seen that Harry was speaking before a Chamber of Commerce dinner tonight from an announcement on a lobby sign. A perfect time to search Harry's room. Not that I expected to find anything—the police had surely been through it. But we were sneakier than most people.

Whoa! Maybe Mother and I were more alike than I wanted to believe.

Gag me.

We'd planned to bribe a front desk clerk for a key to Harry's room, but the strangest thing happened. That afternoon I noticed a keycard lying on the carpet in our entry. Someone must have shoved it under the door. I tried it in our lock. Nope, it didn't open our suite.

I tapped it against my hand. "Mother, are you thinking what I'm thinking?"

She snorted. "I'm thinking if they believe giving us some random key means they don't have to place chocolates on our pillows, that's pretty chintzy."

Please, tell me I'm adopted.

AS I'd hoped, the key opened Harry's suite. Was someone on the staff on our side, or trying to set us up?

Together, we tipped the mattress, but Harry hadn't hidden anything beneath it. Naturally, it fell to me to re-make the bed exactly as the maid had, since Mother hadn't made one herself since Adam and Eve were in high school.

While searching a nightstand, I noticed one drawer seemed too shallow inside for the size outside.

"That's a false bottom!" Mother declared. "I had them put in my dresser when you were little. You were so precocious, I didn't want you happening onto my…more intimate items."

I didn't have the heart to tell her I'd figured out how to open them when I was just a tot. My school's sex-ed was always light-years behind what I'd learned at home.

In Harry's hidden compartment, we found printed-out emails from someone named Jill. Pretty steamy stuff, too.

"So Harry did have someone on the side." Mother snorted knowingly.

"He must have deleted these emails from the computer, making sure Lorna wouldn't see them, but he printed them out so he could keep reading them."

Since our time was running short, we hastily took pictures of the emails with our phones.

At the door, Mother said, "I'll be back," in a spot-on imitation of Arnold Schwarzenegger.

See? She knows nothing outside of films.

† † †

THE next day Harry held an impromptu press conference. Had Mother's threat made him nervous? From the stage set up in the parking lot, he didn't say anything especially convincing.

"I'm innocent," blah, blah, blah. And, "I didn't kill my wife," more blahs. Ending with, "The police cleared me," blahs to infinity.

He had assembled a larger crowd than I expected, though not much press. I noticed a Phoenix TV station had sent a small crew, along with a reporter for the local newspaper. But the crowd was mostly filled with spa guests and employees. And, judging by the sprinkling of Southwestern hippie duds, nosy locals.

Ringing the parking lot were foxglove shrubs. The plant that produces digoxin. Not exactly desert greenery, but they grew everywhere. Had someone clipped those bushes to poison Lorna?

Still-messy Officer Roddy ambled over. With a nod, he asked, "You ladies finding your way around?"

He had to know we'd been there lots of times. Why was he asking? He gave me the old gesture for "I'm watching you," two fingers pointed first at his eyes, then mine.

After Harry's blahs wound down, he thanked some people. "My old friend, Academy Award-winning actress, Martha Collins, is here." He offered her a *namaste*-type bow. Naturally, he didn't acknowledge me. "I also want to thank our executive chef, Peter

Cortero, for his support."

The chef was a skinny dude with a dishwater blond ponytail. Given his scowl, he seemed less-than-thrilled by Harry's acknowledgment. Beside him was a tiny woman on crutches, whose foot was in a cast.

"And Peter's wife, Dani, is also here, even though it's hard for her to stand. She slipped off a rock on a hike."

"I didn't slip, I was pushed," Dani shouted in a cantankerous voice.

Her husband shook his head no, contradicting her.

"Of course, Dani." Harry couldn't have sounded more patronizing. He did the *namaste* routine with her, too.

Chef Peter slipped a necklace out from under his T-shirt. A stone, on which someone had painted a heart.

Mother whispered, "That was Lorna's necklace. One of the women she'd helped made it for her. Why does he have it?"

Good question. Peter kept flipping the heart-painted stone with his fingers. What was that about?

Suddenly, it all came together, hitting me like a thunderbolt— the necklace, foxglove, and even the woman who'd been pushed during a hike.

"Mother, we need to talk." I glanced uncomfortably over my shoulder. "But not here."

WE took a walk on a dusty red dirt trail. "It's like the old Hitchcock movie, *Strangers on a Train*. Both Harry and his chef wanted to get rid of their wives, so they swapped murders. Peter killed Lorna when Harry was alibied." I explained about the foxglove shrubs. "Harry was expected to kill Peter's wife, doubtless when Peter had an alibi. Except when Harry gave her a shove, all Dani got was a broken foot." I couldn't explain why Peter had Lorna's necklace—maybe Harry gave it to him—but I'd bet anything that Peter was signaling Harry he hadn't fulfilled his part of the deal.

Mother beamed at me with momentary admiration. "Tracy, you solved Lorna's murder." Then, she directed a nasty grin my way. "But you figured it out because of a movie plot. Maybe that's all you know, too."

Jeez, no! Was it all in the genes?

† † †

I spent the next morning on the phone with an IT person from the company that manufactured the wireless microphone Mother had "borrowed." She visited a vitamin shop in town, loading up on a substance we'd need. After she returned, room service delivered a tea service for three. And Harry came to our suite, since Mother had given him to understand we wanted to make nice.

He spread his arms wide. "Martha and Tracy, we've been friends too long to squabble. Let's bring our differences to an end."

Harry took a seat, and Mother poured his tea. He gulped a mouthful of the strong Earl Gray, grabbed one of the little chicken salad sandwiches from a platter beside his cup, and took a big bite. Beside my untouched cup, I'd placed an unfurled cloth napkin.

"Harry, let me run a theory past you." I laid out the crisscross scheme for him as I had for Mother. He'd always been a show-off. I counted on his wanting to brag.

While he listened, the anger splashed across his fine features became more pronounced.

"Phones." He threw out his hand. "Give me your phones. You're not going to record me."

I handed them over. "We never considered recording you on our phones."

He snorted like he didn't believe me, and took another gulp of tea and chewed through a second sandwich. When Mother replenished his cup, he drank that as well. "You'll never be able to prove anything." We waited for what seemed like an eternity. Finally, he said, "Lorna kept giving more of our money to her charity cases. I didn't work to make other people's lives better. Besides, I...I met someone."

Jill, of the racy emails. Harry drank more tea.

I cleared my throat. "So you arranged with Peter to swap murders?"

Harry shrugged. Not quite the admission we'd hoped for. We needed him to say it aloud.

Mother asked, "What's to stop me from taking Tracy's theory to the police?"

What now? She wasn't sticking to the script.

Every shred of Harry's usual charm vanished when he

snatched Mother by the collar of her Chanel blouse and yanked her across the table until they were nose-to-nose. "Don't threaten me, Martha. You're not in my league. Remember, I've already committed one perfect murder. It wouldn't require much effort to pull off a couple more."

Yes! An admission, not to mention a threat.

Harry threw Mother back into her chair, before knocking back another cup of tea. She might have radiated a little fear at that point. Even if she didn't feel it, that should have been an easy feat for an actress of her caliber. Instead, while calmly patting her collar down, she looked positively serene.

Now I had to punt. "Peter must be unhappy with you, Harry. You didn't hold up your end of the bargain."

"Hey, I pushed his annoying wife off that cliff. It's not my fault she survived." Harry tossed his napkin on to the table.

"I don't think you'll manage another perfect murder, dear man," Mother said with unflappable ease.

Fury overtook Harry's features once more, but when he rose, he became so woozy, he almost fell down.

"You see, Harry, we dosed you with some of what Peter gave Lorna. You'll be dead in no time." Mother smiled.

We hadn't actually given him digoxin. He felt dizzy from the Kava Mother had bought at the vitamin store, which we loaded into the tea and sandwiches. Harry was a strong man—we thought we'd need him in a more hobbled state.

"No! You can't have." He collapsed back into his chair. For the first time he appeared to notice the sound system wasn't playing its usual flute music. His eyes traveled to the built-in speaker. "What...?" That was the echo of his voice coming through.

I whipped away the napkin beside my cup to reveal the power pack of Mother's mic, which the tech guy taught me how to hook into the spa's speakers. "As I said, Harry, we never considered recording you *on our phones*. Instead, we sent your confession out to the entire resort."

Our door lock clicked, and the door carefully opened. Officer Roddy entered, gun drawn. He didn't look so sloppy now in a different uniform, that of the Arizona Department of Public Safety. The state police force. "Harry Rafferty, you're under arrest for the murder Lorna Rafferty and the attempted murder of Dani Cortero. We've already picked up your chef. You have the right…"

Mother leaned in close and put the full force of her wrath into a nasty, triumphant grin. "You're not dying, you poor fool. You'll live to spend decades in prison."

Officer Roddy gave me a wink. I wished I'd understood what he'd tried to convey earlier. When he told me he'd be watching me, what he meant was that he'd be looking out for me.

Mother glanced around uneasily. "This place really is notorious. Let's head to the bar. Some moments call for more than tainted tea."

Occasionally, she had the right idea.

OVER drinks in a quiet corner of the bar, Mother grew unusually pensive. "Tracy, what I find the hardest to grasp is how the love of two couples could go so badly awry."

A woman with six marriages and five divorces didn't get that? Was my mother growing up?

She popped on her desert fedora once more, and sent a steely stare at any villains who might be nursing cold beers.

Growing up? I stifled a smile. Not a chance.

† † †

KRIS NERI's latest novel, *Hopscotch Life*, was a New Mexico-Arizona Book Award winner. She also writes the Tracy Eaton mysteries and the Samantha Brennan & Annabelle Haggerty magical series. Kris has published some sixty short stories, and is a two-time Derringer Award winner and a two-time Pushcart Prize nominee. She teaches writing online for the prestigious Writers' Program of the UCLA Extension School, as well as other organizations. She and her husband make their home in Silver City, NM, along with two pushy terriers. KrisNeri.com

A BURN THAT REACHES BONE
KAREN ODDEN

LIVING with my father's like driving a bad road. As his kid, you're completely in the dark, and the potholes surprise the hell out of you, but when you're coming up on thirty years old, it's more like driving by a single weak headlight. You know about the potholes, and how deep they are, so you're wary, not wanting to crack a rim or blow a strut.

If I had to guess, I'd say his rotten temper comes from working for fifty years in the restaurant business, starting at age twelve. Bussing tables in a cheap steakhouse, paid in quarters under the table. Slaving sixteen hours a day as a sous-chef in Vegas. Drinking booze with customers till closing and downing coffee to function at opening. Having to beg the last ten thousand from his brother Joe to buy his first restaurant in Phoenix. Talk about a bad road. Although Dad's seven restaurants, sold two years ago to an up-and-coming restauranteur, are thriving. Of course, now my father wishes they'd fail.

There's a new edge to my father's spitefulness since he went into the hospital. He's not just dying of cancer, he's using it as an excuse for abusing the hospital staff. They don't fight back, obviously; they just smile, "in that mocking way," he says, which pisses him off even more. He's scheduled for another round of chemo, a last-ditch attempt to beat it back, but after this, it'll be hospice. I feel shitty admitting it, but there's part of me that will feel relieved when he's gone.

This morning, he sent for Sarah and me, so I drive in from Gilbert to the Scottsdale hospital near his house. I park my rebuilt Mustang between two palo verde trees to avoid the birds that would crap on it.

Sarah is waiting for me across the hospital lobby. She's thirty-two, three years older, and a better person in pretty much every way. After our mom died, she'd text me to stay at a friend's because Dad was raging drunk. After she started at ASU, she helped me graduate high school. I tried college for a while but couldn't stick with it. She's got a Master's degree, a sweet kid, and a great husband, only he found out recently that he's having some health issues. Not sure what, but as I come close, I can see Sarah has that white, weary look around her eyes that means she's not sleeping.

"Hey, Robbie." She smiles wanly.

"Hey." I throw an arm around her, drop a quick kiss on her cheek. "Any idea what he wants?"

She shakes her head.

We take the elevator up and find his room, with MARIO D. on the whiteboard beside the door.

He's in bed with a metal skeletal contraption to the side, one of its arms holding a bag of fluid that's dripping by tube into the crook of his elbow. His once-dark hair has peppered, puffing over his ears. He squints at us, and Sarah crosses to the window to adjust the shade, softening the fierce July sunlight.

We greet him, and Sarah asks, "How are you feeling today?"

"Like shit," he spits.

"I'm sorry," Sarah replies, and we sit in the two chairs. This puts us below bed level, and his body loses some of its tension.

"So I need to tell you," he begins.

We wait expectantly. The doctors told us they're seeing some dementia veering toward paranoia. All of Dad's ugliest impulses are surfacing, including a nasty anti-Semitism that Sarah simply won't sit for. Last time he burst out about the "Jew doctor who hasn't done crap," Sarah left the room and didn't come back, even though he screamed for her until the nurses had to sedate him. We're not sure if Dad's forgotten that Sarah's husband David is Jewish, or if he remembers it perfectly well. Either way, our father has been acting worse and worse. So today I'm ready for him to pop out with just about anything.

He looks at us sideways. "I got a favor. One last thing you can do for your old man."

"What is it?" Sarah asks with a show of patience.

He raises a hand to tell us he's in charge, and the ask will come later. We both stiffen, knowing this stalling is a bad sign.

"Thirty years ago, what'd I do?" he asks.

Not quite in unison, Sarah and I reply, "You opened *Buongiorno.*" Not that we remember; Sarah was a year old, and I wasn't born yet. But we know the script.

He nods, his right hand fingers tapping the tray in front of him, and I notice two yellow envelopes. One for each of us, I suppose.

"Your uncle Joe came to see me last week. Reminded me how he got half the equity for ten thousand dollars. Laughed the whole time. Rotten bastard."

I flinch at my uncle's name. My father wasn't the only one my uncle Joe mocked in a moment of financial need. I haven't seen him in years. He bought a McMansion on the golf course at Grayhawk, with his fourth wife, Margo. The one time I met her, she seemed like a nice person. Nicer than he deserved.

"I built that business myself," my father says. "All seven restaurants!" His eyes narrowed. "Do you know what *he* did?"

I reply solo: "He was a manager for a pharm company."

"Damn straight! And he went behind my back," he says, his hands making a clawing motion, first to the left and then to the right. "Snatching up profits, lying and telling people—"

"Dad, what's the point?" Sarah cuts him off.

His two hands land on the envelopes. "You need to put an end to him."

There's a long silence, and then I give a half-laugh. "You don't mean—"

His face twists with disgust. "Jesus. How did I end up with such a puling idiot for a son?"

"Shut up, Dad." Sarah's voice is flat. "He's not an idiot just because he still tries to find some decency in you."

I swallow hard as I understand that my father means he wants his brother dead.

He ignores Sarah. "I have two wills." His hand taps the left envelope. "One leaves everything to you two—*everything*," he barks and breaks into a cough that brings tears to his eyes. I hand him a tissue, and he wipes at them. "Ten million each."

My chest tightens. There's a gas station and garage I've wanted to buy for four million, but I can't get a loan unless my father co-signs. He's outright refused. And now he's dangling the money like *this?*

"The other will leaves everything to charity." He pats the other envelope. "This one's signed and notarized, for now."

Sarah squints. "Which charity?"

He cackles a bit. "The N.R.A."

"That's not a charity." Sarah despises the group, and he knows it. Her friend Beth teaches at a school in Nebraska where some crazy-ass gunman shot three kids before he was tackled.

My father shrugs, and the pale blue hospital gown shifts and buckles, revealing the wrinkled olive skin with a dusting of curly gray hair below his collarbone. "You do this for me, and I sign the other will. Your choice."

Jesus, he's lost it, I think.

"We're not killing Uncle Joe," Sarah says.

His eyebrows lift. "Then tell me how you're going to help that husband of yours. He could die without treatment," he says triumphantly.

I spin toward her. "Sarah?"

Her green eyes flash at him, and her expression hardens. "He's not going to die."

"That's not what I hear," my father says with a grimace. "Besides, you'll *want* to kill Uncle Joe when I tell you what he did."

"No, we won't," Sarah says sharply. "Come on, Robbie, let's go."

I know she's trying to get me out of there, but curiosity gets the better of me, and I plant my feet.

"I'm not going to kill him, but what did he do?" I ask.

"Robbie, come *on,*" Sarah insists, behind me.

My father's gaze pins me. "He raped your mother in the back room opening night," he says, his voice rough as tires on gravel. "Told me last week, right here." He slapped the bed. "Said he took her, same as he took my restaurants."

I stare openmouthed. My uncle's an asshole, but my father lies, and I don't believe this. It's too much.

"He gets away with everything," my father rasps. "But *I'm* winning at *this.* He dies first. Not me. *Him.*"

Sarah picks up her bag from the chair. "I'm leaving." Her voice is toneless. "And don't scream this time."

"Bye, Dad," I say.

He points. "Don't take long. I might die in a week."

"Selfish bastard," Sarah mutters as we get on the elevator.

"He's wacked," I reply. "But what's going on with David?"

"Oh…they're not sure." Her face is bleak. "They're still testing. The doctors at Mayo think it's a growth in his pituitary."

That doesn't sound hopeful.

The doors open, and we cross the lobby. "Sarah, why didn't you tell me? You've got to be scared shitless."

"There's nothing you could do." She shakes her head. "Can we not talk about it?"

"Okay," I agree, somewhat reluctantly. We approach her car, and she clicks the unlock button.

"The thing about the will," I say. "Legally, is Dad even competent? I mean, he has some dementia. Now he's making shit up and trying to get us to kill someone. I'd say that counts as crazy."

Sarah draws her sleeve over her fingers to protect herself from the metal handle and pulls the door open. The car air comes at us like a sweltering exhale. She turns toward me. I can't see her eyes through her sunglasses, but she's biting her lip hard enough to whiten it. At last, she says, "He's not making it up, Robbie," and there's a note of something like pity in her voice. "I've got to go. I have an appointment at the office." Then she gets in, starts the car, and I'm left standing there, dumbfounded, watching her drive away.

I get in my car, turn the air conditioning on high, and text her:

DID MOM TELL U?

No reply.

I text again:

HOW DO YOU KNOW?

Again, nothing.

And suddenly, from some corner of my brain, a memory rises. Sarah, maybe fifteen years old. Long-legged, her blonde hair mussed. Hurrying away from the casita during one of Dad's crazy parties. She rushes past my friend Jack and me, slurping vodka under the pool umbrella. Her face is strange, her skirt crooked, her step uneven as if she's lost a shoe, which is odd enough that it registers, even though I'm pretty smashed. A few minutes later, my uncle Joe walks past, smoking a joint, which strikes us as hilarious.

It has taken me fourteen years to understand what I saw.

For once our father isn't lying to make his brother look worse than he is.

Despite the blowing A/C, I feel a searing heat, like sun on a black car, fierce enough to burn down to my bones. Remembering how timid Mom was, I know why she wouldn't report the rape. But *Sarah*? Did Sarah not tell *anyone*? Yeah, Mom had died, and Dad would've laughed it off. But what about the police? Or a friend?

And why not tell me, all this time?

I text Sarah a few more times, saying that we need to talk, that I believe her, but she doesn't reply, and I figure it's because she doesn't want to answer questions about what Uncle Joe did to *her*.

† † †

A few days pass, and I plan to drive over to her house after I fix the brakes on Carl's Harley.

I'm in my garage by eight-thirty that morning, with the 1960s swamp cooler trying to keep the temperature below eighty. The brakes are fried, and I'm listening to Sirius XM when the side door squeaks and Carl walks in.

It's not even ten.

"I'm nowhere near done," I say.

"Yeah. I figured I'd see if you were okay."

I look up, questioning.

His expression changes to comprehension. "Man, your uncle Joe died. They found him this morning. It's on the local news." He pushes a few buttons on his phone. "Here, they're still talking about it." He turns it toward me, clicking the volume up.

The blonde newscaster speaks from the sidewalk in front of Uncle Joe's house. "If you're just joining us, this is what we know so far," she says, her eyes wide and serious. "His wife Margo was in Sedona visiting friends, and she arrived home this morning to find her husband dead in bed with no evident cause. Mr. D'Augustino, a former Scottsdale City councilman, has been a lifelong resident of Arizona. He has a record of heart disease, and he was receiving treatment..."

Waves of panic rise from beneath my ribs. *Sarah? Was this you?*

I grab my phone and stand there with my thumbs poised over the screen.

I text and backspace, text and backspace, finally settling on:

DID U SEE THE NEWS?

The three blinking dots show up and vanish. No words appear, and I imagine Sarah in her kitchen, turning on the TV, drinking her coffee. Her daughter Katie has swim camp. David'll be at work. She'll be alone.

But how could she have even gotten to Uncle Joe? Sarah has never stepped foot inside his house, so far as I know, and makes no secret of despising him. She skipped all of his weddings, claiming travel for work. Had Sarah known that Margo was going to be away? Or had she watched the house? But my uncle has cameras and alarms everywhere. My brain has latched onto "no evident cause," leapt to *poison*, and is searching for some way that Sarah could enter his house and convince him to drink or eat something she brought. Utterly implausible.

Is there any chance he died naturally?

"Hey, man, are you okay?" Carl asks. "You look sort of freaked out. I thought you hated him."

"Yeah," I say. "But..."

"Still a shock." He nods understandingly.

Carl keeps me company, talking Diamondbacks baseball while my unsteady hands reassemble his bike. An hour later, he leaves, after handing me two hundreds.

I call Sarah; her voicemail is full. Her email kicks back an Out of Office message. She's traveling until Thursday.

† † †

THE cause of death is ruled accidental overdose of his heart medication, and the funeral is Friday. With us being Catholic, there's a wake Thursday afternoon, and, my stomach in knots, I attend. Sarah is there with David—who looks thin—and Katie, fidgeting with boredom but trying not to be rude.

I approach Margo, who stands stoically, tearlessly receiving condolences. The sunlight blazes through the window above, and coming close, I can see under her makeup the telltale signs of a black eye. I stiffen, remembering that Uncle Joe's second wife had filed a police report for domestic abuse. I mutter how sorry I am, and her lips barely move as she thanks me. I wonder if there will be any money left for her; I've heard his first three wives pretty much sucked him dry.

And I start thinking, maybe for once the universe has actually balanced the scales of justice without anyone rigging them. Uncle Joe dies of a rotten heart, David gets the treatment he needs, I get the garage, Margo escapes while she's still young enough to start over, and my father can die in peace.

Still, my eyes don't leave Sarah, who stands across the room with friends and a distant cousin who drove up from Tucson. She catches sight of me and nods. What am I looking for in her expression? A sign of guilt? Secret relief? Joy? Regret? Panic? I can't find anything except a smile for Katie, when she slips her hand into her mother's.

I am almost convinced that Sarah had nothing to do with it.

"Are you Michael?"

I turn to find an older woman I don't recognize. She's short, and I adjust my gaze. "No, he's over there." I point to my cousin, who stands near the coffin. "I'm Robbie. Joe was my uncle."

"Goodness, you're the spitting image of Joe at your age." She smiles, revealing tiny, yellowing teeth. "Same eyes, same chin."

I shrug politely. "Well, the brothers look a lot alike."

Still, her words unsettle me. And as she walks away, it strikes me that I was born around ten months after Buongiorno opened.

My heart thuds in my chest, and I shuffle to a folding chair to think, to comb back through my life with this possibility in my head.

Is this why Sarah tried to drag me out of my father's room?

When everyone is gone but family, I draw Sarah to an empty corner. "How did you know about it?" I ask quietly. "The rape."

Her eyes skid away from mine and return. "Aunt Marjorie told me before she died."

My mom's only sister. Of course.

I keep my voice even. "Did Mom tell you I was Joe's?"

She winces. "No. She couldn't be sure."

"Sarah?" David approaches, looking pale and sweaty. "I need to get home."

My sister squeezes my arm. "I'm sorry, Robbie. I didn't want—" She halts and takes a ragged breath. "We'll talk soon, okay?"

She holds David's elbow to support him, and I follow them to the open door, watching them go. Margo descends the stairs of the funeral home, graceful in her heels. She falls in beside Sarah, presses her fingertips briefly into Sarah's free hand as she passes, and walks on.

And I step into the searing sun, with the cold knowledge that my sister has taken care of me, yet again.

† † †

KAREN ODDEN earned her Ph.D. in English literature from NYU and subsequently taught literature and critical theory at UW-Milwaukee. She has contributed essays to numerous books, written introductions for novels by Dickens and Trollope for Barnes & Noble, and edited for *Victorian Literature and Culture*. Her published historical mysteries are all set in 1870s London. *A Lady in the Smoke* (2015, Random House/Alibi) was a *USA Today* bestseller. Her second and third novels, *A Dangerous Duet* and *A Trace of Deceit* (2018 and 2019, William Morrow) have won awards for historical fiction and mystery. KarenOdden.com

HOME IS WHERE
R K OLSON

"SHE looks sort of soft, like…delicate." He glances at me. "Feminine."

"Oh." I throw back one final slug of beer. "So, I'm what…the manly sister?"

He hands back the snapshot. "Ah jeez, don't get sore." He shrugs, grabs a towel and wipes his way down the bar. "I just meant she looks…graceful."

Graceful. She can't even run without kicking herself.

I snort and put the photo in my bag and dig around for my wallet, a black leather tri-fold—not exactly feminine.

"Don't be mad. You have a pretty sister." He tosses the rag on the barback. "How's that an insult? You're good lookin' too."

I tuck a five under the half empty glass and swivel away from the counter. I have bags to pack.

"Hey," he calls after me. "Where you goin'?"

"Home." I toss my handbag over my shoulder on my way out the door.

† † †

WHEN I reach the outskirts of Phoenix the dread I've been tamping down rushes in on me, anxiety building along with the heat as I drive through the city. I wind up the side of Mummy Mountain, the house not exactly looming—more like listing—above.

My family used to be pretty well-off before my father disappeared on my mother, my older sister, and me when I was ten. Our property backs up to the north side of the mountain, where streams and rivulets from infrequent, but often heavy, rainstorms wear ragged paths that wind through the cacti and sage.

In its prime, the house had been a masterpiece of southwest architecture. Fine craftsmanship, old adobe blocks, *vigas* and *latillas*. One of the oldest properties in the wealthy enclave of Paradise Valley. Originally it sat on 25 acres but, after Daddy left us, Mother sold off the land, one five-acre parcel at a time to keep us afloat. By the time I graduated from high school there was nothing left to sell, except the home and the last five-acre parcel it sat on, which was tied up in trusts for my sister and me. Mother wouldn't have sold the house, anyway. She lived in a world where this place and her twenty-year-old Mercedes were signs of prosperity, oblivious to the fact that one was crumbling—the other rusting—out from under her.

The lower gate stands open and slightly askew. I make my way up the steep drive between the once-white stables, spattered with dust, and the shack we called the pumphouse, a massive untended prickly pear standing sentry over its entrance. Imagining the cobwebs and vermin inside, I shudder. My *graceful* sister locked me in there when I was eight, triggering a claustrophobia I deal with to this day. There'd been plans to tear the pumphouse down and build a guest house, but those plans died, along with everything else, when Daddy left.

I focus on the driveway, cracked and buckled, leading to the grand front drive. I leave my Wrangler in the roundabout, nose into the once glamorous fountain. Bone dry now, surrounded by weeds.

Grabbing my cap, I make my way to the elaborate weather-worn front door and ring the bell. Nothing. I knock and run my fingers over the ancient carving, the way I had as a child. Long-buried memories rise to the surface. My emotions bounce all over the place. Melancholy. Homesickness—for the time when this place had been an actual home—and more than a little fear.

I take a breath of hot, dry air and make my way through the overgrown desert landscape to the back of the house, which looks down on the stables below. They'd stood empty until Daddy bought Jet for me from a trainer. He'd served his usefulness as a show jumper and was headed out to pasture before we brought him home. I spent as much time as possible with him. As an awkward ten-year-old, he was my best friend. After my father left, he became my solace. Living proof that I'd been loved once. When Jet died, it was like losing Daddy all over again.

I swing myself under the gnarly old orange tree. I have to climb down through the yard, then back up to the patio, to try the back doors.

More than once I sidestep a cactus. I haven't forgotten the pain of jumping cholla spines embedded in skin, but concern grows as I realize how far things have deteriorated in the decade since I left. I fan myself with my hat before jamming it back on my head.

"Hey!"

I stop in my tracks.

"Hey!" Again. I see her now, in an old one-piece bathing suit, sprawled on a plastic lounger up on the patio. She raises the brim of a large sun hat.

"Mother?" I say tentatively. Like I'm not sure.

I'm sure.

"Oh, the prodigal daughter returns. Or should I say son?" She laughs at her own joke. "You chopped off your beautiful hair, didn't you? Take off the hat. Turn around," she says, giving me a lazy finger twirl.

I obey both demands and she scoffs.

"And put on a few pounds."

Just like that, I become a child again.

"Tanty called," I say, trying to explain my sudden appearance after so many years.

"Tanty." She says it like it's a curse. "She was here, nosing around a few days ago. Snoopy biddy. I sent her packing."

Tanty is Mother's sister. *Tante* means aunt in French.

We aren't French, just pretentious.

"Here Mommy, your screwdriver." A childlike voice sings out from inside the house. The *graceful* sister appears and trips on the threshold of the sliding glass door but manages to keep the drink upright. "I picked fresh oranges and squeezed— Oh!" She stops in her tracks. "You're home." She glances at our Mother who snaps her fingers, arm outstretched.

"Yes, yes, she's home." She snaps again. "Gimme," Mother says, her fingers motioning with impatience. She sighs as soon as they're wrapped around the sweating glass. "You girls go play with your dolls while Mommy gets some sun."

I roll my eyes and follow my sister.

"Do you have a boyfriend?" she asks as soon as we're inside. "I had a boyfriend. He used to pick me up in his car, but Mommy made him go away."

"I remember." It'd been the summer she turned seventeen. The same summer our father left. Mother had hated him on sight. Accused him of being after *our fortune.*

I look at her now. She hasn't aged, her skin as smooth as twenty years ago. It's as if time—while gradually destroying all other elements around us—has stood still for her.

I find myself distracted as we walk through Mother's bedroom. The same silk draperies hang in shreds, deteriorated from the sunlight. The same heavy-upholstered bed, now shabby, half unmade because Mother only sleeps on the left side since my father left. I glance in at the master bath, still clad in white marble, now chipped and stained.

We walk into the hallway past what had once been a workout room. The same granite counter spans its width. Holding a small sink and built-in refrigerator meant for "power" shakes, the space seems to have become a makeshift kitchen. A folding table holds the remnants of the Screwdriver, along with a microwave and a variety of canned foods.

"Who does the shopping?"

"Gardener." She opens a cabinet next to the refrigerator and waves a hand like Vanna White. More cans, cracker boxes. She opens the fridge. It's full, too. Vodka. "He comes once a week." She shrugs at her own image in the mirrored wall, as if they share a secret. "Mother calls him with a list."

Tanty must be paying the gardener/caretaker out of her share of their inheritance. She didn't tell me that when she called to ask if I'd try to persuade them to leave this house and downsize into something manageable.

I catch my own reflection. Like always, I see a younger version of my mother and have to curb the urge to slap myself in the face.

In an effort to keep my hands busy, I pick up an orange from the table and peel it.

"That reminds me." She holds the barre and drops into an

artless *plié*, her eyes still glued to her own face. "We need more cream for the coffee." She holds the barre and leans into the hallway. "Mommy!"

I wander past the living area on my own and head down the bedroom wing toward my old room. Not much has changed except a layer of dust, along with a mysterious golden stain on the corner of the ceiling. I peek into the other rooms, all dusty, unused. Not surprising that things have deteriorated to this point.

"I don't sleep in here anymore."

I jump. "Oh, you startled me." I put a hand to my chest, inhale. "Where...?"

"I'll show you." We retrace our steps to Mother's bedroom. She flings open the closet door. Twirling on one toe she tips into the closet, grabbing the doorway to brace herself. "I sleep here!" she announces.

She settles herself, lounging on the thread-bare velvet chaise lounge. True this room is larger than the average bedroom, and still boasts a lovely chandelier, but it's a closet. I reach up to run a finger over the lowest crystal pendant. Only one wall holds clothes now, all dated and musty. Alongside the chaise is a twin bed from somewhere.

We weren't allowed in here as children, but I snuck in a few times to toss a boa over my shoulders or try on a pair of Louboutins. I pick up an old pair and turn one over in my hand. A glint catches my eye as a partially wrapped object falls to the carpet. I grab it and unwrap a turquoise ring. I roll it over in my hand.

My father's ring.

A pale, slender arm reaches in front of me and my fist closes around the ring in reflex. Looking up, I find my sister standing over me, arm still outstretched. Ignoring her silent demand, I shake my head. "This was Daddy's. He never took it off." And he'd promised it to me. "How'd it get in Mother's shoe?"

The shrug again. She smiles at her reflection in the full-length mirror. I catch sight of myself behind her. Two younger versions of my mother stared back at me. The taller, slender one tips her head to avoid my gaze.

"Did Daddy come home?" I shout at her back.

"You girls quiet down!"

Like hell.

I charge out to the patio. "Mother, did Daddy come back here?"

She raises the brim of her hat and turns to stare at me, a steely look I'd been terrorized by in my youth. And still am.

"I haven't seen your father since the day he left me here," she says through clenched teeth. "With you two," she adds as an afterthought.

"So, he didn't take his ring?"

"What are you..." She narrows her eyes. "What ring?"

I hold it out, show it to her.

"Where did you get that?" She tries to grab it, but I hold tight, heart hammering in my chest.

I can't stay here. I need to think.

I walk through the house, back to a spare bedroom where I'd seen a two-door filing cabinet. The top drawer holds nothing but a dusty, long-forgotten bottle of vodka. The other is stuffed with a haphazard array of papers. I grab the entire lower drawer and carry it out to my Jeep.

† † †

I'M glad I had the forethought to book a room at the Camelback Inn, on the other side of Mummy Mountain. I settle the drawer on my luggage stand and order room service.

On top is the deed to the house, paid in full long before Daddy left. Next is Daddy's life insurance policy. Ten million dollars—useless and unclaimed.

I skim through his will. He left everything to Mother and then to my sister and me. Rifling through the pile, I don't see any overdue bills or outstanding debt.

I tuck the documents in my suitcase and—patience not being one of my virtues—dump the rest of its contents onto the bed. At the top of the heap is Daddy's pistol—an ugly, snub-nosed handgun. He kept it loaded. Used it for rattlesnakes. Thinking hard, I try to remember a time I'd ever seen him without it on his hip. I can't. Same for the ring stuffed in my pocket.

I open the pistol's cylinder, dumping its contents into my hand. Three bullets.

Three spent casings.

My heart ricochets around my chest. My mind bounces to the ring he never took off. Not even once.

Jamming the spent casings into my pocket, I finger the carved silver band.

I yank my hand free, snap the gun's cylinder closed.

Time for bed.

† † †

A surprise shower dampened the desert floor during the night, leaving this morning's air humid and filled with the earthy scent of rain on dust. I will myself to focus as I wind through the backroads around the base of the mountain. It takes all my strength to go back to the house. I'm packed up and ready to head home, papers and pistol held securely in my lockbox. Tanty's on her own. Coming back after all this time has shown me I don't belong here. I never have, and nothing binds me to this place now, except a new and urgent need for answers.

My mother sits propped up in bed, her nightgown drooping to expose most of one sagging breast. Someone locked the front door, so once again I make my way through the back to the expanse of sliding doors outside her room. I watch her for a moment, then slide one door open.

"Don't you ever knock?"

"This is my home, isn't it?" I say, finding my voice.

I recognize the disgruntled growl from the back of her throat. This place hasn't been my home, or anyone's for a long time now and we both know it.

"Mommy, there's no cream, you need to call Gardener—" My sister stops short when she sees me. Goes quiet.

"Doesn't he have a name?" I ask with more than a little annoyance.

"Dom…Domino." My mother huffs.

"Domingo?" I venture.

"Gardener." Her voice rises. "Domingo. Domino. Does it matter?"

"Yes," I say, matching her stare. Finally standing up to her. For a man I've never met. "It matters."

The growl again. "Why are you here?"

"I need answers," I say, looking from one to the other.

"*Answers?*" My mother rakes her glare down my frame, taking in my jeans and baggy T-shirt. My hair, self-trimmed. My beloved, well-worn baseball cap. "What you *need* is to lose a few pounds and stop dressing like a boy."

I close my eyes, take a deep breath and let it out slowly. "When did Daddy come back?" I ask, refusing to be derailed.

"Back?" Mother waves a dismissive hand in the air between us. "Your father never came *back*."

"He must have," I insist, eyeing my sister. Watching her as carefully as she's watching me. "Unless he never left."

"Are you crazy?" Mother spits at me. "He left—he's gone. Isn't he?"

I ignore her. Focus on my sister. "You took his ring." I reach into my pocket and pull it out, along with the spent cartridges from our father's gun. Raising them between us, I show them to my sister. "Tell her," I say. Her eyes go wide. "Tell her now. Or I will."

"Tell me what?" Mother sits up. "Tell me!"

The delicate sister sticks her chin out and taps it with a finger, chewing on her lower lip. "*Fine*," she mutters and rolls her eyes. "She's right. Daddy never left."

I look at my mother. Our eyes meet. For once she seems almost speechless. I shake my head. I'm done. The rest is up to her.

"All right..." Mother clears her throat and turns toward my sister. "Maybe you'll tell us where he is?"

In answer she raises a slender arm and points. I walk to the window, survey the yard. The overgrown prickly pear catches my eye, its flat, green paddles, nearly twice as big as my hand, all but blocking my view of the pumphouse door. A feeling far worse than claustrophobia grabs at the pit of my stomach as some distant memory forces its way to the surface. "The pumphouse?" Turning, I grip her bony shoulders, ready to shake the truth out of her. "Daddy's in the pumphouse?"

She nods at me, a slow smile spreading across her smooth, ageless face, like she's glad I finally figured it out. "I followed him." She makes a gun with her thumb and forefinger, holds it to her head. "It was easy. I told him I saw a rattler…" She looks at our mother with a hatred I'd never seen before. "You got rid of *my* boyfriend," she says with a shrug. "So, I got rid of yours."

† † †

"THE usual?" he asks, sliding a pale ale in front of me. I sit on my stool, feeling something like a comfortable embrace in the smell of stale beer and the background sounds of corny country music. He sets the bar mop down and leans forward, both elbows on the counter. "How was your trip to Crazy Town?"

I twirl my father's ring on my thumb and looked into the eyes of the closest thing I've had to a friend since my horse died. "Crazy." I run a finger through the icy sweat trickling down my beer mug and sigh. "It's good to be home."

† † †

Award-winning short story author, and lifelong logophile, **R K (Roni) OLSON** has altered her lifestyle to indulge her love of all things written. A past-president of the Sisters in Crime Desert Sleuths Chapter, her short stories have been published in numerous anthologies. A transplanted native of the Pacific Northwest, she enjoys life as a frustrated minimalist in Scottsdale, AZ. Ronisays.com

NIGHT SHIFT
D. R. RANSDELL

BY the time Kique called me, his sister was being transported to Tucson. They'd been staying in Nogales, which was only sixty kilometers away. I left work as quickly as possible and rushed to Emergency, but Meli had already been given a private room. She even had a window.

My cousin was still asleep. She'd been knocked around so hard that she had multiple bruises on both arms, but what stood out was the bandage that stretched from the top of her ear, across her cheek, and down to her neck.

Underneath the gauze was a deep cut. I was lucky to have missed seeing the effects of the knife. Kique's description had been vivid enough.

She was only twenty-eight, one year my junior. I was on one side of her hospital bed; her brother was on the other. After spending countless summers together, we were more like siblings.

"Rachel, she's waking." Kique said. He kept his cool no matter the circumstances.

Mentally, I braced myself. When Meli opened her eyes, she saw me first.

"Am I dead, Rachel?" she asked in Spanish.

"No," I said.

"You only wish you were," Kique said flatly.

"Kique," I said sharply.

"Well, it's true."

Meli raised her hand toward her cheek, but Kique grabbed her arm and lowered it. "If you can't leave the bandage alone, they'll tie you down."

"Things will be all right," I said. "The surgeon is on call. Right now, there's too much swelling. As soon as it goes down—"

"That's nice."

She didn't care. Her face meant nothing to her. At one time, her marriage had meant something. By now it didn't.

"Kique said that Seba took you by surprise," I said softly.

She nodded as if answering a routine question. "Never thought I'd see him again. He knew about the restraining order, not that he cares about the law."

"Go on."

"Jumped the back gate. Kids in the living room watching TV. Suddenly he's in my kitchen."

She paused. I hated to press, but a best friend had to know.

"So stupid. Had a knife in my hand. Crying while I cut onions. Couldn't even see him. Recognized the sound of his walk."

Seba was a solid man with a beer gut. When he marched into a room, it trembled.

"Then what?"

"Said I was his wife, so I owed him."

"That's when he hit you?" Kique asked.

"No. When I said I'd rather die than take him back. Bad choice of words." Meli paused to catch her breath. Speaking sapped her strength. "Jabbed him with my knife after the first blow. I hurt him?"

Kique patted her hand. "You probably did."

"Knife slipped from my hand. Don't remember anything after that."

Better not to remember. The evidence was clear. Seba had used her own knife to zigzag his way down her cheek.

Though only six and eight years old, children were well trained. At the first hint of a fight, they'd run next door to Uncle Kique. By the time he secured them, Seba was gone and Meli was on the floor, unconscious.

A young nurse entered the room. "You have to leave," she whispered.

"My sister doesn't speak English." Kique lied as coolly as a criminal. "We need to stay with her."

"No English at all?"

"Do you have a translator?

The nurse addressed me. "Only close relatives are allowed."

"She's my half-sister," I lied.

"I'll ask the supervisor."

"She'll need help with the bathroom too," I said. "In case you're short-staffed—"

I knew they were short-staffed. All the hospitals were. Now that the pandemic was over, they were crazy busy with surgeries.

"We'll wait right here." When Kique smiled at the nurse, she smiled back. I wasn't surprised. Kique had a way about him. He could get away with anything.

KIQUE and I spent the night watching over Meli, but she mostly dozed. The next morning Kique went out for supplies, and I sat next to Meli pretending to read magazines. In between I fielded texts from my mother and sister, who lived across town, and some of Meli's many relatives down in Mexico. Initially everyone wanted details. After I mentioned the ninety-seven stitches, they stopped asking.

Despite efforts not to, I kept imagining the scenario. Meli in her own kitchen, preparing dinner for her children. Horrible ex-husband coming around to prove—what? That he was strong enough to subdue an unsuspecting woman?

No wonder my grandmother had left her hometown in Durango, Mexico, when she had the chance. Over the years the laws had shifted slightly, but society was still quick to blame women. If married men took lovers, it was because their wives didn't pay them enough attention. If kids didn't like their dads, it was because mothers turned the kids against them.

Or, in Meli's case, the philandering husband had impregnated two other women during the same time period and expected Meli to look the other way, which meant she nearly had to look backward. But after the third or so time he came home angry and beat her up for no reason, she left him for good. After she won the divorce, he started in with threatening phone calls. Then she got the restraining order. As an added precaution, she and Kique moved to Nogales for the summer. Result? Seba hunted her down to teach her a lesson about freedom. I wanted to kill him myself.

"Water," Meli said weakly.

I jumped up to fill her glass.

"Did I sleep through the night?"

I nodded.

"I'm okay, right? Except for my face?" She drank carefully, through a straw.

"Three bruised ribs. A sprained wrist. By the time you arrived, you were dehydrated."

"The surgeons are so much better in Tucson?"

"It was the only way to protect you."

"I'm not here under my own name?"

"For attempted murder, Holy Trinity has an arrangement."

"Insurance?"

"Under control."

Meli's eyes danced. "Seba can't find me?"

I shook my head. "I left a description at the front desk just in case. If they see him, they know to call the police."

Meli nodded so slightly I barely noticed.

"Find my cell phone?" she asked.

I fished it from her purse. "Anything else?"

"If there's a choice, for dinner I'd take beef."

"I thought you were going vegetarian."

"Yes. But first I'm building my strength." As if to prove her words, she settled into a deep sleep.

Kique entered the room with a big plastic bag. "I found the coolest thing. Meli's going to love it."

He took out a hefty wooden box whose sharp corners were reinforced with antique brass. "The Goodwill down the street is fantastic."

I must have given him a funny look.

"Can you guess what it is?" he asked.

"No.

"A chess set." He opened the heavy lid, which became half a chessboard. Although the wood was somewhat battered, the metal playing pieces were intact. They'd been neatly secured in a red felt bag.

"You couldn't have bought a deck of cards?"

"She's always wanted to learn to play chess," Kique said. "Now she has extra time."

Meli had never played chess. Nor did she play that day. She

dozed on and off, and Kique and I took turns watching her. That night we left the TV on, but we ignored it, lost in our own worlds.

I'd met Seba when I went to Durango for the wedding. I'd never disliked anyone so instantly. Instead of acting the happy groom, he resembled a cocky rancher acquiring a stable. He was a rich-kid mama's boy who loved only himself. I questioned Meli, but her infatuation was complete. Kique warned her too. And her parents. She never listened.

She enjoyed the wedding, at least. And the honeymoon lasted several months. Then, the same old story. A child is born, a husband feels ignored, and he excuses himself for straying. Instead of learning her lesson the first time, Meli had learned it with a second child. The rest of us had seen it coming.

THE night nurse entered so quietly she startled us. She apologized for bringing dinner so late, but the night shift was understaffed. Meli smiled and thanked her cheerfully. She used the steak knife to cut the meatloaf into tiny pieces that she ate one painful bite at a time. I couldn't bear to watch her struggle.

When Kique went out for a cigarette, one of his few vices, Meli bolted upright for the first time since she'd arrived in the hospital.

"What's wrong?" I asked.

"Seba."

"You're safe. He can't find you here. And they're watching for him downstairs."

"I sense him, somehow," she said. "As if he were right around the corner."

"Maybe you need another painkiller."

"No."

"You're under protection. You're not staying under your own name."

"Right, right. But if he somehow finds out—"

"Kique and I will protect you."

"Love you guys for taking care of me."

"Of course. You don't have to worry."

"Not anymore."

But I worried plenty. After Kique came back, I recounted Meli's feelings. He pooh-poohed the idea as silly but suggested a trip to the nearest Walmart. While pepper spray was rarely lethal, having a small can in my purse gave me the illusion of safety. At the very least, I could play bouncer long enough to slow somebody down. That would give Meli enough time to run away.

Nothing else would matter.

† † †

THE next day was a repeat. Same nurses, same routine. While Meli slept, Kique and I paced as caged animals protecting a cub. To keep busy, I washed the blood out of Meli's clothes while Kique brought up snacks from the lounge.

"You can go home, you know," Kique said after dinner. Meli had dozed off.

"I'm all right," I said. "I just need some exercise."

"You could run around the building."

"It's a hundred degrees out there." Tucson had broken eight records that month, and we'd only reached mid-August. We were praying for monsoons.

"You can handle it."

"Are you trying to get rid of me for good? Last month they found two armed vagrants in the parking lot."

"Good point. Go run up and down the stairs a few times. I'm the only one who uses the stairwell."

He was right. I did three dozen sets of stairs without spotting another soul. When I returned to the room, Kique broke out the Brandy Presidente he'd smuggled in. We giggled as we added some to our Coke cans. We might have been teenagers again.

IT was three a.m. by the time I stood up and stretched. Meli had tossed and turned without waking up.

"You could go home, you know," Kique repeated. "None of the other patients' visitors spend the night."

"You already said that. Why do you keep trying to get rid of me?"

"I'm not. But nobody would blame you for wanting to sleep in your own bed."

Even my beat-up mattress sounded enticing, but I would never forgive myself for abandoning Meli. "Thanks, but I can't."

Kique nodded. He knew I wasn't going anywhere. I couldn't. Neither could he.

We lay in the dark and recalled our favorite times together. As kids we'd spent carefree vacations on either side of the border. Barbecues. All-day picnics. New Year's Eves where we'd danced until dawn. My regular visits stopped after Meli married Seba. It wasn't fun to visit anymore. Meli and I couldn't have a conversation without Seba listening in, waiting for the chance to criticize. We couldn't spend any money because every peso she saved had to go to the children, or to him.

Kique and I also whispered about Meli's marriage. She loved her children, but they had come at a price. At the moment they were with the neighbors, but my aunt and uncle were on their way to fetch them. They would be all right for the next few days, but what then? Should Meli prevent them from seeing their father again?

"If I were Meli, I would never forgive Seba," I murmured. "Ever."

"Marriage takes faith," said Kique, the confirmed bachelor. "You swear for better or worse and then learn to live with it. Or else run so far, they can never find you. And then you have to forget."

"You think Meli can do that?"

"She'll have to."

"She can't."

"Shh."

"You don't believe me?"

Kique was on his feet, tapping his index finger against his lips. "Shh."

Heavy feet *clomp clomped* down the hall.

The night nurse didn't walk like that.

"Janitor?" I whispered.

Kique shook his head.

"You don't think—" I let the question trail off in the air. Seba here? Not possible. He couldn't have followed us. Meli was under a false name. Nobody knew where she was, not even her parents. And yet.

The steps came grew closer and louder. Kique flattened

himself against the wall beside the door and motioned for me to copy him.

As I trembled, I took the pepper spray from my purse.

Kique picked up the chess box and held it above his head.

We waited one long second. Two. Ten.

Then the door slowly opened.

I shrank into the corner as a man stumbled in from the well-lit hallway.

Seba.

I would have known his outline anywhere.

For a pregnant second he stood getting his bearings, but the bed was easy to find even in the dark.

Why were all hospital beds draped in white? Nurses didn't need neon signs to find their patients. The colors might have been soothing: a deep rose to imitate flowers in summer, a cheerful aqua to suggest a shallow lagoon. But no. Hospital sheets were always white, as if the world itself were black and white, as if you were either sick or you were well, as if there were an answer as to what to do when your husband abused you because of his own inadequacies and then blamed you for having done so.

I rushed Seba, spraying his eyes. Meli reached for the steak knife under her pillow and buried the metal in his chest as Kique slammed the corner of the chess box into his brain.

Seba slumped to the floor as if his final act had been to deliberately slink from life without a fuss. Had we succeeded in taking care of him? Were his children finally safe?

Kique softly closed the door, leaving us with the faint light that slipped in from the window. For a moment we were silent. I listened for footsteps. I imagined my cousins did the same.

There was nothing.

I emptied the rest of the spray up Seba's nose while Kique gave him a final whack with the box. By the time we stepped back, Meli had stumbled around to the foot of the bed. She threw her weight on her knife, driving it further into the lifeless hulk until the handle submerged below the flesh.

Kique took out his cell phone to help illuminate the room. "We have to go."

As Meli rose, we saw the blood on the gown. "Your clothes

are in the closet," I said. "Put those on."

"Gather anything personal," Kique added.

"What about—" I pointed to the body.

"Stairwell," he answered.

We peeked into the hallway. Bright, but deserted. Using every muscle, Kique and I dragged Seba across the linoleum. *Swoosh*, pause, listen. Repeat. When we made it to the stairwell, Kique held the door open with one foot. Seba's boot clicked as it scraped against the doorjamb, but we didn't stop until we closed the door behind us.

We stood, panting. Kique pointed to the floor above. That would be the best way to run.

But nobody came. After Kique pocketed Seba's wallet, we bounced him down two flights of stairs. I wanted to bounce him down a dozen more. Lifeless or not, he deserved every thump.

By the time we returned to the room, Meli sat on the edge of the bed, waiting. She'd gathered everything together, but her face was tight and pale.

We took the elevator to the lobby. The night clerk, a young woman, was naturally surprised to see us. "May I help you?"

"Everything's fine," Meli said. "I decided against the surgery."

It was a small hospital. "But they said your cheek is badly—"

"I decided I needed the reminder."

We thanked the woman before she could think of a reply. We continued toward the exit as if this were a normal day and Meli a normal patient. While I waited with her on the curb, Kique fetched my car.

Kique drove up as the sun snaked over the horizon. I helped Meli into the passenger seat and climbed into the backseat. Kique drove off at a steady pace. We might have had all day.

"Your place?" he asked me.

"Of course."

The hospital faded from sight.

"You're sure they don't know who we are?" Meli asked.

"They don't know."

Meli nodded. "Then it was perfect."

"Perfect?" I shouted. "The hospital let Seba in! They didn't try to protect you! We should file a complaint!"

"Or not," Kique said quietly.

"Meli?" I asked.

"You said the hospital doesn't know who we are."

"Right," I said.

"The chess set was a smart touch," she said. "And I wouldn't have thought of the pepper spray."

"You didn't put the knife back on your meal tray," Kique said. "That's when I knew."

And suddenly I knew too.

"You asked for your phone. You texted Seba yourself, didn't you?" I tapped Kique's shoulder. "And you wanted me to go home."

Kique turned right on Sixth Street. "Good thing you didn't. That guy weighed a ton."

Meli lay back against the seat. "Like I said, it was perfect."

"I wonder which of us killed him," Kique said.

Although we were alone in the car, I lowered my voice. "We'll never know. Maybe that's best."

"I wonder what the staff will think," Meli said. "Seba slipped past everyone. He played right into our hands."

"It happened at the change of shift," Kique said. "That's good, actually."

I snapped my fingers. "Of course. The night shift can blame the day shift."

Meli laughed. "And vice versa."

Perfect.

† † †

Originally from Springfield, Illinois, **D.R. RANSDELL** now resides in Tucson, Arizona, where she can hang out at the pool after she's done writing for the day. She writes a mystery series about mariachi violinist Andy Veracruz and travel-based fiction about Rachel and Gina Campanello. Her latest mystery, *Substitute Soloist*, won a regional Independent Publisher's award and an Arizona Author's Alliance award. A violinist herself, her musical memoir, *Secrets of a Mariachi Violinist*, won the 2019 New Mexico/Arizona Award for Biography. DR-Ransdell.com

TRY AGAIN
KIM RIVERY

"SOMETIMES it's scary not knowing where my child is," Trina's mom said. She paused her kitchen counter cleaning to shoot her older daughter the look. After moving the vase of dahlia flowers from the countertop, she continued wiping. Her eyes focused downward as she said, "And sometimes it's worse when I do know."

"Mom, I'm fine." Trina threw her long black hair into a bun.

Trina hadn't seen a single teardrop, but her mother wiped her eyes as though she'd been crying.

"You have to protect yourself. Are you carrying mace?" Her mom attacked the counter with more disinfectant.

"Dad made me get the handgun. I carry it with me. I'm fine."

In Phoenix you don't see a lot of women in their twenties carrying guns, and you wouldn't see Trina either, because even though the state didn't require it, she had a concealed carry permit.

"It's a dangerous world out there..."

Before her mom could spiral, Trina grabbed her mom's hand. "*I'm fine.*"

Her mom finally heard her words. Not the fine part, though.

"A gun! I know your line of work can be scary, but do you really need a *gun?* Because if you need a gun maybe you should do something else." Her mom's eyes began to water. She tucked the cleaner under the stainless steel sink where she kept all the chemicals. "You'd think it'd get easier when your children are adults, but no," she said to herself.

"Did Chellie get here yet?" Trina changed the subject. She sat at the round kitchen table looking around for evidence of her younger sister. But as usual, nothing was out of place. The only spot that could be considered messy was the front of the refrigerator. It held photo cards of distant cousins, magnets Trina brought back from her work trips, and Chellie's accomplishments. In the center was a photo of their family at the top of North Mountain.

"Your dad's picking her up. You know the shuttle from Tucson takes a bit longer so close to holidays."

"I don't know that," Trina said, the resentment creeping through her body. "You guys always made me take the Greyhound."

This time it was her mother who changed the subject, "Go put your things down. You're going to stay with your sister in her room."

Trina carried her duffle bag and purse to the room. When Chellie left for college, their parents kept her room just as it had been growing up. They had turned Trina's room into an office as soon as Trina graduated from high school. She thought it would have been nice to sleep in her old room, but her bed was long gone, and her father's desktop didn't appeal to her.

Tossing her bag across the threshold of Chel's room, Trina sighed. *When Chel graduates college, will her room become a shrine to her or a home gym?* Knowing the answer, she flipped off the light and headed back to the kitchen.

AFTER dinner, Trina cuddled a cup of tea, and her sister read a book while sitting in the chair next to her. Though it was called a living room, the soft recliners, and the decorative pillows with matching throws turned the room into a cozy reading space. Their mom came and kissed them on the heads. "I'm going to bed. Love you girls."

"Love you," they both said.

As soon as she was gone, Trina looked at her little sister. Same curly brown hair. Same reading glasses. But something was different. Off. "Chellie, you okay?"

Chellie gave a shrug, folding her legs under her. "It's just tough right now."

Trina put her mug down. "Just keep studying, you'll get it."

Her first month of college, Trina struggled and got the lowest test score of her life, 78 percent. "The first semester is tough. And engineering is difficult."

"I'm sure studying forensic science wasn't easy for you. But, it's not that." Chellie picked at her cuticles. She'd already chipped all of her nail polish away on the ride home.

"What's going on?" Trina asked.

Chellie nibbled on her lip.

"I can help you. Whatever it is." Trina leaned toward her sister and lowered her voice. "Are you pregnant?"

"What! No." Chellie almost cracked a smile. "Why would you say that?"

Trina shrugged, glad to have pulled her sister out of her mood a bit. "I'm just trying to figure out what would be so difficult for you to tell me."

"You were so popular in school. You always had friends, so you won't get it."

Trina put her hand on her sister, "You're my most important friend. I'll always have your back. What's up?"

"Just some girls." Chellie shook her head. "It's nothing."

"Your roommate?" Trina probed. "You get along?"

"She's okay… She's friends with Shannon." Chellie chipped away at her nail polish. "CHS Shannon."

"Oh." Trina sipped her tea to camouflage the clench in her gut. "How'd they meet?"

Chellie's green eyes narrowed on her sister in suspicion. "Are you using your investigative skills? Because there's no story here."

"Chel, I'm not trying to write a piece on you."

Chellie sat in silence and bit her lip again.

Trina sighed. "I'm meeting friends at The Parlor on Camelback. You want to join?"

"No. Thanks."

"Come on." Trina tried to entice her little sister. "You love their watermelon salad."

Chellie groaned and shook her head. "We already had dinner." Fidgeting with her bookmark, she added, "Not really a people person these days."

"My investigative skills tell me that's the first real thing you've said." Trina joked.

Chellie's silence broke with short breaths that always preceded crying.

Panicked, Trina reached for her sister's hand. "I'm just joking Chel."

"I thought when I left high school, I was leaving the problems behind but they followed me. *She* followed me." Chellie wiped her eyes.

She is Shannon. Trina didn't have to ask.

"I got the high score on two tests in Intro to Engineering, so she started a rumor that I was sleeping with the professor," Chellie blurted out.

Trina slammed her cup of tea down. "What the hell?"

The careful lid Chellie had on her emotions popped off. "My shuttle wasn't running late like I told Mom and Dad." Chellie squeezed her hands together. "I had to rewrite a paper." She reached up swiping the tears streaming down her face. "It was due today, and when I pulled it up this morning to review it before submitting it was blank except for *Try again*. "I know my roommate must have had Shannon over when I went to dinner."

"It's okay." Trina pulled her sister into a hug. "I don't have to go. I'll stay home tonight."

"No, I'm fine." Chellie's face hardened. "Shannon lives by The Parlor, maybe I *should* go."

"That's a bad idea." Trina stroked her sister's hair, the way their mother used to when they were kids. "Let's sleep on it, and come up with a plan in the morning."

In the bedroom, Trina slipped on her jeans and rifled through the desk to find earrings. Chellie had left her laptop open. A message popped up as Trina put her earrings in. The reporter in her had to see who it was. Chellie was in the bathroom. The notification couldn't be heard from there. Trina clicked.

A message from Shannon Brighten.

TRY AGAIN

She exited the message, hoping her sister wouldn't see it.

The words swirled in her mind. *Try Again.*

In high school there had been a rumor that Chellie tried to kill herself after bombing a test. The truth was, she bought sushi from the gas station on 15th Avenue and got food poisoning. She stayed home the next few days, and when she went back to school, she looked terrible. Shannon had started those rumors too. Told everyone Chellie took a bunch of sleeping pills and had to be under observation in the psych ward. Someone carved CHELICIDE into Chellie's homeroom desk. Shannon called her Chelicide until the day she walked across the stage and accepted her diploma. Chellie barely made it through high school. College was a do-over. Things would be different. Better.

But nothing changed.

It was all starting again.

Trina wasn't sure Chellie would survive another four years of Shannon's torture. The words continued on repeat in Trina's mind.

Try again, Chelicide.

Last time, Trina had been away. A piercing pain came to her stomach every time she thought about her sister's loneliness in high school. Chellie wouldn't be alone again.

She grabbed her purse, knocked on the bathroom door and said, "I'm gonna take off."

"Thanks, Trina. Sorry about the trouble."

"How do you always find a way to apologize?" Trina laughed even though it wasn't funny. "It'll be fine tomorrow. We'll figure something out."

"Love you Tri," Chellie called out.

Trina laid her forehead against the door for just a second. "I love you too," Trina said before she walked out the door.

"BUT have you tried it here?" Trina asked her friend, Jaz.

"It won't matter. All brick oven pizza is burnt."

"I guess you should order a salad then," Trina said.

Jaz adjusted herself in the booth. "Does anyone have an Advil?"

Trina dug in the oversized purse. "I'm sure I have something in here."

"How can you carry that huge suitcase around?"

"It's a purse! As a reporter, you never know what you'll need," Trina answered. "Gotta be prepared."

"Wow. Do you carry a change of clothes?" Her friend laughed.

"I have a shirt."

"What's this?" Jaz fished out a small packet with picture warnings printed on it and showed it to Trina.

"Oxygen absorber." She snatched it and tossed it into her bag before her friend could get a closer look.

"Why do you still have that?"

"It's good for my camera. Never know when that packet will come in handy." Trina closed her purse and set it aside. "I still have my pandemic gear in there—gloves, mask." She shrugged. "Other stuff."

Jaz laughed again "You are so 2020. Clean out your purse."

THE house looked dark, but Trina knocked on the large wooden door anyway.

Chellie was right.

She didn't live far from The Parlor.

A brunette girl with high cheekbones and the posture of a ballerina answered the door. "What are you doing here?"

"Came to talk," Trina said. She placed her keys in her purse.

"Um, okay." Confused, Shannon moved away from the door.

Trina peacocked in. Her posture stronger than the ballerina. "Parents out of town again?"

"When are they *in* town?" Shannon smacked her gum.

"You must be lonely to let me in."

"Or maybe I'm curious." She pulled the gum out of her mouth and twisted it around her finger. "What do you want?"

How juvenile.

Trina held her purse close. "You're harassing my sister again." She looked straight into Shannon's eyes.

"Harmless fun." Shannon blew a bubble with her chewing gum, letting it pop before she broke away from Trina's gaze. "Little Miss Perfect needs to learn how to take a joke," she said.

They walked to the only room with the light on, the kitchen.

"Can I have some water?" Trina asked Shannon.

Shannon grabbed a glass and filled it from the fridge. She placed it on a napkin in front of Trina.

"You have a straw?" Trina put her nitril gloves on.

"The pandemic is over. You don't need gloves for a glass of water," Shannon put a plastic straw in the glass.

"Never can be too careful," Trina said. "You're taking things too far with Chellie." Ignoring the water, she crossed her arms. "You need to stop. *And* apologize."

"No, I don't." Shannon laughed. "It's not my fault she jumps on anyone with a red pen."

"Okay..." Trina's hands cranked into fists as though she was going to punch Shannon so hard it would reshape her perfect bone structure. "Okay. It seems you need a lesson in understanding," Trina said.

"A lesson?" Shannon took a few more chomps of her gum. "You're going to teach me a *lesson?*"

"I'm going to try." Trina forced herself to smile. "Grab a paper and pen. It'll make sense in a minute."

To Trina's surprise, Shannon complied.

While her back was turned, Trina pulled a small packet from her purse and dumped its contacts into the glass of water. The powder dissolved before it hit the bottom of the glass.

Shannon dropped her gum in the garbage and placed the paper and pen on the counter.

"We're going to write down some feelings."

Shannon rolled her eyes. "Are you like a psychologist or something?"

Trina laughed. "No, but let's start with you being alone this weekend. How do you feel that your parents left town again? Write in complete sentences."

"Oh, now you're an English teacher? You going to give me a grade?" Shannon flicked at the pen's end like it was a cigarette.

"Grow up." Trina knew girls like Shannon could be ruled by pressure from someone they thought was socially superior. "Just do it."

The marble countertop allowed for a smooth writing surface, no need to move to the office. Trina bet Shannon's parents had at least one office, probably a home gym, and still had Shannon's room intact.

With a sigh, Shannon put the tip of the pen to paper and let it move.

I used to think it was so cool to have the house to myself. Parties if I wanted, peace if I didn't. But being

*alone every holiday is sad. I thought for my first
holiday home from college my parents would actually
be here. But I'm alone. Again.*

"Good. How did that feel?" Trina asked.

"Kinda cathartic, actually."

"Now write about the things you've done to my sister."

Shannon slammed the pen down.

"I'm not doing that."

Trina's face flushed. "Pick up the pen."

"No." Shannon shook her head, jaw stiff. "I love my parents. I don't give a crap about your stupid slutty sister."

"Pick up the pen." Reaching into her bag, Trina grabbed her gun. Pulling it out, she pointed it at Shannon. "Now." She said it with more confidence than she felt.

Hand shaking, Shannon picked up the pen.

"Write down what you did to Chellie. I know you *don't give a crap* enough to put her name. You don't want to write it, that's fine."

"I don't have to?" Shannon looked at her as though she'd lost it. "You're pointing a gun at me. What the hell is wrong with you?"

"Just write." Trina motioned toward the paper with her gun. "All of it."

Shannon recounted the rumors she started, the messages she sent, the paper she deleted, and the time she laced Chellie's food with laxatives so she'd miss a test. Trina hadn't known about the food.

"Now that you see it written, do you see how you've crossed the line?" Trina asked as she held the gun.

"The only thing I *see* is the gun you have stuck in my face." Shannon pointed her silver tipped gel nails at the firearm. "Your sister needs to stop messing things up for me."

"You're not learning anything, so let's wrap this up. Last lines..." Trina paused. "I told my classmate to kill herself. I told her to *try again*. Write that."

Shannon cleared her throat as if it removed her fear. "No."

"Write it." Trina put the gun closer to Shannon's head and watched while she complied. "Now write *but it's me who needs to try again*."

After she wrote it, Shannon dropped the pen. "What are you going to do with this anyway? Post it? Show it to your weak, pathetic sister?"

Stunned that not even a gun to her head could make Shannon think before she spoke, Trina said, "You need to wash your mouth out." She grabbed a napkin from the counter and lifted the soap bottle from the sink and set it next to the glass of water.

"Screw you!"

"Drink it." Trina pushed the glass in front of Shannon with the tip of the gun.

Shannon lifted the glass and crunched her nose in distaste at the bottle next to it. "You put soap in this?"

"That's how a mouth gets clean." She motioned with the gun. "Swallow."

Shannon scoffed "I'm not your sister."

"You're pushing it." Trina growled through clenched teeth. "And I'm losing my patience."

Shannon gulped down a few sips. "Aren't you supposed to spit when you clean your mouth out with soap?"

"What you're an expert on cleaning mouths? Keep drinking."

Shannon glared at Trina and chugged it like a beer.

"I'm gonna call the cops as soon as you leave, you know."

"You don't get it."

Shannon squinted her eyes. "You're throwing your life away to get a stupid apology note for your sister?"

Trina shook her head. "You wouldn't understand sisterly love because you're an only child whose parents couldn't care less about her."

Trina prepared to duck and dodge the glass Shannon would throw at her, but it never came. Shannon slammed it back on the counter instead. "Are we done here? Can you get the hell out of my house now?"

"Not quite yet."

AWHILE later Trina walked out the front door, turning the lock on the inside before closing it. She took off her gloves and said, "I guess it is time to clean out my purse."

† † †

TWO days later, as they ate cereal at the kitchen table, the two sisters watched the local news.

The caption read, CYBERBULLY TAKES OWN LIFE TO REPENT.

The newswoman began, "Nineteen-year-old Shannon Brighten took her own life after writing a note explaining her loneliness due to absent parents, and the bullying she'd inflicted on a classmate…"

"Oh my gosh! It's Shannon!" Chellie shouted. She dropped her spoon.

"Shannon?" Trina asked.

"CHS Shannon. The one I told you about."

"Oh, yeah," Trina said. "Sorry."

Chellie picked up her spoon. "Ugh! You never listen."

Trina pulled Chellie into a hug. "I love you Chel."

† † †

KIM RIVERY is the author of "Try Again." It is her first short story publication. She is a teacher by day, and writes in the middle of the night when her children and husband are asleep. Unless she's writing side-by-side with her daughter, who also enjoys telling stories. Kim loves Arizona sunsets and the smell after the rain— thank you to the creosote bush. Kim is thankful to her family for supporting her dreams, and to all the authors and editors in this SoWest Anthology.

EVERYTHING
Elena E. Smith

THANK God it wasn't too hot. Eighty-five to ninety degrees I could handle. The A/C blew straight at my face as I climbed Highway 68 toward Golden Valley, Arizona. Sixty-eight, just can't wait. Passed the rock that saluted me like a middle finger. Blasted punk rock music from the late seventies and screamed out lyrics at the top of my lungs. Took a shot of tequila between verses. Did everything that would piss off the hubs if he got wind of it.

Doug. Douglas. Dougl-ass, as I called him when I cursed him in my head. Never to his face. To his face, I was the loving wife. We portrayed the perfect couple, but it was a farce. I'd heard years of "Jack Sprat" comments from my in-laws, beginning with their reference to me as a "cornfed beauty" when he'd introduced me to them. I'd endured this since our wedding, right after high school graduation. Put on the wax lips when they harped on our childless marriage. Now, I was in my fifties. He was only a few years older than me but with his fitness routines it looked like I'd be deprived of the experience of widowhood. I was sure to die first. From stress if nothing else. Croak croak croak, not a joke joke joke.

That's why I had to go for a drive. To get away from him for a while. Lied about where I was going. Like I always did. So what if he looked at the odometer? It wasn't like I was having an affair. I was too old and too fat for that. Who'd want me? I wasn't even sure why Doug still did. *If* he did. During every big fight I suggested a divorce but he didn't believe I was serious. Nope, I was stuck. Stuck stuck stuck, like a duck duck duck.

In the twenty minutes from the Laughlin Bridge to Golden Valley I climbed three thousand feet toward a dull dusty town that was ten degrees cooler. Under a light breeze. At the crest, I passed a historical marker, whose significance I didn't know, then coasted the short downhill stretch into a town I'd heard of but hadn't yet visited. It hugged both sides of the highway. Some gas station mini-marts, eateries, a few buildings, swap meets, a school, a small medical plaza. I slowed to look for the Everything store.

I'd seen a write-up in the *Mohave News*. The owner was a gal about ten years older than me who looked like she belonged in a comic strip. She had round red curls, purple-framed glasses and a dangling cigarette with an inch of ash. Her slogan was *Everything but the kitchen sink*. She must have been doing well with the business because the picture in the article showed her standing in front of a mini mansion, a rarity in our county.

One of the ongoing disputes Doug and I had was what I could and couldn't live without. I liked to buy collectibles because they retained their value and were pretty to look at. Doug didn't think so. He spent our money on stockpiling foodstuffs for an impending disaster. This morning, he'd brought home a box load of canned tuna. I kept telling him there was an expiration date on the cans. Same old argument that went nowhere. Fight fight fight every night night night. I needed an escape. Going on a mission for a Roseville vase at bargain basement pricing always put me in a better mood. Maybe I'd see Carnival Glass or Fenton that was undervalued. Or a Fiestaware color I didn't have enough of. She'd said, "Everything..." Was it true?

I saw the old building, slowed down for a tight turn into the narrow dip in the pavement. Got honked by a semi-truck driver. Beep beep beep, you creep creep creep. The store was long and low, made from slatted wood, built in the 1930s. Rooms had been added on—by hand—a little at a time until maybe the 1950s. A windbreak at the top, like old west saloons had, featured the store name in black calligraphy.

When I got out of the car, a breeze lifted my oily brown hair and set it back down. Tickled my neck. I adjusted the heavy glasses that depressed the top of my nose. Pulled a tissue out of my purse to wipe them with. Put on the COVID mask my insurance company sent me by mail.

Walking through the soft dirt to the front of the store, I wondered what I would find inside. The thrill of discovery and the shots of tequila made my stomach flutter. I mounted two wood steps onto a long handmade porch with loose slats. My cowgirl boots tap-tapped a rhythm as I approached the entrance, featuring a grungy homemade screen door from the Depression era. I walked in the door. Spring hinges squeaked as it flapped shut behind me.

The owner was at the front counter, radiant as a stockbroker meeting a new investor. We nodded hellos and checked each other out. Me in my elastic-waist jeans and T-shirt. Her in an old-fashioned house dress, a lavender flour sack print that harmonized with her purple glasses. Our face masks color-coordinated with our clothes.

"Looking for anything in particular?"

Sellers always ask that. Some even scream "Welcome!" at me when I walk in. Ever since the Great Recession happened, they want to know if you're a looker or a buyer.

"I'll know it when I see it," I said.

Her eyes crinkled above a mask that hid her smile. "Well, let me know if I can help you."

My eyes dilated as they adjusted to the sparkling displays. Lamps, sandwich glass, refrigerator dishes. She even had some Vaseline Glass in a locked cabinet with a black light over the display. Their neon green glow proved they were authentic. I shuffled forward slowly, mesmerized by all I saw.

"This is my glass room," she said.

Well, duh.

"The next room is pottery."

I wouldn't inquire about Roseville. When a seller wasn't savvy, I didn't want to tip them off that I was. Better to play dumb and comment on how "cute" something looked. I'd once, for three bucks, picked up a Roseville bud vase that was selling on e-Bay for ninety-five. Dealin' Deena was my name and getting the best price was my game.

I walked through a doorway into the pottery room and quickly spotted a small Roseville display. From the corner of my eye I could tell she was watching me, so I pretended not to notice them. I moseyed through the room, mindful not to get too close to the shelves. Had to avoid the old *you broke it, you bought it* routine where the price went way up if you were the unfortunate one whose purse swept by a knickknack they hadn't been able to sell.

She had several pieces of Roseville. That was a lot, really. I'd concluded a while ago that there wasn't much in circulation. The originals were beautiful, airbrushed and hand-painted to artistic perfection. But you had to know your stuff, like I did, to avoid getting swindled. China had bought the original molds and started turning out replicas that showed up in the U.S.

I browsed, pretending to notice something unfamiliar for the first time. To my disappointment, the prices were affixed to the bottom of the items, so I wouldn't be able to see them unless I got into a yoga position. That wasn't easy with my girth.

"I see you have expensive taste."

She was right behind me. I almost jumped. Was she trying to make me break something so she could charge me?

"I have great taste," I agreed. "But the hubs is stingy. Know what I mean?"

Maybe she'd negotiate on her prices, whatever they were.

"Oh, you still have one of those?" Saw the surprised look in my eyes and guffawed. "Hopefully you won't have to wait too much longer."

She'd found my hot button. My blood pressure rose. "What do you mean?"

Forgetting about the COVID threat for a moment, she reached her hand out to pat my arm. Then remembered. Withdrew it. Kept her six-foot distance.

"You'll find out soon enough." Moved her hand up to straighten her mask. "When he kicks the bucket. Your life will get so much better."

No duh.

Could she read my feelings from the look in my eyes? How much of my dissatisfaction did I show? Maybe I was part of a big club of women who all wanted their freedom. This was nothing unusual by a certain time of life.

"Do you like holidays?" she went on. "In the back is my Halloween room. It's special. Not everyone gets invited to see it." She winked at me. Wink wink wink, where's my drink drink drink?

I traipsed after her to a narrow 1920s 4-panel door with a glass knob. Watched her use a key. The padlock slid off the hasp into her hand and she said, "You can take a look around by yourself; I have to get something out in the mail today."

She backtracked, careful not to bump any of the precious goods on display. I looked in the open doorway. A lot of black and orange going on. Ducked under a faux web. Almost stumbled on the uneven stoop. My eyes hit the ground. Dang! There were gaps in the boards, just like on the second floor of the Oatman Hotel. Well, I guess it contributed to the haunted house theme.

The room lights dimmed. That gal sure knew how to create atmosphere. I walked further in and stopped to let my eyes adjust. Bookshelves lining the walls and glass display cases in the middle of the room were filled with tombstones, skulls, and plastic spiders with red rhinestones glued to their bellies.

I walked in further and my cell phone buzzed. Damn. Hubs texting.

WHERE ARE YOU?

Ignore him or not? I'd ignore him for now, but I didn't want to get startled again around any high-priced merchandise. I silenced the phone.

I took another step and my boot knocked into something, almost tripping me. I braced myself against the wall and looked down. I'd almost stepped on a life-size model of a coiled rattlesnake. Gasped louder than I meant to. I heard Mrs. Purple Durple leaving the register to head my way.

And that was when I saw it. Maybe she knew I would find it on my own. Next to the rattler was a missing board. Between the slats I saw a certain shade of white. Bone white. Part of a skeleton. My hand was still on the wall and I balanced against it as I lowered myself on stiff stocky legs. Peered through the opening. A cool blast of air brushed my face. Pushed my glasses up on my nose, awkward with the cell phone still in my hand. A skeleton. Good idea for decoration, but maybe it should have been out in the open instead of hidden. Not all of us have strong tickers. Tick tick tick, don't get sick sick sick.

"Oh, I see you found Gordon," she said.

"G-Gordon?"

"My dearly departed."

I laughed weakly. She'd named her skeleton. How cute.

"You think I'm kidding." Her bulk filled the doorway as she

peered down at me, house dress still fluttering around her knees from her sudden stop. No way out for me. Stuck stuck stuck.

"Getting rid of him was the best move I ever made. My Gordon was a real a-hole."

"I know the feeling," I said.

"Yep. I saw it on your face the minute you walked in. And I could tell by the comments you made. That's why I showed you this special room. You need to be released from that burden."

I laughed, an involuntary bark that spewed out like a hunk of snot after a dust storm.

"It's a lot easier than you think."

I was interested. And, since she was a saleslady, I'm sure she realized it.

She relaxed. Slanted her eyes away from me. Her voice lowered. "It just takes a little money, that's all. I got a fat mortgage payment on that new house. And I'm sure you can get your hands on what you'll need. Everyone can." She paused. "Go ahead and look through the crack. Gordon's not the only one down there."

I didn't want to look. I felt vulnerable enough wavering on my XXL calves knowing I'd lose my balance if I stayed this way much longer. I mean, how could I be sure those skeletons were all really from men? Maybe there were some ladies down there, too. The room felt closed in. Warm. Suffocating. Greasy sweat formed on my forehead. A rivulet oozed down my cheek. I pushed hard against the wall and with all the strength I had, eased myself into a standing position.

"How much money?" I asked.

She told me. She was right, I could afford it. I had some savings, and I could replenish that if I sold off a few antiques.

"How do we work it?"

She folded her arms across an ample bosom that reminded me of cow udders. "Just invite him up here. Today, if you want. I can close the store early. I do the job, you pay me, and we're done."

"How do I know you won't get caught. Or I won't get caught?"

The way her eyes crinkled behind her glasses told me there was a wide grin beneath her face mask. "My brother's the sheriff. And, you know, lots of people disappear in the desert. They go on a short hike without water, start to dehydrate, lose their sense of direction. Fall into a ravine and get eaten by coyotes. Some missing bodies are never recovered. Like what happened to my poor Gordon, may he rest in peace."

We talked about what we'd do with Doug's car afterward and how to erase any of my fingerprints that might appear where they shouldn't be. She nodded to the silenced phone I still held. "Go ahead, call him. Invite him up here. Tell him I have...whatever it is he likes."

I nodded. "Doug," I said, my words breathy with excitement. "I'm up in Golden Valley where this lady has a surplus of prepper supplies." Listened. "Yes, she has that." Listened. "She has that, too." Listened. "It's easy to find. Just come up Highway 68 to the Everything store."

Yep, she had everything all right. Including dead bodies.

I disconnected from the hubs and turned the phone off before I slid it into my back pocket. If I butt-dialed him right now it could really screw things up.

The store owner's eyes transmitted satisfaction above her COVID mask. "You made the right decision," she cooed.

Yes, I did.

Soon I'd be free free free.

† † †

ELENA E. SMITH has had four noir short stories published: "Trunk" and "The Answer" (2016, *Café Noir* anthology, CHWG Publishing), "Toil and Trouble" (2017, *Darkness Brewing* anthology, CHWG), "Service Providers" (2020, *The Absurdist* online) and a non-fiction piece "The One Percent Cat" (2016, *No Wasted Ink* online). You can join her at her Facebook group, MAHUENGA.

EDITOR BIOGRAPHIES

Lead Editor: MAEGAN BEAUMONT is the author of the award-winning Sabrina Vaughn thriller series. Her debut novel, *Carved in Darkness*, was awarded the 2014 Gold Medal by Independent Publishers for Outstanding Thriller as well as being named a Foreword Book of the Year Finalist and Debut Novel of the Year by *Suspense Magazine*. When she isn't locked in her office, torturing her protagonists, she's busy chasing chickens (and kids), hanging laundry, and burning dinner. Either way, she is almost always in the company of her seven dogs, her truest and most faithful companions, and her almost as faithful husband, Joe. MaeganBeaumont.com

Co-Editor: DEBORAH J LEDFORD - "As a Past-President of the Desert Sleuths, it is an honor to be associated with the finest Sisters in Crime chapter in the nation, and to provide my editing talents for many of the DS anthologies. It has been a pleasure helping to cultivate established, as well as new talent."

Deborah is a professional developmental editor and First-Reader for a number of published authors. She is also the author of the award-winning Inola Walela and Steven Hawk suspense thriller series, including: *Causing Chaos* and *Crescendo*, both Anthony Award Finalists for Best Audiobook. DeborahJLedford.com.

Co-Editor: SUSAN BUDAVARI - "*SoWest: Love Kills* is the seventh Desert Sleuths anthology I've had the pleasure of co-editing. Coming from the non-fiction side of writing and editing, I've enjoyed my journey in fiction. Each anthology experience has been so different yet equally exciting. I've worked with dozens of talented authors and continue to marvel at the ideas they come up with for markedly diverse short stories set in Arizona. I'd like to also acknowledge my colleagues on the various Desert Sleuths editorial teams who have given so generously of their time and talent to produce each volume."

EDITOR BIOGRAPHIES

Co-Editor: R K "Roni" OLSON - "Having spent a lifetime indulging my passion for the short story, sharing the editing duties for our 9th anthology, along with five other talented women, was a collaborative labor of love. It was a joy to work with this year's writers, some new, some veterans. Together I think we teased the best out of each story. Thank you, authors, for allowing me to share the experience."

Co-Editor: SHANNON BAKER writes mysteries about strong women in dangerous situations. Her books are set in the iconic landscapes of the American West, from the Colorado Rockies to the Nebraska prairies, to the deserts of southern Arizona. Now a resident of Tucson, Baker spent 20 years in the Nebraska Sandhills, where cattle outnumber people by more than 50:1. She is proud to have been chosen Rocky Mountain Fiction Writers' 2014 and 2017-2018 Writer of the Year. *The Desert Behind Me* was 2019 New Mexico/Arizona Book Award winner. Shannon-Baker.com

Co-Editor: MEG E. DOBSON'S short stories have appeared in national anthologies like Malice Domestic, Poisoned Pen Press, and SinC Desert Sleuths. Additional award-winning shorts were honored twice by the Tempe Community Writing Forum. Her flash fiction placed top-five three times at Writers' Police Academy. Her young adult crime fiction novel, *Chaos Theory*, a Kami Files Mystery, was published by the Poisoned Pen's imprint press. Meg is honored to edit for Sisters In Crime and lives by their mission statement—promote the ongoing advancement, recognition and professional development of sister/brother crime writers. MegEDobson.com

Cover Designer: MAEGAN BEAUMONT is an accomplished cover designer in multiple genres, and was named a finalist in 2020 for her work on the 2019 Sisters in Crime Desert Sleuths Chapter anthology, *So West: Ladykillers* from the New Mexico-Arizona book awards. Check her work out on Facebook at MW Designs.

Praise For Sisters in Crime Desert Sleuths Chapter Anthologies from DS Publishing

SoWest: Ladykillers (2019)

† BEST ANTHOLOGY 2020 FINALIST AWARD:
~ New Mexico/Arizona Book Awards ~

"This excellent and diverse collection of well-crafted mystery short stories is just what you'd expect from professional writers who call themselves Sisters in Crime. In addition to treating the reader to a killer buffet of sinister mayhem, the stories highlight Arizona's geographic variety from the muddy streets of frontier Bisbee to artsy Scottsdale, a dystopian future Phoenix and beyond."

~ ANNE HILLERMAN, author of the bestselling Leaphorn, Chee, Manuelito mysteries.

SoWest: Killer Nights (2017)

"SoWest: Killer Nights showcases twenty southwest crime tales filled with suspense, tension and action. A great read."

~ Clive Cussler, International Bestselling author

"The southwest comes blazingly alive in SoWest: Killer Nights with stories that are so hot with crime, mystery, passion and suspense that you'll feel the desert heat rising from the page might burst into flames. Warning: don't read this book without protection."

~ Lee Goldberg, #1 New York Times Bestselling author

SoWest: So Deadly (2015)

† BEST ANTHOLOGY 2016 FINALIST AWARDS:
International Book Awards ~ International Readers Favorites Awards
~ New Mexico/Arizona Book Awards ~
USA Best Book Awards

"The Wild (South)West has never been so much wicked fun. This exceptional collection showcases new and exciting talent, while exploring the Southwest in all of its magnificence...and malfeasance."

~ HILARY DAVIDSON, Award-Winning author

SoWest: Crime Time (2013)

"Suspenseful, surprising and sometimes even hilarious! This twisty and entertaining collection of revenge, retaliation, and diabolical deeds not only showcases the gorgeous and unique southwest—but also the skill and originality of these incredibly talented sisters in crime. Loved it!"

~ HANK PHILLIPPI RYAN, Agatha, Anthony, Macavity, Mary Higgins Clark Award-Winning author

Praise For Sisters in Crime Desert Sleuths Chapter Anthologies from DS Publishing

SoWest: Desert Justice (2012)
† *Suspense Magazine*'s Best Anthology of 2012 Finalist
† New Mexico-Arizona Book Awards Finalist -
Best Anthology 2012

"Arizonans and all who love their mountains and deserts spiced with danger are in for a treat. The Sisters in Crime Desert Sleuths have put together another anthology of stories that powerfully evoke all the beautiful (and deadly) aspects of their state: white water rivers, hidden caves, steep mountain trails, blast-furnace deserts and yes, diamondback rattlers. Visit at your own risk!"
~ MARGARET MARON, Award-Winning author

SoWest, So Wild (2011)
† *Suspense Magazine*'s Best Anthology of 2011 Finalist

"Arizona proves hot, dry, and deadly in this anthology. There's something for everyone to enjoy here, in tales of murder ranging from the humorous to the macabre."
~MEG GARDINER, Edgar Award Winner, and *New York Times* Bestselling author of *The Nightmare Thief*

"An old time sheriff only had six bullets loaded into his gun to take care of the bad guys—with *SoWest So Wild*, twenty different authors take aim and each one hits the bulls-eye. You'll never look at the Wild West the same way again."
~ TONI L.P. KELNER, co-editor of the *New York Times* Bestselling Anthology, *Death's Excellent Vacation*

How NOT to Survive a Vacation (2010)

"Like a macabre travel brochure, these chilling mystery stories take you on a grisly tour of choice vacation spots, except instead of Mai Tais, they serve murder."
~REBECCA CANTRELL, *New York Times* Bestselling author, and Award-Winning author of the Joe Tesla series

How NOT to Survive the Holidays (2009)

"Stuff your stocking with this string of holiday sparkles, ranging from the chilling to the decidedly wacky."
~ RHYS BOWEN, Agatha and Anthony Award-Winning author of the *Molly Murphy* and *Royal Spyness* mysteries